TALES FROM WHERE
THE ROAD ENDS II

Kevin F. McCarthy

ISBN: 197818932X
ISBN 13: 9781978189324
Library of Congress Control Number: 2017916840
CreateSpace Independent Publishing Platform
North Charleston, South Carolina

These are works of fiction. Names, characters, places, and incidents either are the
product of the author's imagination or are used fictitiously, and any resemblance to
actual persons, living or dead, businesses, companies, events, or locales is entirely
coincidental.

Books by Kevin F. McCarthy

Tales From Where The Road Ends

Tales From Where The Road Ends II

TABLE OF CONTENTS

THE SONG REMAINS THE SAME

Chapter One

The guy selling the car was full of shit and he knew it, and Bob knew he was full of shit too, and the guy knew that Bob knew he was full of shit but he didn't care. He just kept waxing poetic about the Chevy like it was a long lost love instead of a really old car parked in his driveway and baking in the sun.

"They just don't make them like this anymore," the guy said. It was the fifth, or maybe the sixth cliché he'd used in the past five minutes; Bob had stopped counting them.

"The price is a little steep don't you think?" Bob said.

"Well that depends, doesn't it? That depends on how much you're willing to spend on history, how much you're willing to spend to drive a classic example of Detroit rolling iron. It's not like you can leave here, drive to the nearest Chevy dealer and just buy a 1966 Impala, is it?"

Bob agreed that it wasn't.

"Was this your first new car then?" the guy asked him. "You're looking at it like it was."

"I was nine when this thing rolled off the production line," Bob told him.

"Well you owned one later on then, I can tell by the way you're eyeing her. Lose your cherry in the back seat of a '66 Impala did you."

"Still have my cherry," Bob told him, "I don't get out much."

The guy responded with just about the phoniest laugh Bob had ever heard and slapped the front fender of the Impala. Some rust flakes fluttered down out of the wheel well.

"I'll give you fifteen hundred for it," Bob said, "and that's really the best I can do. I mean, it needs body work, the engine sounds kind of choppy, and the seats need to be re-upholstered."

"Fifteen hundred!" the guy was genuinely insulted, his honor had been impugned. Bob may have even insulted the United States of America; the car guy couldn't be sure. "That's kind of an insult," he informed Bob, "to me and the car both."

"Look," Bob said, "if it had a 327 or a 427 in it things would be different. But it's a 289. The 289 doesn't put out more than 195 gross horsepower."

"The small block 289 was the workhorse engine at General Motors for thirty years my friend, they run forever, you can't kill them, just like the old Chrysler 318's, same deal, it's a great motor." The guy's tone of voice now said that he was dealing with the heathen and that Bob had for all time revealed himself to be totally ignorant about cars and car engines both. And he still wasn't sure if Bob had insulted the United States of America.

"Eighteen hundred," Bob replied, "and only if I'm able to drive it out of here."

"Well you sure as shit ain't going to fly it out of here now, are you? Eighteen-fifty and I'll throw in all the spare parts I have for the car, they're in the trunk anyway and I don't feel like pulling them out," he cackled at the joke as if it was the funniest thing he'd ever heard himself or anyone else say.

2

"And you do have clear title right?"

"Said I did, didn't I? It's right there in the glove box."

"Ok, eighteen-fifty. There's a bank down by the mall, I'll shoot down there and be back in twenty minutes."

"Cash," car guy said. "Don't take those certified checks or cashier vouchers or any such things."

Twenty minutes later Bob was back with eighteen one hundred dollar bills and one fifty, no certified checks or vouchers or any such things. The car guy, while still full of shit, did indeed have the title to the Impala. He signed it over to Bob and handed him four keys, two for the ignition and two for the doors and trunk. Bob had forgotten that you needed different keys for each with old cars. He'd also forgotten how small car keys used to be; they were about the size of his house key, maybe even a bit smaller.

So, paperwork done, Bob slid into the front seat and put both hands on the enormous Bakelite steering wheel. He looked at the metal dash that seemed impossibly long, and hard and flat, then out of habit he reached for a shoulder belt that wasn't there.

"Weren't invented yet," the car guy cackled. "Even the lap belts were an option back then, only reason this thing has em is because the original owner paid for em."

"Do you know who the original owner was?" Bob asked him.

"Some asshole down the Cape, car was bought new from a dealership in Hyannis, that's all I know."

Bob nodded and slid the very small key into the ignition that was located on the dash, not the steering column. He pumped the gas pedal several times and told himself that if the car didn't start he was going to ask for his money back but when he turned the key the 289 V8 rumbled to life. He revved it a few times and it sounded ok, probably need a new exhaust before too long but it was ticking over nice and steady.

Car guy slapped him on the shoulder through the open window and stepped back away from the car. "Enjoy her," he said, "I'll bargain she's going to be more fun than you think." With that he cackled one final time and started up the driveway toward his run down split ranch.

Bob slowly dropped the gear arm down to D; just two gears here, low or 1st gear and drive. They used to call it a hydro-glide tranny and Bob had a vague idea that they were worth some money these days. The Chevy began to roll down the driveway on its own, he tapped the gas pedal and it picked up speed. When he reached the street he pushed down fairly hard and the car accelerated with alarming quickness. He took his foot off the gas pedal and tapped the brake pedal to slow down a bit, brakes worked, that was good, and probably something he should have checked right away. With that in mind he twisted the wheel from side to side a few times to be sure the front tires responded and nothing was broken up there. Another thing he'd forgotten about these old cars, when they said power steering they meant it, he could spin the over-sized steering wheel with one finger and the car would turn. It almost felt like the steering wheel wasn't actually connected to anything.

By the time he got across town and pulled into his auto mechanic's shop he felt like he'd been driving the Impala for years.

Chapter Two

A week later, on a Saturday, he took the Chevy out for a spin. His mechanic had fixed a few minor things on the car and then given it a clean bill of health. Bob had plans to have the front seat re-upholstered but that meant leaving the car with the shop for at least a week and he wanted to have fun with it for a while first. He'd just bought it after all.

He was sitting at a traffic signal at the edge of town waiting for the light to change when he turned his attention to the radio for the first time. It was obviously the original radio that the Impala had come off the production line with, an on/off/volume knob on the left, a tuning knob on the right and in between a long narrow analog radio dial that only showed AM stations because in 1966 that was all there was. And under the tuning window seven black push buttons to pre-set particular stations. Bob seriously doubted that the radio still worked but he reached out and twisted the left hand knob anyway and…the car was filled with static. There was a speaker in the center of the dashboard and a second imbedded in the top center of the rear seat, that one was covered by a silver grill emblazoned with a leaping Impala. He turned the volume down then, for the hell of it, pushed in the first pre-set button and the static changed to Paul Revere and the Raiders singing *Kicks*.

The light changed and he drove on, listening to music and thrilled that the radio still worked. The AM signal was coming in more clearly than it ever had on the stereo in Bob's SUV, the speakers were a bit tinny but he could always install new ones, and more of them. It was all good.

Twenty minutes later he was cruising a two lane country road, windows down, one hand on the wheel, the other arm resting on the top of the door, wind in his hair, digging on the oldies station that someone had programmed on button one, not knowing where he was going and not caring. The song on the radio ended and *Reflections of My Life* came through the speakers, a classic oldie but goodie by The Marmalade and then something happened. He wasn't sure what it was but it was something because he felt it, a kind of rippling sensation that passed through the car, and through him. And then everything was normal again, the Impala humming along, Dean Ford still singing away on the radio, no worries.

A car appeared around a bend up the road and headed toward him and it was another classic car, a big old Buick sedan. As it passed Bob waved to the driver because that's what you did, two classic car guys passing one another on a weekend cruise; you waved. The driver waved back and that was fine, until Bob recognized him. The guy driving the Buick was Mr. Pal, the manager of the Rexall drugstore on Main Street. And that wasn't at all fine because Mr. Pal had been dead for twenty years and the Rexall had been closed for even longer than that. There was some fast food place there now.

Bob looked in the rear view mirror and watched the Buick disappear around another bend in the road then he pulled over onto the shoulder to think about it. He'd just seen a dead guy tool past him in a car that had probably been junked decades ago, and even if it hadn't, who cared, a dead guy had been driving it. He tried to recall if Mr. Pal had had a son, someone who might look just like him but that didn't fly because he remembered that Mr. Pal had only had one child, a girl, and she had looked just like Mrs. Pal which had been a fortunate turn of events for her.

He dropped the Chevy into gear and pulled out, did a U-turn, and headed back toward town. If long-dead Mr. Pal was tooling around in his long-dead Buick Electra Bob wanted to see if the Rexall had also suddenly re-appeared. Or maybe on the way back to town he could catch up with the Electra and see where dead Mr. Pal was headed. He pressed down on the gas pedal and pushed the Chevy up to fifty.

He never did catch up to dead Mr. Pal but it turned out to be not all that important because as he started to get into town a whole bunch of new stuff started to happen. All the cars he saw, parked or sharing the road with him, were classic cars. He didn't see a single car that was newer than maybe 1974 but the thing was, they all looked new, or most of them did anyway. He reached the outskirts of town now and that's when things really started to get weird, not that long-dead pharmacists driving old Buicks wasn't weird enough.

Buildings started to appear on either side of the road that shouldn't be there. He had stopped at a strip mall just that morning for something or other and now in its place were three houses. Thing was he remembered those houses; a high school friend of his, Tony Swenson, had lived in one of them. Tony's family had moved away during their junior year and maybe five years later the house had been razed, along with its two neighbors to make room for that icon of modern America; a strip mall. Yet there was Tony's house, just as he remembered it, and then Tony himself, all of seventeen years old, came out the front door and Bob almost drove the Impala up onto someone's lawn. He straightened the wheel out and kept going because he didn't want to have a conversation with seventeen-year-old Tony Swenson, he honest to God didn't.

He kept driving toward the little downtown area, passing more buildings that no longer existed, trees that were smaller than he remembered them being, people on the sidewalks wearing lots of polyester, and forty-year-old cars that looked brand new. On the radio Chuck Berry had given way to Bo Donaldson and the Heywoods singing *Billy Don't Be a Hero*, a one hit wonder if ever there'd been one. He passed a gas station and thought about pulling in to fill the Chevy's enormous gas tank, hard to pass up premium at twenty-seven cents a gallon, but then he realized that they probably wouldn't take his credit cards and if they happened to notice the dates on the bills in his wallet he may find himself talking to law enforcement. He drove on.

At the center of downtown, all four blocks of it, was a little park with a statue of a civil war soldier flanked by a couple of cannons. Bob swung the Impala over to the curb and put it in park. He hesitated shutting it down because what if it wouldn't start again, did that mean he was stuck there? Finally, he turned the key and the big V8 went quiet, it would start again, the car was in great shape. And that was when he noticed the newspaper dispenser at the curb; he leaned across the seat to see the front page of the paper in the dispensers' window or more specifically, the date on the front page. It was June 15, 1975.

He looked around the little square remembering things: his mother taking him to the park to play when he was little, hanging out here with his friends in high school before any of them had driver's licenses or cars, sitting on a bench before or after seeing a movie at the little theatre that was now a paint store. The park hadn't really changed that much from what he could see; there were more benches than he remembered, it seemed cleaner, but other than that...it was the surrounding buildings that were so different. The only one he saw that was still the same in 2016 was the convenience store on one corner. Well, it was almost the same; the store he was currently looking at was family owned and run, while in 2016 it was owned and run by a national conglomerate.

Two young women came out of that store and crossed the street toward the park. They were holding sodas and bags of potato chips and were talking away, a mile a minute. Bob recognized them instantly, Diane Roby and Kathy Werner. Both had been a year ahead of him in school, he'd had a crush on Kathy until she went off to college and he never saw her again. So if the newspaper he'd just seen was real then it was 1975, just around the time he'd graduated from high school. If that was right, then Diane Roby over there had only a few months left to live because she was killed in a car accident out on County Road the year after she'd finished high school. He watched the two of them sit down on one of the benches, still chattering away and suddenly he felt very creeped out. He was watching a girl who'd been dead and in the ground these forty odd years sitting in the sun on a park bench talking to her best friend and sipping on a soda. He had the sudden urge to get out of the Chevy, walk over to them and tell Diane that whatever else she did she needed to just stay the hell off of County Road. Instead he started the car, dropped it into gear and got the hell out of there.

It just didn't feel right; the nostalgia he'd started off feeling had begun to fade when he'd seen Tony Swenson be-bopping down his front steps and it left him entirely after watching long- dead Diane

Roby sitting on a bench drinking orange soda and eating chips. He drove back out of town the way he'd come in and began cruising up and down the rural road where he'd first seen Mr. Pal and... nothing happened. Several cars passed him going in the opposite direction and all were like-new 70's models, the driver of one was an old high school teacher of his. He pulled over to the shoulder and just sat there and it occurred to him that he might be stuck there, stuck in 1975 for the rest of his life. Then The Marmalade was back on the radio singing *Reflections of My Life* and he felt the rippling sensation again and two minutes later a brand new Toyota Camry, as in a 2015 Toyota Camry, passed him heading into town. He was back.

Chapter Three

When he got home Elaine was in the back yard working on her flowers. She spent a great deal of time working on her flowers. Bob had begun to suspect that she spent so much time working on her flowers as a way to avoid being around him. That was bad enough but what was worse was that sometimes he hoped he was right. But then he would think that it was normal for two people who'd been married for so long to want their own space, it was probably even healthy. They couldn't spend every minute of the day gazing lovingly into each other's eyes, now could they?

He got a beer out of the fridge and went outside to say hi. On the way home he'd juggled the pros and cons of telling Elaine what had happened to him and as he'd swung the Impala into the driveway he'd decided that there really weren't any pros, just cons. So when he got outside he just said hi and asked how the flowers were doing even though he didn't care at all. Elaine said they were doing fine and asked how the Impala was even though Bob knew she didn't care at all how the Impala was. She'd stood back while he spent the money to buy the car and fix what needed fixing on it partly because she did want him to indulge in his passion for classic cars, but also because it gave him something to do to keep him out of her hair which just brought him back around to his original thought.

Elaine had ridden in the Impala with him a few times but he could tell it was to indulge him, that she didn't see it as anything other than a relic from a bygone era, and not a very safe one at that: no airbags, metal dashboard, steering column that would happily impale you upon impact. The first time she'd sat in it her only comment had been that you could probably play tennis on the hood it was so wide.

So he said the Impala was doing fine and left it at that because yeah, the Impala was doing fine and get this Elaine, apparently it's a goddamned time machine! Can you believe that? Pretty good deal for less than two grand, right? How'd you like to go back forty years or so and check out how dorky we looked when we went to the senior prom together?

So he sat on the patio and they chatted for a bit while she worked on her flowers and then he went inside to watch the game and it was all good.

Chapter Four

The next time it happened was the following Saturday. He took the car out for a spin and tuned the radio to the same station he had it on the previous week and for thirty minutes or so he just cruised around town, occasionally waving to people he knew. And then The Marmalade was back on the radio and the rippling sensation came, just like the last time. So he wasn't at all surprised a few moments later when a brand new 1975 Plymouth Duster passed him going in the other direction. It was painted an almost fluorescent lime green color that no car maker in 2016 would even consider putting on a car.

Once he knew that it had happened again he swung the Impala around and headed for downtown. He had an idea.

He'd realized after the last little trip that, when he got to the past, the time of day had been the same as when he'd left the present, his present anyway. He was counting on that holding true again and it did. By the time he got into town it was just coming up on 3 pm. And it was 1975 because he was assuming that the car had brought him back to the same year as his first trip. In 1975 Elaine had worked at the Rexall drug store on the square and on Saturdays her shift had been 10 am to 3 pm. So, he planned to park just down street from the Rexall and get a look at his wife when she was seventeen years old and smoking hot.

As he parked the Chevy along the curb, just down the street from the drug store in a spot that Elaine would walk right past, it occurred to him that since this was 1975, there must be an eighteen-year-old version of him around somewhere. He immediately rubbernecked around checking out the square, looking for himself. He couldn't remember many times that he'd meet Elaine when she got out of work, not many at all he thought; but what if today was one of the days he did just that? What would happen if the eighteen-year-old version of him encountered the 59-year-old version? He had no idea but he had a sneaking suspicion that it would be bad so he kept an eye on the square.

At five past three seventeen-year-old Elaine walked out of the Rexall right on schedule and she looked fantastic. Bob actually remembered the skirt and blouse she was wearing; he'd taken them off of her enough times in the back seat of his car, one too many times as it turned out. He really wasn't concerned about her recognizing him as she walked past the car because while he still looked like himself he had a fraction of the hair he had in high school, it *was* the 70's after all, and his face had forty years on it. But she didn't walk past the car; instead she turned the other way and began walking in the opposite direction. That threw him for a moment, her house was in the direction he'd parked and she would always go home right after her shift on Saturdays to do the chores her mom had set for her so she could go out with him on Saturday night. Then he thought she probably had an errand to run before she went home, no big deal. He pulled away from the curb and drove slowly to the end of the square, passing her as he did so. Then he pulled over again with the corner of the square just ahead. She could either turn left to stay in the square or keep going straight out of the square and continue down Whitman Street, the street he was currently parked on.

Turned out she did neither. When she got to the corner of the square she stopped and stood there as if she was waiting for someone. This gave Bob time to admire her legs, the same legs he'd seen this morning at home only…younger. And then something happened that was going to change his life forever, even though it was something that happened over forty years ago.

A black Plymouth 'Cuda swung in to the curb at the corner and Elaine got into it. Then the car pulled away with a chirp of tires and sped off down Whitman Street. Bob hadn't needed to see the driver; he knew who it was because that car, and that driver, had been the bane of his existence in high school. Vinny Tessler had been one of the class bullies from elementary school on up and decades before anyone even thought of zero tolerance he'd gotten away with a lot of shit. He'd actually dropped out of or flunked out of school his junior year but he hadn't gone anywhere. He was still around town terrorizing kids, either behind the school while he hung out with his shop buddies or after school right there in the park. He also always seemed to show up at parties uninvited and no one had the stones to ask him to leave. Bob's last run in with him had been toward the end of the summer before his senior year, there'd been a bunch of kids hanging out down at the lake and Vinny had shown up and started acting like an asshole. After he grabbed one of the girls by the boob Bob had said something to him, which resulted in Vinny putting Bob in a headlock and holding his head under the water until he'd almost blacked out. Tessler had finally let him up and left him lying on the beach gasping for breath while he went over to bother a newly arrived bunch of girls. When Bob had gotten his breath back he'd gotten up, walked over to the group and punched Tessler in the face as hard as he could. That was when things really went south, ending up with Bob in the ER and explaining to his parents how he'd gotten a broken nose and two broken teeth. That led to Bob's parents threatening to press charges and also sue Mr. Tessler who was divorced and the town drunk. He in turn had pointed out that Bob had swung at his son first and besides, he didn't have a pot to piss in so they were welcome to sue him to kingdom come. Then he told them to go fuck themselves and in the end they all let it slide. A few weeks later Tessler was arrested for some other stupid thing and he was gone for a few months. When he returned he acted as if Bob simply didn't exist.

So now Bob watched for a moment as the 'Cuda headed down Whitman Street before putting the Impala in gear and following. He didn't have the first clue what Elaine was doing in Vinny Tessler's car because as far as he knew they'd never said two words to one another.

They headed out of town in the opposite direction of Elaine's house or his house, or Tessler's house for that matter and after a few minutes Bob started to feel a large cold lump growing in his stomach because he began to suspect where they were going. When Tessler swung the 'Cuda off the two lane blacktop and onto a dirt access road Bob knew for sure and for a moment he thought he was going to puke. He went past the access road then pulled over and parked the Impala. He sat there in the car for a long moment and a voice inside of him was screaming at him to drive away, just drive the fuck away because whatever this was, it had happened forty-one years ago, it didn't mean shit now, and he wasn't supposed to be there to see it.

He got out of the car and walked back to the access road. He knew what was up ahead very well because he'd been there himself

13

with Elaine hundreds of times. The access road crossed a narrow grass strip by the roadside then cut in through a stand of trees to emerge at a mile long clearing that ran along the river. The kids had called it The Boulevard back in the day and it was a favorite place to go parking. Many of the instances of him removing the skirt and blouse that Elaine was currently wearing, the one's that he had just minutes ago remembered so fondly, had happened right here. In fact, they had lost their virginity to one another here, or at least he had.

When he got to the forest he left the access road and used the trees for cover. When he reached the clearing he saw the 'Cuda immediately, it was parked at the far left end, nosed in at the edge of the trees. They're not here to gaze at the river, Bob thought to himself and that made him feel like laughing and crying all at the same time.

He made his way along the edge of the forest until he was behind a large tree not twenty-five yards from the car. The 'Cuda had extremely small back side windows that offered a very narrow view into the rear seat of the car but it turned out that that didn't matter because they weren't in the car. Elaine was naked, up against the front fender and leaning forward over the hood of the car. Tessler was behind her, also naked, and he was thrusting into her with a slow steady rhythm that kept slapping the front of her thighs against the fender of the car. Two things that Bob would never forget as he turned away and staggered back through the woods, Elaine moaning with each thrust, and that Tessler's penis was the biggest one he'd ever seen, in or out of a porn movie.

He'd gotten about halfway back to the car when he had to stop. He leaned against a tree and threw up his lunch onto the forest floor. It was a lunch that Elaine had made for him in 2016, and now he was leaving it behind in the dirt in 1975. When he got to the Impala he turned on the radio and cranked the volume and started driving aimlessly. A few minutes later *Liar* by Three

Dog Night came on and that was new, the ripple came, and he was back.

Chapter Five

He didn't go right home; he wondered how he could *ever* go home. So he parked the Impala in the lot behind the mall and just sat staring through the windshield. And as he sat there something else occurred to him, something other than the fact that his entire life had been a lie. Elaine had gotten pregnant just after their senior year in high school and they'd gotten married, something they'd been planning to do eventually anyway. But it had been rushed, an accident, and they'd both had to put off college for a while but Bob never cared because it all worked out, and they ended up with a beautiful daughter they'd named Rebecca who lived in North Carolina now and had a family of her own. Was he Rebecca's father? He took out his wallet to look at a photo of his daughter he'd had for years, taken at her college graduation. She looked like Elaine; everyone had always said so. There was nothing of him in her face but now he studied the photo to see if there was anything of Tessler there. Maybe his nose, or his eyes...he snapped the wallet shut and put it back in his pocket and in that instant he hated his wife, hated her with every fiber of his being. So he sat there some more because he sure as hell couldn't go home yet.

Finally, he took out his cell phone and called home...home. Keeping his voice as normal as possible, and considering how he felt he thought he did a good job of that, he told Elaine that he'd run into some of the guys from the club and they were going to try to get in nine holes then have dinner and a few drinks, she shouldn't wait up. It wasn't something he did very often but it wasn't totally unheard of either and she sounded fine on the phone. Besides, even if she thought something was bothering him he was pretty damned sure she'd never figure out what it was. Then he wondered were Vinny Tessler was these days; maybe Elaine could give him a call and they could hook up for old times' sake. And then that made him wonder if she'd done it after they were married, not with Vinny because he disappeared from town not long after his last brush with the law but with someone else. After all, he'd had no idea about this…all these years, so how could he know she hadn't done it again with someone else. He had an impression of the ground beneath him, beneath his life, shifting and beginning to dissolve.

He drove to a gas station and filled up the Chevy's tank then drove around for hours, thinking. He didn't turn the radio on. Sometime after eleven, when he could be sure that Elaine would be in bed asleep he went home. As he lay next to her he stared at the ceiling and thought about the idea he'd finally come up with, about whether he was willing to go through with it. He decided that not only was he willing but that he needed to get started on it right away.

So he went back more times, always just before 3:00 p.m. and always on a Saturday. Five more times he went back, and on three of his trips he watched Vinny Tessler pick Elaine up in his Plymouth 'Cuda and drive to the Boulevard. They never went anywhere else, just there. Then something occurred to him and he went back earlier, in the morning, and sat across the street from Elaine's house and twice he saw her, once shaking out a rug in the back yard and once through the big picture window, vacuuming the living room. Yeah, she always did the chores her mother put out for her *after* work on Saturdays, because she liked to sleep in, unless of course she had a date after work with Vinny and his freakishly big penis.

The 'my life is over' lump in his stomach that was making him ill began to give way to the anger he'd felt that first day, and that anger began to replace all else. And he had started to wonder who else had known about this and wasn't that was a really fun new wrinkle that he couldn't get out of his head. Did her friends know, did any of his friends know? It wasn't like they had tried so hard to hide it; he was picking her up right on the street corner and dropping her off at her house when they were done. Did everyone in the entire fucking town know about it? He decided he'd seen enough and it was time for part two of his plan.

Chapter Six

He picked a weekday for his next trip; it didn't really matter what time as long as it was before 3:00 in the afternoon so he went in the morning.

Driving back to his old high school felt both surreal and routine at the same time. The school had been torn down and replaced with a new one on the same site two years after he'd graduated so it was gone not long after he'd finished there, not that he would have ever had a reason to return anyway. When he swung the Impala into the student parking lot on the left side of the building he looked around for some kind of security even though he never remembered there being any and of course there wasn't because it was 1975, the advent of school shootings was still far in the future.

His senior year in high school he had owned a beat up old Dodge Polaris, a faded blue land yacht that had gotten three miles to a gallon which only worked because gas had been 27 cents a gallon back then. He still remembered where he used to park, last row over under the trees so the car wouldn't be hot from the sun when he came out to head home. He found the Dodge right where he remembered it would be and pulled in a few spaces down from it. The parking lot was deserted, rows of cars quietly baking in the sun. He got out of his car and walked down to the Dodge, amazed at how wide the thing was. He circled around to the driver's side, took the envelope out of his pocket and placed it under the windshield wiper. Then he returned to the Impala and got out of there.

The note in the envelope was short and to the point, from a 'friend'. All it said was that his teenage self really needed to know that the love of his young life was banging Vinny Tessler like a drum and all he had to do to verify this was to watch her when she left work at the Rexall the following Saturday. Done deal.

As soon as he left the school he snapped on the radio, the third song up was *Reflections of My Life* again and he was back in the present, the new present. He drove straight home and there were two strange cars in the driveway so he parked down the street a bit and waited. He had no doubt that Elaine was living there, she'd loved that house since they were kids and when it had come on the market after they were married she'd insisted that they had to buy it, that it was her dream house. Oh yeah, she would be living there; the question was with who.

As if on cue, Elaine appeared at the head of the driveway carrying a recycle bin. As she walked to the curb to put it out he noted that she looked pretty much the same, she looked like his wife. But who else was living in the house with her, whose wife was she now? Because he was pretty sure it wasn't going to be him. Elaine got into one of the cars and drove off toward town. He followed her and for one insane moment he was worried that she'd spot him because she knew the Impala.

She drove downtown and parked in front of the bank. Just as she got out of the car a man emerged from the building to meet her and they walked off together toward the park. He parked and followed on foot. He hadn't gotten a very good look at the man she was with but he did look familiar. When they got to the corner of Whitman Street he thought, 'remember that corner Hon? That's where Vinny used to pick you up for your little river-side sex parties'.

They went into the Parkview Diner, which had been there as long as Bob could remember. He waited a few moments then walked in himself. They were seated along the wall and before he could think about it he walked right up to their table. As he approached Elaine glanced up at him and a look came over her face that he'd never seen before; recognition, sadness, dread, other things he couldn't find words for. He almost turned and walked out but he didn't because she'd seen him, so he approached the table trying to smile.

"I thought that was you," he said to the woman he'd woken up next to that morning in another world. "I just came in for a coffee and I saw you over here, thought I'd say hello." He turned to the man still smiling and he did know him, his name was Dennis Linskey, he'd been a year ahead of Bob in high school. He'd hit on Elaine a couple of times when they were all in school together and Bob had wanted to fight him but Elaine had said she'd take care of it. She had told Linskey that she was in love with her future husband so he was wasting his time. Linskey hadn't bothered her again. Or at least that's what she'd told Bob.

"Hello Dennis," Bob said, barely missing a beat. He suddenly wondered if he should even be there, in that world. Did he still live in town? Was he married? Hell, was he dead? "You guys are married huh?" Should he have already known that?

"Hello Bob," Dennis said and he was friendly enough, "How's life out on the left coast? Surprised you could bring yourself to come back to this little berg."

"Just visiting," he replied. He lived in California? He turned to Elaine and she was still looking at him that way. "Hey," he said quietly, "how have you been?"

"I've been fine," she replied "I never thought I'd see you back here again."

"Just visiting, like I said," he replied and suddenly all he wanted was to get the hell out of there. But there was one more thing he had to know. "You guys make a great couple; you have any kids?"

"We do," Dennis said and he was already reaching for his wallet, the proud father, and the picture he held up was of Rebecca and then Bob really needed to get out of there. He looked once more at the picture just to be sure then told Dennis she was beautiful and he wondered if Dennis knew. He looked at Elaine one more time and she looked like she was holding back tears so he said it was nice to see her again and then he did get the hell out of there.

He drove around to the other side of the park and pulled over to the curb. And he just sat there. In this world he had dumped Elaine after finding the note on his windshield. Had he followed her first to make sure and seen? He would have had to; he would have had to be sure before walking away from her...because they'd been in love since they were kids. And then she had hooked up with Dennis and married him. She would have had to do it fast; just the way she had done it with him since she was pregnant with Vinny Tessler's kid. Because the picture he'd just seen was of his daughter, his and Elaine's, only here it was Dennis and Elaine's. But Becky still looked the same because either way, in either world, she still had the same parents didn't she. And she'd mostly taken after her mother anyway. Did Dennis know? Maybe not, not if Elaine had hooked up with him immediately after they'd broken up, let him have her right away then told him she was pregnant. He sure as hell hadn't known, had he? But hey, it was small town America in a different time and a girl's gotta do what a girl's gotta do. Right?

They came out of the diner just then and walked back toward the bank. Apparently Elaine had lost her appetite; Dennis was carrying a doggy bag. He watched them walk to the bank then stand and talk for a few moments then Dennis kissed her and went inside. Elaine just stood there for a minute then turned and looked around the park. Bob slid down in the seat and he didn't think she saw him. Finally, she got into her car and she sat there with her head down for several minutes before she started the car and left. He watched her drive away.

He sat for a while thinking then he reached back and pulled his wallet out of his back pants pocket and opened it. His driver's license had been issued by the state of California and he lived in a town called Boonville, wherever the hell that was. He found an appointment card; apparently he had a doctor's appointment at the Anderson Valley Health Center next week, in Boonville. Next was an employee card for Donelly Creek Vineyards…it didn't say what he did there.

Was there a woman in Boonville looking for him right now? His wife? Somehow he knew there wasn't. He went through the photo sleeves in the wallet and there were no pictures of a wife, or kids, there was nothing. This morning there'd been photos of Elaine and Rebecca there. He wasn't married because he had never gotten over what happened with Elaine, was that it? He thought it could be, there was a good chance it could be. And he couldn't stop thinking about the look on her face when she'd seen him in the diner just now, after not having seen him for years. He'd never seen a look like that on anyone's face before. And the two of them, her meeting her husband for lunch, Dennis Linskey…seeing them sitting there smiling and talking just before she'd seen him. Did he want to live in Boonville and let Elaine be married to Dennis Linskey? He didn't think he did. But could he live with the alternative, could he go back and live with Elaine knowing what he knew? She already suspected something was wrong, after the past few weeks of him taking off in the Impala every weekend and barely talking to her. And what about Rebecca? She wasn't his daughter; how could he live with that?

He stared out through the windshield for a while and tried not to think about it all, tried to just feel what he was feeling. He started the Impala, put it into gear and pulled away from the curb.

Chapter Seven

As he pulled into the high school parking lot at 2:40 p.m. he remembered that school let out at 3:00 p.m. It was going to be tight and he wondered what the hell he would do if he came face to face with his eighteen-year-old self. He was cutting this too damn close, but it wasn't his fault because ironically, he'd just lost track of time.

He'd left the park and driven around for a while thinking, then driven by the house again. Elaine was back at home and he wondered what she and Dennis had planned for that night, what they'd done yesterday, what they were doing tomorrow, what they were doing for the rest of their lives. As he was doing that the memories finally started to seep in, the memories from *this* life. He remembered the confrontation with Elaine, decades old but once the memory came it cut like it had happened yesterday. He remembered deciding to leave, just days after that, not wanting to stay in town and see her, see Vinny, see anything that reminded him. And he remembered packing up his car in his parents' driveway, saying goodbye, promising to stay in touch, and as he pulled out and started down the street seeing Elaine standing on the sidewalk looking at him, calling out to him. He couldn't hear what she was saying and he didn't stop to ask; he was angry and hurt and humiliated and it was her fault. He'd glanced in his rearview mirror as he drove away and she standing there watching him go and it was the last time in this life that he'd seen her until that afternoon. His mother had told him later that after he was gone Elaine showed up at the house and when they told her about California she'd collapsed on the steps in tears.

Because she had a bun in the oven and no one to bullshit into marrying her, he thought, but he knew that wasn't true; looking back at a memory that he'd never had until today and remembering that look on her face in the diner, he knew that wasn't true.

And it started to scare him because as the new memories came he began to lose the memories of what he still thought of as his real life. He started to forget about being married to Elaine, the vacations they'd taken, the challenges they'd faced together and overcome together, how good a partner she's always been, that they were best friends. He began to think about this being his life now and to wonder just what the hell he'd done.

So he turned the radio on and he drove around for what seemed like forever and the song didn't come, a lot of other golden oldies but not the one he needed and he began to think that the car was done, that it was wasn't going to take him anywhere anymore because he'd messed around with things too much. And then finally *Reflections of My Life* was playing and he was back in 1975 again.

And now he was cutting this too damn close. He swung the Impala into a space three down from the Polaris and he remembered that Elaine used to call it the blue whale. As he opened the Impala's door he heard the class bell go off inside the school, but no one was coming out of the school yet, he still had time. He walked quickly toward the Dodge and the doors to the school flew open, disgorging kids into the sunshine. At the same time several cars pulled into the parking lot and passed him on their way to pick up students. The last one stopped beside him and the driver rolled down his window. Bob looked and knew him immediately, he was a friend of Bob's father, had been at the house all the time when Bob was a kid. His name was Walter Marin. He was probably there to pick up his daughter Joy who'd been a freshman in 1975.

"Good afternoon," Walter said, a slight frown on his face. "Forgive me but do we know one another; I feel like we do but I can't place from where."

"I don't think so,' Bob said and tried to smile, "I just have one of those faces, happens to me a lot."

"You don't live in town do you? Again, I don't mean to pry but you just look so familiar."

"I don't," Bob said, he glanced up at the school and there he was, walking across the parking lot toward them. He was wearing his letter jacket for baseball that he'd given to Elaine and that was still hanging in a closet at home. She wore it sometimes when she was gardening, she refused to throw it away and he suddenly felt, standing there, that he was losing his grip on reality. Walter Marin was saying something else and Bob looked down at him again.

"I'm sorry?"

"I asked if you were from town, but you're not because it's a small town and I'd know you. You must be related to someone I know though; do you have family here?"

"I don't actually, I was just inside interviewing for a teaching position. I'm from Chicago. I'm trying to get out of the lot before the kids get in their cars, be backed up for ten minutes once they do."

"Of course, and you're right, it will be, my apologies." He put his car into drive and smiled at Bob, "Have a nice day and good luck with the job." He pulled away and Bob waited until he turned up one of the lanes toward the school before almost sprinting for the Polaris. His young self was only a few rows over now, and Bob realized he wasn't going to be able to reach the Dodge and take the note off the windshield without being seen. He moved to the front of the cars, onto the grass under the trees and sped up. He reached the front of the Polaris just as his young self reached the last lane, the lane the Dodge was parked in. He was going to see Bob take the damn note off the windshield; no way he couldn't at that distance. And then he got a break of cosmic proportions, a girl who'd already gotten her car stopped in the lane and young Bob stopped to talk to her. Bob could only see the back of her head but he thought he remembered the car, it was Laney McLaughlin and they'd been friends since first grade. Laney had gotten married and moved to Boston a few years out of school.

He got around to the driver's side and the note was still there, under the wiper where he'd left it. He snatched it and hurried back for the Impala just as a squeal of tires signaled Laney's departure, she always had driven like a maniac. He glanced back at himself just once more then got into the Impala and just sat there until the lot had emptied out and his heart had stopped racing. Then he pulled out of his old high school parking lot for the last time, forty years after he'd pulled out of his high school parking lot for the last time...the first time. As he turned onto Franklin Street he snapped the radio on and waited for the song.

Chapter Eight

He didn't go right home, he stopped and sat for a while in the mall parking lot, thinking and wondering what the hell he was going to do. After a while he got out, went into the mall and walked around a bit...he didn't want to be in the Chevy anymore.

He had to go home, sooner or later, and he had no idea what he was going to do. When he finally did go home, to *their* home, Elaine was out back working in the garden. He stood in a window for a while just watching her, she didn't know he was there. Then finally he went outside and said hi then sat down in a chair on the patio. She turned and looked over her shoulder at him.

"No beer? That's not like you, one in the afternoon, always."

"I'm watching my girlish figure," he replied and the joke fell flat, just laid there between them, dead on arrival. She studied his face for a moment then got up and went into the house. She came back a moment later with two beers, handed one to him then sat down in one of the other patio chairs.

The image of her bent over the hood of Vinny Tessler's 'Cuda was suddenly in his head and he pushed it down hard. That had been a lifetime ago...hadn't it? Then he remembered the look on her face in the diner again, that look that he still couldn't find words to describe. That had been just this afternoon, in another world but just this afternoon...hadn't it? In that other world was she sitting here with Dennis Linskey right now? Did her garden look the same?

"What's wrong Bob?" she said finally. "Something is, this past month you've barely said ten words to me."

He had thought about this sitting in the car, and walking the mall, and driving home, and he hadn't been able to decide anything. His choices, as he saw them, were to tell her what he knew and then just leave, and keep going. In a way he'd already done that once before, hadn't he. But if he was going to do that why didn't he just stay in that other place, where he had a life already somewhere else. Would the memories of this life eventually simply fade away? He thought so and that felt just as bad as any of the rest of this did. Or he could tell her what he knew and ask her why, because he really wanted to know that, he really did want to know why.

And then there was the question of time, how much time could pass before something like this didn't mean as much anymore, or did that ever happen? And he had to keep reminding himself that for him this had just happened, but for Elaine it was forty years ago. Forty years that she'd spent with him building a life together. And that led to the question that he most needed an answer to, even more than why; was she with him because Vinny had rejected her and she needed a father for her baby? He had trouble believing that because their marriage had been a good one and he thought he knew his wife. Then again, considering recent events, maybe he didn't know her at all.

"I'm thinking about leaving," he told her abruptly before he could think about it.

"What, what do you mean?" she wasn't particularly concerned yet because she wasn't sure what he was saying.

"Don't ask me how, but I know about you and Vinny Tessler, all of it. And I know that Rebecca is his daughter. So I'm thinking about leaving."

She definitely got it now, and she looked like someone had just punched her in the stomach. She actually jolted back in her chair and for a moment he was afraid she was going to faint, or have a heart attack. Then abruptly she got up, turned her back to him and faced her flowers.

"Do you care if I leave?"

"How can you even ask that?" she said.

"Because I'm not sure of anything anymore Elaine, that's how."

"How long have you known."

"A few weeks."

"Who told you, it had to be Vinny because no one else knows."

"I haven't seen Vinny Tessler in forty years. Apparently you two weren't very concerned about being seen, he would pick you up right by the park, and the Boulevard in broad daylight?"

She wrapped her arms around herself, "So who then? Who do I have to thank for this after all these years?"

"I think you've got things backwards Elaine; you have yourself to thank for it because no one would have been able to tell me if you'd never done it." He stood up too. "I want to know why Elaine, for God's sake why? And I want to know if you married me because he wouldn't and you needed a father for his daughter."

She turned to face him and she had a blank, shocked look on her face that scared him a little, "I wouldn't have married Vinny Tessler if he got down on his knees and begged me."

"Really, because apparently you had no trouble going down to the boulevard with him and fucking like rabbits whenever he wanted to."

That made her recoil a bit but she held eye contact with him. "I was seventeen and I was stupid and I thought it was glamorous that the town bad boy wanted me. I wondered what it would be like with someone else because I'd never been with anyone but you. I was a fool and after the first time I didn't want to anymore but he said he'd tell you all about us so I'd better keep letting him so I did because I was just a kid and I didn't know what else to do and I was terrified that you'd find out and I would lose you. I know you probably think that makes no sense but that was how I felt. And he wouldn't use protection and when I told him I thought I was pregnant he said it had to be yours, not his, and he never came near me again. And all these years I've thanked God every day that you never knew, that I was lucky enough to get past it without you finding out, and that I was lucky enough to still have you. I've been thankful of that every day of my life Bob. And Rebecca is your daughter, you're the first person she saw when she opened her eyes and you raised her and she's everything she is today because of you. No matter what happens with us here today you have to know that. Don't make her pay for my mistake. You're her father and she doesn't ever need to know anything else. You've been the best father she could have ever had and the best husband I could have ever had, even if I've never deserved it.

"So the past forty years, they haven't been a lie?"

"Would I have stayed with you if they had been? I could have provided for Becky myself. I'm here because I love you and I always have, since the day I met you. Just think back about our life together, you must see that."

Bob sat back down in the chair and lowered his head. He reminded himself again that it was forty years ago for her, she doesn't know about the car, that damned car.

"I wish I knew how to say how sorry I am for this," Elaine said softly, "I've lived with it all these years, lived with the fear that you'd find out. I wish I knew how to make it so it didn't happen because I wish it never had. But it did give us Becky; she's something good that came of it at least. Please see it that way Bob, and see that we belong together, we always have."

He looked up at her, "I need a little time with this," he told her. "You've had forty years to put this behind you but for me it just happened."

"Just don't leave," she said and her voice hitched a little.

"Is there anything else I don't know, any other secrets? If there are I can't imagine them being bigger than this one."

"There are no other secrets, not one, and there never will be. You've always been honest with me and I swear I'll always be honest with you."

"That's not exactly true," he said, deciding, "you're right, we shouldn't have any secrets, so there's something I have to tell you." He looked up at her, "It's about the car".

Epilog

Bob was standing in his driveway talking to a guy named Stanley. Stanley was a car guy and he was looking at the Impala like he'd just hit the lottery.

"She's in terrific shape," Bob was telling him, "you won't find a better '66 anywhere."

"I can see that," Stanley said, "So, everything works?"

"Everything except the radio," Bob said, putting a hint of regret into his voice. "I'm afraid the radio is shot, totally fried."

"Well that's no big deal," Stanley replied, "I'll just get a new one."

"Yeah," Bob agreed, "I think that would be your best bet."

20 minutes later he stood at the end of his driveway and watched as the Impala disappeared down the street with Stanley, the car guy, at the wheel as its proud new owner. And that was that. He turned and started up the driveway toward the house, his and Elaine's house.

A few weeks before, about the same time he'd listed the Impala on line, he'd did a little Internet search for Dennis Linskey. Turned out Dennis lived a couple of thousand miles away in California so, no worries there.

REVENGE IS A DISH BEST SERVED COLD

One

Brian Howe, Howie to his friends and he was friends with just about everyone, had been running Emersus Laboratories for more than ten years. Science in general, and the lab in particular, was his life. He'd never married or had children; he hadn't even taken a vacation in over six years. He held PHD's in Biophysics and Neuroscience and his sincere goal in life, as corny as it may sound when he told people, was to help mankind.

Emersus was a research laboratory and while it was privately owned and wasn't a non-profit, its mission statement was to move medical science forward through research with the goal of improving quality of life for one and all. It was something that the majority of the eighty-seven employees at the lab took seriously. That they'd had six drugs make it through to FDA approval in the past five years provided strong motivation for them to continue their good work. And if those drugs brought in a healthy profit in the process then that was just the icing on the cake. Emersus did not suffer from a lack of funding and since it was mostly self-generated, everyone was happy. On the rare occasion that a position became available at the lab Howie was flooded with resumes from some of the best research scientists in the world.

⇒+ +⇐

"It looks like we may have a spot opening up in neuro soon," Jean Happ told Howie as they walked down to the cafeteria. Jean Happ was Howie's executive assistant.

"Really, why, I thought everyone was happy down there."

"They're deliriously happy," Jean replied, "Maisie Cooper is expecting again, it's her third and I think she's going to decide to be a stay at home mom."

"Well that's unfortunate," Howie said, "Maisie is a top notch researcher. I hate to lose her."

"We can't stop people from procreating," Jean pointed out.

"That is true," Howie agreed.

"Word is already getting out, I've received seven resumes just this morning and we haven't even posted the position yet."

"I want that Dutch guy, the one who was here last year and has been sending emails ever since. He would be a perfect fit."

"Alard Van Dijk," Jean said.

"That's him, let's give him a call."

"Do you want to post the position and see who else may be interested?"

"I don't know," Howie said, "why don't we see if Alard is interested first. I'd hate to interview a whole bunch of people and then have to tell them someone else got the job, it makes me feel bad. I always end up wishing I could hire all of them."

"All right," Jean smiled a bit, "I'll get in touch with him and see if he wants to sit for an interview."

They reached the company cafeteria and began greeting employees. Every Friday afternoon during the summer months the lab put on a catered BBQ for the staff. It had been Howie's idea when he'd first come on board as a way to end the week and kick off the weekend on a fun note. It was very popular and always well attended and many employees would linger in the cafeteria socializing well past one o'clock. That was something that had almost never happened before the BBQ's began and was exactly the result Howie had been hoping for. Research scientists tended to be solitary creatures, focused on their work and shut up in their labs. Getting them to talk and share ideas and compare notes was always a good thing. It also made for a happier, friendlier and more productive work force which didn't hurt either. Howie wanted Emersus to be a place that people looked forward to coming to every day. He would have been gratified to know that almost all the employees did just that...almost.

"Oh my," Jean said, "it appears that the dragon lady has deigned to grace us with her presence. That *is* unusual."

Howie looked over at the corner of the cafeteria that Jean was nodding to and smiled when he saw Marjory Root, one of his senior research scientists, sitting at a table. "Well it's definitely progress that she's here," he commented. "I think it's a first. And stop calling her that because someday you will slip and say it in her presence."

"I try never ever to *be* in her presence, and definitely never alone," Jean told him and he laughed.

Two

Marjory Root was not a pleasant person. She was not a nice person. She was tall, thin as a rail and of extremely stern countenance. And while one or two of her braver co-workers may at times consider asking her how much she charged to haunt a house not one of them would ever dream of calling her Margi. Like Jean Happ they mostly just tried to stay away from her.

Marjory Root was an extremely gifted research scientist though, and her career may have reached great heights on the strength of that talent were it not for a few inconvenient character traits. Marjory did not take instruction well and she accepted constructive criticism not at all. She held PHD's in biomedical sciences and neuroscience. She was one of the few people on site, other than the director, who held two PHD's, something she seldom let her co-workers forget. Marjorie was always right, even when proven wrong and, when she lay her head upon her pillow at night she slept the blissful sleep of the self-righteous.

On that particular Friday afternoon, she had descended from her lab in a rear corner of the top floor not because she craved BBQ, or wanted to bond with her fellow scientists, or because she cared what people said all the other times that she didn't show up. She was in the cafeteria for the sole purpose of buttonholing Victor Frobel. Victor was the director of facilities at Emersus and while his title made him sound like the guy who oversaw the cleaning staff he was actually more a director of operations, a job that included control of equipment supply. That meant that if you wanted pretty much anything of note for your lab Victor was the one to talk to. Marjory Root had a long list of things she wanted for her lab, all of them of note as far as she was concerned, and she was accustomed to getting what she wanted.

Victor had made the mistake of sitting down at an empty table after getting his lunch, giving Marjory a perfect opportunity at buttonholing. He hadn't even started eating when she slid into the chair across from him, folded her hands and gave him the baleful stare that she was known for, the one that made those brave employees consider asking her that question about haunted houses.

"You're not eating?" Victor asked her, looking down at her empty hands.

"I do not eat carbonized animal flesh." Marjory informed him. "What you have on your plate will probably kill you before we complete this conversation."

"Fingers crossed," Victor replied.

"I ordered the new equipment for my lab months ago Mr. Frobel," Marjory said. "When can I expect it to arrive?"

"Never Ms. Root, you can expect it to arrive never. I've told you time and again that this company is not purchasing an 8 petaflop computer for your personal use. I don't even know why you need one. What is it that you're working on that requires that much power?"

"That is really not your concern, is it?" Marjory told him, "I require it, that is all you need to concern yourself with. And I grow weary of asking."

"Then I suggest you speak with Howie about it, which I believe is what I've told you the last three times we've had this conversation, because unless he OK's it I'm not going to purchase a piece of equipment that expensive for your exclusive use. And I'm quite sure he will not OK it."

"Do you feel a glowing sense of contentment each night when you take your pedestrian mind home to your pedestrian wife and regale her with tales of how you've once again thwarted your intellectual betters in their quest to improve the world in which you both exist?"

"It's what I live for Ms. Root," Victor replied.

With that Marjory got up and stormed off across the dining room, bumping into several co-workers before reaching the exit. Victor sat and thought about it for a moment before he turned in his chair and started looking around the room for Howie.

Three

The following Monday morning Howie sent an email to an employee named Josie Miller asking her to come by his office as soon as she had the time. Josie Miller had been Margaret Root's lab assistant until Ms. Root had driven her from the lab in tears and then stormed into Howie's office insisting that he fire her immediately for being impertinent, insubordinate and an imbecile. Instead Howie had assigned Josie to another lab where she was now flourishing.

Josie entered his office with a scared rabbit look on her face and he smiled and asked her to sit down.

"You're not in any trouble Josie, please relax. I just wanted to ask you a few questions about your time working with Ms. Root."

Josie did sit down and did look a little better but not by much… invoking Ms. Root's name tended to have an adverse effect on people.

"I did the best I could for her," Josie blurted out before he could ask a question, "I honestly did Mr. Howe, but she was always screaming at me, and sometimes she would throw things at me, mostly pens and pencils but once it was a beaker that hit me in the shoulder and left a bruise."

"That's terrible Josie, why didn't you tell someone about that? We can't have that sort of thing going on here."

"She said that all she had to do was tell you to fire me and you would, she said that…" Josie stopped and looked down at the floor.

"What did she say Josie?"

"I'd rather not tell you."

"It's all right, you can tell me anything. I'm well aware that Mr. Root can be a bit acerbic at times."

"She said that you were a weak and ineffectual boss and you would do anything she told you to do, including firing me."

Howie could actually feel his face turning red. He shuffled a few pieces of paper on his desk while Josie continued to look at the floor.

"You're not though," she said finally, "you're a great boss, everyone else says so all the time. And she was wrong about you firing me because I'm still here." Josie glanced up at him, "She asked you to though, didn't she."

"That doesn't matter," Howie smiled at her, "Ms. Root doesn't run this company and in any event, you've been doing very well in your new position so she was obviously wrong about you as well, wasn't she."

Josie nodded but didn't say anything.

"I'd like you to tell me what she was working on," Howie went on, "what type of research, exactly, she was focused on when you were up there."

Josie looked up at him and the frightened expression had returned to her face. "Will she know I told you?"

"She will not, I promise your name will never come into it. She's working on something up there she shouldn't be…isn't she."

Josie nodded again.

"Is she working on digital emulation, is that what she's doing?"

Josie shook her head, "She was for a while but she decided that it wouldn't work, or that it wasn't exactly what she wanted."

"I don't suppose she ever mentioned that I had forbidden her from continuing down that path, did she?" Howie asked.

Josie shook her head again.

"So what has she moved on to then?"

"I can't say for sure because that was about the time that I left. She said that digital emulation wasn't good enough and I asked her why anyone would want to do that anyway. I thought I was agreeing with her but she started screaming at me and throwing things at me. Then she came down here to see you."

"So you don't know what she intended to move on to then?"

Josie hesitated for a moment, "I don't know if I should say Mr. Howe because she hadn't actually started the research when I left, she'd only talked about it."

"So what did she talk about? I think I know Josie because it's the next logical step after moving on from digital emulation, if you can actually call that line of reasoning logical, but I need to hear you say it."

"She'd said once that the only right way to do it was to keep a person's actual brain alive after they'd died. That it would be better, and even easier, than trying to transfer their consciousness to a machine by digital emulation. She said that you'd have to reproduce the brain's biochemical reactions artificially but you should be able to do that with electrical impulses...actually she said it more than once."

Howie closed his eyes for a moment and shook his head. He could feel his face turning red again but for a different reason now; he was angry, an emotion that he didn't experience often and didn't like. "Have you told anyone else about this?" he asked Josie.

The girl shook her head and managed to look even more miserable. "I was afraid to Mr. Howe, after she threatened me. And I thought she was just kind of thinking out loud, you know? I mean no one would actually try to do that, would they? That's like something out of a bad horror movie. Even she wouldn't actually try to do it."

"I'm sure not," Howie told her reassuringly. "I'm sure she was simply thinking out loud, just as you said. But I want you to continue to keep this to yourself just the same. Can you do that?"

Josie nodded her head eagerly and a few moments later when Howie wrapped up their conversation she practically flew out of his office, through Jean's office and into the hallway.

He knew that Marjory always worked late...and often came in on weekends. She had no family, no kids, had never married, so she had no pressing business to go home to. He was similarly unencumbered in his life and had often worked late himself, although he did so much less frequently now than he once had. Her work habits did explain how she could sit up there in her private lab after everyone had gone and conduct the very research that he had expressly forbidden her from conducting.

So he waited her out. After Jean left for the night and the building emptied he stayed, using the time to catch up on some paperwork, and when he'd exhausted that option, watching videos on YouTube. Finally, a little after 10:00 p.m. he heard an engine start up in front of the building, crossed to his window and looked down to see her car leaving the lot. He waited several minutes to ensure that she hadn't forgotten something and was going to return and when he was sure, he retrieved a master keycard from a locked desk drawer and left his office.

Four

Howie waited until the following Friday afternoon, getting his ducks in a row and preparing himself for what was sure to be a very contentious meeting. He told himself he needed the time to prepare and that was part of it, but another part may have been that he just wanted to put it off for as long as possible.

Marjory Root was in her lab on the top floor, rear corner, working on the project that was not only unauthorized but one that she had been explicitly told not to pursue...more than once. But of course Marjory knew best, she always did; what she was working on would allow the human race to leap ahead hundreds of years in its development. And that was just one of the incredible things it would do. It would also make her very rich and very famous, Nobel Prize famous. And when that happened everyone who had ever derided her work, and everyone who had ever passed her in the halls and averted their eyes, well then they could all just eat it.

She was actually much further along than Howie would ever have guessed because she had been staying late, very late, and coming in early and on weekends. She had pretty much reached the point that she would normally start doing trials to see if her theories were valid, if the methodology held up. The problem was that she was working on a non-sanctioned project, a big one. Another problem was that she didn't have any test subjects to conduct trials on and wasn't likely to get any, not in any first world country anyway. She was sitting in her lab thinking about this problem and how she would surmount it because no problem was insurmountable, when her phone buzzed. She looked at the screen, saw Brian Howe's name and snorted derisively as she let it go to voicemail. She did the same thing the next three times it rang. But then it occurred to her that if he was that insistent he may just decide to come up to her lab to talk to her in person so she picked up the phone and punched in his extension.

"You were looking for me?" she said drily when Howie picked up… I'm extremely busy Brian, I'm sure this can wait until a more convenient time…All right, there's no need for you to come up here, I'll come down there but I will warn you, I can only give you a few minutes of my time." She hung up without waiting for an answer, got up and left her office.

Jean had already left for the day so she stormed right into Howie's office. Howie was seated at his desk looking grim, he was alone. Marjory stomped across his office and sat down in one of the two wing backed chairs facing his desk.

"I really do hope this is important because my work is at a crucial stage right now," she said tightly.

"Would that be your work with digital emulation," Howie asked her, "or have you already moved on to trying to preserve a brain in a sentient state?"

She simply sat and looked at him for a moment before her lips curled up into a slight smile. Howie wasn't sure what he'd expected as a reaction from her but a smile certainly wasn't one of the contenders.

"Whom have you been listening to," she asked him, "That half-witted dolt they gave me as a lab assistant. I wonder that that girl can find this building each morning. I am surprised that you would listen to anything she had to say about anything."

"I went to your lab last Friday night after you'd gone home for the evening," Howie replied, "and I saw for myself what you're working on."

Margery sat and looked at him for another moment only this time she wasn't smiling; this time her face was slowly turning to stone right in front of him. *This* was definitely on the list of reactions he'd been expecting.

"How dare you," she said finally in a quiet voice that really creeped him out. "How dare you sneak into my lab and snoop through my research. I doubt you actually understood most of it but that's moot, you have no right to look at my work without my permission which I most certainly did not give!"

"Of course I do," Hugh replied wearily, "as director of this facility I have the right to do just that at my discretion. It's in your contract Marjory, perhaps you should read it."

"I DON'T HAVE TO READ MY FUCKING CONTRACT!" and suddenly she was shrieking at him, spittle flying from her mouth. The instant change in demeanor settled any doubts he'd had going into this meeting, settled them for good and all.

"I've spoken to you about this numerous times," Howie said calmly. "You've blatantly ignored both my directives and the policies of this organization, multiple times on multiple levels."

"I'm doing research that will change the world we live in, and that will make this company famous in the process," Marjory said to him. She was no longer yelling, now she was effecting a tone one would use speaking to a five-year-old. "I don't for a moment expect you to understand that but I do expect you to stay out of the way, shuffle your papers, and allow those of us with vision to move forward."

"The data shows that only roughly one percent of the population would be interested in preserving their consciousness after death," Howie said, "I checked."

"The one percent who are worth saving no doubt," Marjory replied, "and once it becomes a viable option that number will increase tenfold."

"I'm not going to debate the ethics or viability of it with you," Howie said, sorry that he himself had taken the conversation down that road. Now he just wanted to end it. "In fact I see no reason to continue this conversation at all. You've violated your contract by conducting prohibited and highly questionable research after being warned on numerous occasions. I'm afraid you've left me no choice but to terminate your employment with this organization."

"You can't do that; you don't have the authority!"

"Actually I do and I have done it. You were warned repeatedly Marjory, and yet you continued on. You've left me no other choice here."

"I'm the only decent research scientist you have! Compared to me the rest of your employees are knuckle dragging Neanderthals and you know it."

"I know no such thing but sadly I'm not surprised to hear that that's how you perceive your co-workers. That's neither here nor there however, I will give you some time to clear out any personal effects from your lab and then I would ask that you leave your access badge on Joan's desk and kindly exit the building. You can come back in on Monday and meet with HR to complete the necessary paperwork." He stood up from his desk.

Marjory continued to sit in her chair and glare at him, "I intend to take this up with the board on Monday," she informed him, "this will not stand. My work is far too important to be stopped by a paper pushing cretin like you. When was the last time you even attempted to conduct research…Howie?"

"You may take it up with whomever you like," he replied, "though I doubt anyone on the board will listen after hearing what you've been doing. To be blunt here no one on the board likes you Marjory, some of them don't like you a lot."

"I will speak with them on Monday and we shall see."

"You can speak with anyone you like on Monday but right now you're going to go upstairs, collect your things, and then you're going to leave this building. I will give you thirty minutes and then I will be forced to call building security to escort you from the premises."

She stood up abruptly, looked at him for a moment then turned and left the office. He'd thought she would slam the outer office door…for effect…but she didn't, she closed it so softly that he barely heard it at all. He sat back down at his desk and stared at the wall. His hands were shaking.

An hour later he was still sitting at his desk, going through the motions of doing paperwork but really just waiting. His hands had stopped shaking. Finally, he stood up and walked to the windows to check the parking lot. The only two cars in the lot were his and Marjory Root's. He swore under his breath and started for the door. He'd always hated confrontation and really hated firing people but now he was just angry at the woman for forcing him to have to deal with this.

Marjory's lab was at the far end of the corridor on the sixth floor and as Howie got off the elevator and turned that way he could see that the door was standing open and the lights were on. She was going to force him to drag this out as long as possible and why was he even a bit surprised at that, because it was just who she was. He had to admit that it would be a rather large relief just to have her out of there and off of his staff. It would be like a breath of fresh air, a whole lot of breaths of fresh air actually.

He stepped into the lab and she was standing there facing the door, waiting for him because she must have heard the elevator doors.

"You're timing is impeccable," Marjory said to him and smiled, "I'm just about ready for you." She stepped forward and before he could react she plunged a hypodermic needle deep into the side of his neck and depressed the plunger.

Part Two

One

Brian Howe still knew that he was Brian Howe and he was aware of where he was and how he had gotten there. But there wasn't much more than that...other than the passage of time.

Two

Emersus Laboratory had moved twice to larger facilities and currently occupied a building outside the city in an industrial park. Employees at other companies in the park had very little if any idea of what actually went on at Emersus. And while they sometimes speculated about what type of research might be going on right next door to them none would have ever guessed what the real company secret was. Even many of the people who actually worked at Emersus didn't know a lot about what was on the top floor and those few older employees who did generally kept their mouths shut.

━╋ ╋━

"How long has the company occupied this building?" Claire Cooper asked.

"Just two years, I'm afraid we're already outgrowing it though," Douglas Stanfield replied.

It was Claire's second day as the new director of Emersus Laboratories; Doug Stanfield was the Chief Science Officer and had been acting as her guide as she began her assimilation. They were making small talk about office space because they were on their way to the top floor and the longer they talked about office space the longer they could put off discussing what was on the top floor. When they got on the elevator and it was empty Claire decided she might as well stop avoiding it so she broached the subject first.

"All right," she sighed, "I think I know the basics but why don't you tell me the story, from the beginning. He was the Director here ten years ago?"

"He held the position for almost ten years; it's been eighteen years since the incident."

She gave him a moment because it was obvious he found the subject distasteful but when he didn't continue she waved her hand a little to urge him to keep going. It was a gesture of hers that he would come to know well.

"There was a research scientist here named Marjory Root, she'd been here before Howe came in as Director, all told she worked here for thirteen years."

"Did you know her?"

"I didn't, I started not long after this all happened. There are a number of employees still here that did though, who knew both Marjory and Howe. I'm told they used to call him Howie."

"We should probably touch base with those people at some point," Claire said then motioned him to continue.

"Ms. Root became interested in digital emulation, the preservation of human consciousness in an artificial medium, a computer."

"I know what it is," Claire said, "I also know that it's illegal."

"Yes well, it wasn't at the time, primarily because no one had thought it possible. Ms. Root eventually came to pretty much the same conclusion so she moved on to the next step, keeping a human brain alive and sentient after a person's death. That is also illegal now by the way and this incident had a lot to do with it becoming so."

"And Howe discovered what she was doing."

"He did, first about the digital emulation which he forbade her from pursuing, several times in fact. We still have the paperwork on that by the way. And then he apparently found out that she had moved on to the second part of it. It doesn't appear that he had any idea just how far she'd progressed though."

"Or that she was insane," Claire added.

"Or that, right. When he confronted her about her activities and terminated her employment he seriously misjudged the situation, he seriously misjudged her. He terminated her late on a Friday afternoon after everyone else had gone home, and he gave her time to go back to her lab to pack up her personal belongings. When she didn't leave he went looking for her."

"And he found her," Claire interjected, "to his lasting dismay I would imagine."

"She drugged him and dragged him into her lab," Doug continued, "Then she removed his brain while he was alive and installed it in a support chamber that she had already constructed for that very purpose. He'd presented her with a specimen at the exact time she was ready to accept one and maintain it."

"Christ," Claire said under her breath.

The elevator doors slid open and they stepped out onto the top floor. There was just one lab up here, the rest of the floor was utilized for storage and records retention. Doug turned right down the hallway and Claire followed.

"She tried to bluff her way through it," he continued as they walked. "She said he'd suffered a massive coronary while they were talking. The drug she'd used to incapacitate him actually did induce one so that jived. She'd also forged a release document she claimed Howe had given her stating that if he died she had permission to try to keep his brain alive until a cure for whatever killed him was found. Of course no one in the organization at the time bought her story for a moment. They all knew what Howe's opinion of Root really was and that he would never do such a thing. Howe's assistant, and a lab intern, both testified that Howe had found out about her research just that week and was livid about it. Ms. Root was arrested and the DA decided to charge her with manslaughter. Her attorney argued that she couldn't be guilty of manslaughter because, technically, Howe wasn't dead. They finally ended up charging her with a slew of other felonies, all of which she was found guilty of in a jury trial."

"And only served six years," Claire interjected, "I couldn't believe it when I read that."

"Yes, and in a minimum security facility. But her career was finished. She went to South America for a while but for all intents and purposes she was done. I heard that she eventually moved back here."

"Where is she now?"

"No idea and I suspect no one here is particularly interested in finding out." They had reached the lab door a moment earlier and stopped to talk. Now Stanfield unlocked the door and they entered.

It was a small room, not more than twelve by twelve feet square with equipment along the right hand wall and a work station along the left. At the rear center of the room, almost as if it was on display, was a lab table on top of which sat a life support system of sorts. The main component was a large stainless steel box. There was a half dozen wires and tubes protruding from the box and snaking off in different directions to connect to various equipment around the room. The box was solid so there was no way to see what it contained. Claire considered that a blessing.

The lab tech sitting at the work station had stood up and faced them as they'd entered the room. Claire was surprised to see that he was older, late middle age probably. It didn't seem like a job for a senior person.

"This is Harvey Crane," Stanfield said to Claire, "he's technically retired from Emersus but he still pulls shifts here every week." Crane smiled and held out his hand which Claire shook.

"How long have you worked here Mr. Crane," Claire asked.

"Just about forty years now ma'am," he replied.

"Then you must have known Mr. Howe."

"I did, I knew Howie well. He was a great boss and a good man."

"He's still a good man," Claire said.

"Yes, yes I suppose he is." They all turned to look at the box on top of the table.

Three

They'd moved down to a conference room on the second floor and been joined by a number of other Emersus employees as well as several people from outside the company.

One of those was Daniel Simmons, the laboratories chief legal counsel. Two others were doctors from the local hospital, Mark Welby was chief surgeon at the hospital and a renowned neurologist. Eustace Killian was also a neurologist in addition to being a transplant specialist.

"Legally we're covered," Simmons told them. "We've obtained the necessary permissions from the pertinent regulating bodies, there is no next of kin to consult. Mr. Howe has basically been a ward of this company for the past eighteen years which has made things a good deal easier. So there's nothing stopping us, at least from a legal standpoint."

"And what if it goes wrong and he ends up in a vegetative state or something similar?"

Stanfield asked.

"I don't see how that would be much different than the present circumstances," Simmons replied, "the logistics of supporting him would change, that's all."

"Let's talk about that again," Claire said turning to the man sitting to her left. "How sure are we that there's still anything there to recover?"

"There is solid brain activity, there has been for the past eighteen years," Marcus Gray replied. Gray was the laboratories senior scientist and a member of the board of directors. He was also an MD. "He is actually conscious," Gray said, "after a fashion."

"Well that begs another question then," Stanfield said. "If he's been conscious in that state for the past eighteen years, being able to think but with absolutely no sensory input at all, how can we know that if we bring him back he won't be anything more than a raving lunatic?

And if that's a real possibility, should we do it at all?"

"His brain activity doesn't seem to support that," Gray replied, "but of course there's no way to be absolutely sure until it's done."

"In your opinion what are the chances we'll get back a viable human being?" Claire asked him.

"Possibly no better than fifty-fifty," Gray said, 'but that's not the real question here, at least I don't think it is."

"What is the real question?" Claire asked him.

"This man suffered a fate more horrible than I think any of us can really imagine," Grey said, "a fate that he didn't deserve, brought about by an employee of this company. I think the real question is how can we *not* do this; how can we not at least give this man a chance to get his life back if it is within our ability to do so. I think at the very least we owe him the effort."

"We'd be achieving an incredible medical breakthrough as well," Stanfield said, "Let's not forget that."

"The process is still illegal," Claire pointed out to him, "despite our obtaining permission to perform it. So it will serve no useful purpose to science or to medicine other than us proving it can be done."

"Mr. Howe would likely disagree with you on that," Gray said to her. "I'm afraid I will have to as well. The useful purpose here, as I see it, is making Mr. Howe whole again. This is a rescue mission as far as I'm concerned."

Claire turned to the two doctors and raised her eyebrows. "What I've seen from the data suggests that we have solid, positive brain function," Mark Welby said. "EM imaging didn't indicate any damage to the synaptic or nuclear structures. The electrical feeds that have served as replacements for his biochemical impulses have never been interrupted and appear to be substituting nicely. Lastly, there are just no indicators present to suggest that Mr. Howe is suffering from any form of abnormal brain activity. Of course as Doctor Gray has stated, we will never be sure until he can tell us for himself. From a medical standpoint there is a good chance of success; Doctor Killian and I are both of that opinion. We believe it's within the margin of an acceptable risk."

"What if he dies," Claire asked simply.

"Would that be any worse then what he's going through now?" Gray asked her. "Any worse than his consciousness being trapped in that steel box upstairs for the next thirty or forty years? If this weren't a viable option, my suggestion would be to terminate his support systems and legalities be damned."

"I take your point," Claire replied, "and I happen to agree. I just want to be sure that we've look at this from every side." She turned back to Doctor Welby, "I understand that you already have a donor ready for the procedure," she said.

"We do, he's a twenty-nine-year-old male, unmarried, no immediate family and he signed a donor card some time ago. He succumbed to an inoperable brain tumor just last week; otherwise he's in excellent shape. He has zero brain activity and is being maintained on life support until he can become a donor."

"Brain Howe was in his forties when he…when the accident occurred." Stanfield said. "Wouldn't it be better to find a donor closer to that age?"

"We're incredibly lucky to have such a perfect candidate now," Welby told him. "I don't think we should wait until someone closer to the patient's age comes along. That could take years, if it ever happens at all."

"In a way it could make up for the years he's lost," Claire observed, "And there's something else; if this does work and he comes back to the world, the person that looks back at him from the mirror every morning is going to be a complete stranger anyway. *That's* what he's going to have to deal with, not a ten or twelve-year age difference."

"We do plan to provide psychiatric support for him," Gray said, "for as long as he requires it."

"Of course we will," Claire said. She looked around the table at each of them then nodded, "All right, let's see if we can give Mr. Howe his life back."

Four

The first indication Brian Howe had that something was different was a sense of movement. It wasn't an actual sense of movement because he no longer possessed an inner ear, or anything else to signal movement to his brain. And yet he still sensed it, he sensed that something was changing. Not long after that he stopped sensing anything at all and his consciousness, the only thing he'd had for the past eighteen years, faded to black.

When he swam back up out of the darkness the sudden onslaught of sensory input almost drove him mad. Not sight because his eyes were covered, but smell; he could smell the nurse that was in his room, her body lotion, her shampoo. And auditory input, he could hear the swish of her starched uniform skirt as she moved around the room. Hell, he could hear her breathing, and the rasp of her pen as she made an entry in his chart. And he remembered everything.

━╋ ╋━

His rehabilitation wasn't exactly of a physical nature because there was nothing wrong with his new body. It was more psychological, teaching his brain to process all the input that it was receiving again after so long an absence. And controlling the output from his brain required to successfully operate a human body. It came back to him much more quickly than they'd expected it to or had reason to hope it would. He could have explained to them that during all those years in darkness he'd been walking and talking and doing it all in his mind, over and over again. Reliving it from the time he was an infant up to and including his final days. And then past that, into what he imagined his life would have been beyond his final meeting with Marjory Root. It was the only way he had to remain sane through the dark passage of all those years.

And once the bandages were removed from his new eyes and he looked upon the world again it was complete...he was back.

The strangest part of it all was the person who looked back at him from the mirror every morning when he shaved; Claire had been right about that. It took him a very long time to accept that he was that young handsome blond man. And the smile, his donor had had perfect teeth and a dazzling smile which now belonged to him. In his old life women had tended to look right past him then move on, at least those who didn't know him and respect him for his intellect. That didn't happen anymore; the nurses and aids he saw daily were definitely not looking past him now, especially when he smiled.

There were still a handful of employees at Emersus left from his tenure as director and he tried to re-connect with them because they were familiar faces, they were old friends. After a while he stopped though because it became apparent that, try as they might, they just couldn't see him as Howie, not the Howie they had known. Eventually they drifted away and he struck up friendships with the newer employees at the lab, people who hadn't known him before. A few would cast sidelong glances when they thought he wasn't looking but most seemed to accept him. And some were fascinated by his ordeal and wanted him to recount those lost years over and over again. Eventually he ended up distancing himself from those people as well.

He was busy catching up too. He wasn't exactly Rip Van Winkle but there were eighteen years of progress that had happened without him and he worked hard to get up to speed again. He thought this tended to put the senior people at the lab at ease to some extent because it spoke well of his psychological outlook, something they were obviously concerned with. After a time, they seemed to relax and accept that he was assimilating back into a normal life and into the work he used to do.

Once that happened he felt that he was ready to tie up one loose end that he'd been thinking about since he'd first woken up in his new body. And he thought he could do it without raising any red flags with his caretakers.

He began making inquiries about the present whereabouts of Marjory Root. It turned out that she wasn't hard to find at all. In fact, she was less than ten miles from the lab. And when he learned of her current circumstances he was more determined than ever to stop by and say hello.

Five

The facility was up on a hill in a suburb of the city and it had a nice view of the surrounding area. The building itself was constructed of tasteful red brick, surrounded by manicured lawns and well-kept paths for the patients to stroll in nice weather. He knew that the research that went on here must be minimal but he supposed it was better than nothing at all. This was more of a holding facility than anything else but it looked like a nice place to be and he supposed Marjory's options were a bit limited these days.

He had called ahead and made arrangements to visit but he had asked the senior administrator not to let Marjory know that he was coming. He told her that he wanted it to be a surprise. She met him in her office just off the lobby and, like most people he met these days, she responded very nicely to his smile. After a bit of small talk, they left her office and started down a corridor toward the interior of the facility.

"So you and Marjory used to work together?" she asked him as they walked. "How long ago was that?"

"Oh, quite a while ago, almost twenty years. I'm not sure she'll recognize me at all now."

"Oh I'm sure she will remember you," the administrator smiled at him. "You look a bit young to have worked with her that long ago though, if you don't mind my saying."

"I get that a lot," he smiled again.

"You do understand of course that since the stroke she's lost all mobility, along with the ability to speak and see. She does still have her hearing though, she responds very well to sound."

"But you said that she is fully cognizant. She does still have complete brain function; she'll know I'm there."

"She will; she's fully aware. There are times that I almost wish she weren't because she's trapped in her body now and likely to live on in that state for many years. But you can be certain she'll know it's you and that you've come to visit."

"That's good," he replied, "because I'm really looking forward to catching up." He favored the administrator with another one of his smiles.

LAST CALL AT JJ'S

One

It was getting dark and fewer cars were passing him now, probably because it was a weeknight and people were home eating dinner, watching TV, and playing with the kids. He was parked in the lot of a defunct car dealership on a little two-lane road; it'd been a small dealership that had changed hands numerous times before finally shutting down for good. He wasn't interested in the empty dealership although he had bought a few used cars there over the years, a long time ago. It was just a convenient place to park that was out of the way of traffic and gave him a good view of the building across the street.

That building, a New England farmhouse style wooden structure was painted a washed out red with peeling white trim. In front, a large wooden sign hung haphazardly from a protruding black wrought iron arm. Judging from the angle at which it was hanging the sign likely wouldn't make it through the coming winter. The building itself was two stories with a steep roof pitch, nondescript and forgettable. The second floor windows were blocked by drawn white shades that gave them the appearance of giant cataracts. A narrow casement window and a large picture window were the only ones on the first floor that faced the street, both were dirty and dark. The picture window was shaded by a sagging wooden awning that wasn't going to last much longer than the sign.

The entrance at the left side of the building was invisible; completely overgrown by shrubs and weeds. He knew it was there though; he'd passed through it enough times. From where he sat he couldn't read the weathered sign either but that didn't matter because he knew what it said, *JJ's Pub.*

The overall impression was one of abandonment, hopelessness and neglect...it reminded him of his life.

He sat in the car for some time as the traffic continued to thin and the light fade until finally, when it was full dark, he put the car in gear and drove across the street and to the back of the pub's dirt parking lot. The shrubs that had overgrown the front door had also begun to encroach on the parking lot and once he was behind them his car wasn't visible from the street.

He was well aware that what he was about to do was more than a little odd, but he really just didn't give a shit. He got out and walked to the kitchen entrance toward the rear of the building. The vegetation hadn't gotten that far yet. The door was wood and it was locked but it was also similar to the rest of the building, old and decrepit and he had it open in two minutes. He was carrying a thin canvass shopping bag with the name of a discount dollar store emblazoned across it. He pulled a flashlight out of it and switched it on as he shut the door and made sure it was secure. He was in a short hallway that opened onto a kitchen and he went slowly because he'd never been in this part of the building before. The mingled odors of ancient grease and fresh mold hung in the air. The stainless steel surfaces in the kitchen were covered in a dull brown patina and the door of the big walk-in fridge hung half open on rusted hinges. A fryer basket lay on its side on the dirty linoleum floor like a dead animal. He didn't touch anything as he made his way toward the swinging doors that led to the front of the pub.

He pushed through the doors and swung the flashlight around and it all came rushing back. He hadn't stood in this room in more than fifteen years yet it seemed like he'd been here just last night. To his right in the far corner was the front entrance, the one he'd always used. To the left of the door, pushed against the front wall, was a jukebox and to the right of the door a pay phone hung on the wall, an honest to god pay phone with a beat up wooden chair beneath it. It was all still there, just as it'd been the last time he'd walked out that door, or more likely staggered out it.

After the phone were the narrow doors to the rest rooms, then a corner and a blank rear wall leading to the kitchen door he was currently standing in. Directly before him was the bar, a three sided square that butted up against the buildings front wall, support columns at the two corners. At full capacity it would only seat maybe sixteen or eighteen people. The left of the bar was open to the dining area that ran back as deep as the kitchen along that side of the building. Brown leatherette booths lined the walls and scarred tables and chairs ran up the center and pressed right up against the backs of the bar stools on the left side of the bar. The smell here was stale beer and more mold.

He walked around to the left hand side of the bar, the dining room side, because that was where he'd usually sit, where he could look across the bar at the door and see who was coming and going. The bar stools were still there so he pulled one out, middle of the bar, two or three stools to either side of him, and sat down. He put his shopping bag on the stool next to him and pulled out a Coleman lantern. Once lit he placed it on the bar next to the corner post and it lit the room up nicely. It wasn't like the place had ever seen the light of day anyway; it had always been dark in JJ's... harder to see the food that way.

They hadn't taken the stools but other than that the bar had been stripped bare. At the center of the square a large built-in beer cooler sat on the floor, it's double steel lids dull and dented. He didn't bother to go behind the bar and check because he was sure it was empty. Along the wall that made up the rear of the bar were rows of shelves, empty. Above his head were glass racks, also empty. No worries though, he reached back into his bag and produced a bottle of cheap gin and a glass. Next came a small lunch cooler holding a freezer bag of ice cubes. Quite a few had melted already, but he didn't care.

"Think I'm going to drink my gin warm like a fucking barbarian," he muttered to himself as he fished out three cubes, plopped them into the glass and splashed gin over them. He swirled it to chill the liquid then held the glass up to the abandoned bar; "To everyone I ever drank with in here, fuck you all very much!" He took a long hit of gin then placed the glass on the bar's wooden surface, scarred by decades of water rings and cigarette burns. Speaking of which, he took an ashtray from his bag and lit up a smoke. He eyed the jukebox by the front door for a moment but he knew the power was off and it was probably broken anyway, otherwise they wouldn't have left it. Maybe next time he'd bring a radio. He took another drink and started singing *Cherokee Nation* by Paul Revere and the Raiders, oldie but goodie.

He was halfway through the bottle of gin when he heard the outside door open and then close. He froze with the glass halfway to his lips and stared across the bar at the front door. That door opened onto a short hallway that led to the outside door, the one that he could swear someone had just come through, the one that was completely overgrown with vegetation. It was just after one o'clock in the morning. He stared at the door for several minutes and nothing happened. Finally, he got up, walked around the bar to the door and tried it. It was locked. He put his ear to it and didn't hear a damned thing. "Bullshit," he muttered to himself and he went back to his seat to continue drinking. He began having a one-sided conversation with Tom Carling, one of his close friends from high school. He hadn't clapped eyes on Tom in fifty years.

Just after 2:00 a.m., closing time, he packed up his stuff, except for the empty gin bottle, and staggered out to his car, closing the kitchen door behind him. The fact that he made it the six miles to the little run-down apartment building he called home without killing himself or someone else was a miracle.

Two

He was back two nights later, same drill only this time with a bottle of cheap scotch, beer chasers and a bigger cooler. He'd also scraped together the cash for another, smaller lantern. He put it on his side of the bar at the post and the bigger one over by the jukebox. They lit the bar up just enough to remind him of the old days.

For the hell of it he flipped a couple of light switches…nothing, the power was off and he'd known that, didn't know why he even tried. He didn't notice that the empty gin bottle he'd left on the bar two nights earlier was gone.

He was halfway through the bottle of scotch and was staring up at the blank TV screen above the bar, wondering what had been the very last program it had shown before someone had turned it off forever. He had already had a couple of conversations with old friends, nothing heavy, just hi how are you kind of stuff. He was thinking about an old high school girlfriend when his eyes dropped down from the TV to see her sitting across the bar looking at him. A full glass of white wine sat on the bar in front of her. She looked to be maybe a handful of years older than she'd been when they split up and that made absolutely no frigging sense because she'd be in her 80's now, just like he was.

"What the hell are you doing here Jimmy?" she asked him and he just looked at her while he wondered exactly when it had been that he'd lost his mind.

"What...are...you...doing...here...Jimmy?" she asked again. "Place is closed." She always had been a wise ass.

"What are you doing here?" he asked her back. "And why do you look like you're twenty-five years old."

"I'm here all the time," she told him. She ignored the second question.

"You just said the place is closed," he pointed out. He had her there.

"Jesus you got old," she said, "and you don't wear it well Jimmy, I have to say."

"Why don't you look as old as me Janey? Because you are as old as me."

"This is how I looked when this was our hangout. Do you remember when this was our place Jimmy? Of course you do, otherwise you wouldn't be here now would you."

"Why don't you look like you do now, like I do?"

"I died in 1987 Jimmy, so I probably don't look all that great right now."

"Sorry, didn't know, what'd you die of?"

"Natural causes, aggravated by my drunk and stupid husband driving our car into a tree at 80 plus."

"Tom Nunez is dead too?"

"Tom was my first husband; Ray was my third husband, my last as things turned out. But then you never did bother to keep in touch did you Jimmy. You dropped me like a bag of dirt and just walked away. You were hot shit then weren't you, on top of the world. You were one of those guys that peaks when they're eighteen." She took a sip of wine and studied him across the bar. "You don't look so hot shit now though," she said.

"I've had a tough life," he informed her. "Things just never seemed to break my way!"

She laughed and took another sip of wine and that was when he noticed that the level of wine in her glass hadn't changed, even though she was drinking from it. "You ever been launched through a windshield at 80 miles an hour?" she asked him.

"I've had other things go wrong," he said and there was a defensive whine in his voice that he'd always hated.

"So you know what good old Ray said to me after we hit that tree?" she asked as if she hadn't heard him. "He crawled out of the car and stood over me; I was lying on the ground about ten feet beyond the front bumper at the time. He stood over me and told me to hurry up and die if I was going to die because some of his drinking buddies were waiting for him at the Hollow, that was a bar by the way."

"Why'd he say something like that?"

Probably because I'd caught him cheating on me again and had just told him I was going to take everything he had in the divorce. But also because he was a needle dicked asshole; that definitely had a lot to do with it."

"Why didn't you just stay married to Tom?"

"Why didn't you do anything with your life?"

"How do you know I didn't?" There was that whine again. He splashed some scotch into his glass and downed it.

"Because if you had you wouldn't be sitting here right now in a dead bar reliving the good old days and talking to me. Plus, you look like shit. Plus, I know for a fact that twenty years after we all graduated you were still a regular here and that's pretty pathetic all by itself."

"Before the other night I hadn't been in here in years," he informed her.

"Because you'd moved away," she said, "and by the time you moved back it had closed. Nice try though, you always did try to bend the truth to suit yourself."

"You see," he banged his empty glass on the bar, "You see, that's why I dumped you Janey! You were a bitch and you were constantly giving me a hard time."

"I was trying to get you to make something of your life, excuse me for that. And you dumped me because you'd developed a raging case of the hots for Linda Anderson, who you then dumped six months later. You always thought the grass was greener, didn't you Jimmy? You always thought there was something better coming just around the corner. And that's why you're sitting here alone in a deserted bar in the middle of the night talking to me, no family, no friends, just ghosts and the stink of stale beer."

"You just said that you're in here all the time."

"I lied, I've been waiting here to finally tell you what I thought of you and now that I've done that," she got up from the bar, "I'm moving on. Have fun with your walk down memory lane Jimmy."

"Janey wait, you haven't finished your drink. Just stay a bit longer and we can talk about the good memories, we did have some of those you know."

"What, you rolling around on top of me in the back seat of your mom's Plymouth? Always trying to get me to do stuff that I'm sure Linda Anderson had no problem doing? She laughed and headed for the door. "For me that's ancient history Jimmy. For you it's apparently all you have left." She went out through the inner door, the door that was locked, and a moment later he heard the outer door open and close, the door that was covered in vegetation.

"Got lot's more than that left," he said to himself and filled his glass.

Three

Two nights later he was back and this time he noticed that the empty scotch bottle he'd left on the bar was gone but that Janey's wine glass was still there and it was empty.

"Must have evaporated," he muttered to himself as he unloaded his shopping bag. Tonight was bourbon, the cheap kind, and domestic beer. And he'd added a bag of pretzels because he might get hungry. He poured his bourbon over ice and dumped pretzels into a scarred old plastic bowl from his apartment. Then he sat and drank and stared at the wine glass across the bar. When that got old he stared up at the TV some more.

When he looked back down Linda Anderson was sitting across the bar from him.

"Hello asshole," she said and he put his head in his hands.

"And last but certainly not least," Linda finished several minutes later, "you blew sunshine up my ass just long enough to take my virginity and then told your loser friends a bunch of lies that got me the reputation of being this towns biggest slut."

"Sorry," he muttered into his drink.

"I'm sorry, what was that Jimmy? I didn't hear you."

"I said I'm sorry," he said loudly, looking up at her.

"You sure as hell are," she replied and got up from the bar. "You know, I never believed in karma but here you sit in all your pathetic glory so maybe I've been wrong."

"I suppose you're dead too then."

"Eight years ago, cancer, but you know what? You've survived me by eight years and you could survive me by eight more and I'll still have had a fuller life than you, tenfold." She headed for the door, the front door again. "Goodbye Jimmy, here goes another chance you had at being happy walking out the door, the very same door I walked out of sixty-six years ago." And she was gone.

"Women!" Tom Carling said from the seat next to him and he screamed and fell off his stool. Tom helped him up and he felt real which was the strangest thing yet because none of these people were really here, he was holding on to enough of his sanity to know that to be true...probably.

"She always was a bitch," Tom said to him.

"She was a great girl," Jimmy replied and took a hit of whiskey. "You just never liked her because she wouldn't go out with you."

"It's true what she just said isn't it?" Tom asked. "You made up all that shit about her being a slut, about all the things she let you do to her."

"You knew that already," Jimmy said.

"No, no I actually didn't. I believed it because you said it and you were my best friend and you wouldn't bullshit me. Except you bullshitted me regularly didn't you Jim?"

"Maybe," Jimmy replied, "but not all the time, we were teenagers for Christ's sake, we all bullshitted about stuff, it was part of being a teenager."

"I never did, I never made up lies about the girls I dated to make myself sound like a big man. I wouldn't have done that because it wouldn't have been fair to the girl, would it. Besides, you didn't just do it while you were a teenager did you Jim? You've kept right on doing it your entire life."

"Everyone exaggerates stuff," Jimmy said, "to make yourself sound more important."

"Sure," Tom said, "like at our tenth reunion when you told everyone you were a portfolio manager at a big investment firm?"

"I worked there," Jimmy said.

"You did, yes you did, you worked there for about four months as a runner, right up until you were fired for trying to sell inside information to some guy in your apartment building."

"He should have told me he was a broker," Jimmy said. "He set me up."

"You also told everyone at the reunion that your wife was an ex-model and had been in *Playboy*, do you remember that? That wasn't true either, was it?"

"She was pretty enough to be," Jimmy said.

"She was, she surely was, and how do you think that made her feel Jim? You lying about her like that and making her play along, instead of just telling everyone what she really did. What did she really do?"

"She worked in a bank, the assistant manager for accounts for something like that."

"A perfectly good job, right? She probably made a pretty good living; better than you did anyway because you couldn't really hold down a job, could you? So she had to pretend she was a model and had posed naked in a magazine to make you feel more important. Ever occur to you that it also drove home the point to her that you didn't think who she really was was good enough for you. Probably didn't make her feel all that good about herself, huh?"

"Maybe not, but it was just because I thought she was pretty enough to be all that, that's all."

"It wasn't that at all and you know it. She obviously knew it too because, after six years of trying to un-asshole you, she finally realized she was wasting her time and walked away, didn't she?"

"How do you know all this shit?"

"Do we see a pattern developing here Jimmy?"

"What the fuck is all this, am I supposed to be Scrooge and you're all the ghosts that are going to help me redeem myself?"

Tom laughed and slapped his hand on the bar. "That's funny Jimmy, that's a hoot. Redemption? You are so far past redemption that you couldn't spot it in your rear-view mirror with a telescope!" Tom took a sip of his beer then placed the glass back on the bar, same deal as the wine, still full. "No," he said softly, "your last chance at redemption was way back in 1991. Do you remember what happened that year Jimmy? 1991?"

"Lots of things happened that year, how the hell am I supposed to know."

"Oh you know, yes you do. That was it, you got one more shot, you started dating this woman you'd met because you both went to the same supermarket and even though by that point you were really a first class jerk she didn't see it. Wonder of wonders, she thought you were a nice guy! But then again the one thing you were always good at was bullshit wasn't it? At least for a while. Yeah, you could bullshit with the best of them Jimmy. Thing about bullshit is, it has a very short shelf life, it doesn't usually hold up for very long, but it's all you had so when it wore thin..." Tom shrugged and took another sip of beer. "So," he continued, "this really nice woman, what was her name?"

"Nora Wilkins," Jimmy said quietly.

"And what was her father's name?"

"Frank."

"That's right, so Nora apparently sees something in you that she thinks is good and kind, something that wasn't really there at all. She tries to help you; she tries to straighten you out and she talks her father into giving you a job at his company. What kind of company was it Jimmy?"

"It was a building supply company."

"That's right, not a huge company but a pretty good operation, been in the family for a couple of generations, right? So there you are, you and Nora are getting married; already living together and you've got a good job with dad's company with a bright future because Nora is the old man's only child. Not a bad life right? Didn't you think so Jimmy?"

"I guess, yeah, it was a really nice life."

"Sure it was, for most guys anyway, but apparently not for you because you 'borrowed' a whole bunch of money from the family business and invested it in this half ass fly by night business deal that you thought couldn't miss. But it did miss, didn't it Jimmy? Turned out it was just a scam and it missed big time and all the money was gone. You had convinced Nora that she should go along with you too, right? That you were this savvy businessman, which you weren't, and that this was a deal that would double the size of daddy's company and you two could get married and you'd be the family hero. She'd be marrying the guy who took the family business to the next level. You talked her into stealing from her own father didn't you? Because that's pretty much what it amounted to. On something that you knew deep down wasn't much better than betting the horses, but what the hell, wasn't your money was it."

"I thought it would work out." Jimmy said to his glass.

"Truth be told, and that's what we're doing here by the way, telling truths, you didn't really care one way or the other. And what did you do when the shit hit the fan, did you man up and take responsibility and tell the old man you'd talked his little girl into it? Tell him that it wasn't her fault at all. Is that what you did?"

"No."

"So what'd you do Jimmy?"

"I left."

"You left. You packed up without even talking to Nora about what had happened and you were gone, you were in the wind. Leaving her to take the blame and deal with the fallout, to deal with her father."

"About the size of it," Jimmy whispered.

"Yeah," Tom nodded, "about the size of it. So, that was your last chance at redemption Jimmy. This right here, this sure as hell isn't."

"Then what is it?"

"It's whatever you think it is. By the way, since you hit the road and never bothered to call or check back with Nora, do you want to know what happened to her and daddy? Do you want to know how it all shook out?"

"No," he whispered.

"Oh come on, sure you do. You must have wondered over the years, even a narcissistic son of a bitch like you, you must have wondered."

"I never did."

"You know, sadly I do believe that," Tom replied, "but here it is anyway, something for you to ponder while you sit here all alone in this deserted bar. Turns out the family business was just kind of getting by when you came along, doing ok but operating on a thin margin. Would have kept doing ok and maybe even better than ok if you hadn't darkened their doorway. But not after you took all that money. Losing that money lost them the business you see, couldn't pay their creditors, couldn't make payroll. You get the idea. Shut their doors two months after you left. Where were you by then Jimmy? You were in Florida, right? Living it up tending bar at a place in the Keys. Having a great time, not a care in the world. Meanwhile, the company folded and it just about killed old Frank, family business, father, grandfather, all of that. And while he didn't blame Nora, not really, because he blamed you, he still couldn't look at her the same way, try as he might. He could barely look at her at all. And that made her blame herself more and more every day. So do you remember the little hoodsie you hooked up with in Key West Jimmy? The one you spent the weekend with in Miami, screwing and doing blow? Remember that?"

Jimmy just nodded.

"Sure you do; she was a hottie wasn't she. Dumber than a bag of rocks but who cares about that, right? Well that Saturday night, just about when you two were getting busy on your hotel room balcony poor Nora, the woman who gave you your last chance, who saw God knows what in you that convinced her to offer you her world, was sitting in a bathtub of warm water and slitting her wrists. She left two notes on her kitchen table, one to her dad and one to you. Frank threw the one to you away unopened, wouldn't have known where to send it anyway. He read the one addressed to him over a hundred times though and then he died of a heart attack not long after which was probably a blessing because by then he was thinking seriously about putting a gun to his head."

"How do you know all this?" Jimmy shouted at him.

"Just do pal," Tom replied. "And hey, don't blame me, this is what you came here looking for isn't it? And if it wasn't, it should have been. You should have known coming back here that this was waiting for you because what's here after all, just ghosts and a long dead past that you can never get back. Redemption? This isn't redemption Jimmy boy; this is you cashing in the chips you've accumulated throughout your life. So don't blame us if it's not what you want to hear." Tom slid off of his stool and headed for the door. "Maybe I'll see you again Jimmy, if you have the balls to come back here again." And he was gone.

Four

It wasn't two nights later this time; he came the very next night, because he couldn't not come. This time he didn't bother with pretzels or beer, just the hard stuff and a bag of ice because even with it all, he still wasn't a barbarian.

He bought the bag of ice at a convenience store down the street and he'd almost said something to the cashier while she was ringing it up. He'd almost told her that he was having some trouble and he needed help and could she call someone for him? He wasn't sure who, just someone. Because the cashier was real, she existed in the real world, and if she could stop him from going where he was going maybe he could be back in the real world again too. But he didn't do it; he didn't say anything. He picked up his bag of ice, not destined for a backyard barbecue or a birthday party but for another insane drinking session with dead people, and he left the store and drove to JJ's, because he couldn't not drive to JJ's.

He was into his second drink when Tom was beside him again and this time he didn't jump; he didn't even flinch.

"Didn't think you had it in you buddy," Tom told him

"What the hell is there to lose?" Jimmy asked him. "Besides, I don't have anywhere else to go."

"That's got to be one of the sorriest things I've ever heard anyone say."

"Go screw yourself, I suppose your life turned out all sunshine and fairy tales."

"Not quite," Tom replied, "but not far off either. I had a great wife, good kids, and a good job; all in all, it was a great life. Compared to yours it was a stairway to the frigging stars. Course, you didn't set the bar very high now, did you?"

"This is all in my head," Jimmy replied. "You're not even here."

"Now that would be even sadder wouldn't it? Tom said. "That you come back here and spend night after night in a cold dark abandoned bar getting drunk and imagining old friends showing up to tell you what a piece of shit you are? That is some serious psychosis right there my friend! If I were you I'd stick with the ghost thing, it's not a great scenario but it sure beats the thought of you sitting here alone engaged in such severe self-flagellation! Besides, self-flagellation was never one of your talents Jimmy, you're way too narcissistic for that."

"I didn't know you were going to be here or that I was going to have to listen to this shit. I just wanted to remember some of the good times."

"Sure you did," Tom replied, "on some level sure you did! But that's not why you had to come back again is it? It's because you need to face this before the end, who the hell knows why but you do. Otherwise you wouldn't have gotten near this place again after Janey showed up. Oh and as far as 'the good times' go, seems that your memories of the old days don't quite jive with your old friends' memories, do they?"

"We had some fun," Jimmy replied defensively, "We had a lot of laughs before everyone went their separate ways. You and I and Carl and Rudy and the old gang, it wasn't all bad."

"I guess," Tom said and shrugged. He took a drink of beer and the thing with the glass was really starting to bug Jimmy. "What do you think?" Tom asked, "Did we have some laughs?"

"We did," Rudy said from the end of the bar, "but I'll be honest Jimmy, we had more when you weren't around than when you were. Sometimes when you were around the bullshit got so thick I felt like I should've been wearing boots." Tom laughed at that.

"Come on," Jimmy said, we knew each other since first grade; if I was such an asshole why did you guys hang out with me all those years."

Rudy shrugged, "Small town, not a lot to do, not that many options I guess. But ask yourself this Jimmy; once school ended and we all went our own way did you ever hear from any of us? Did we keep in touch?"

"No, but that's to be expected, everyone moved away except for me. People move on, that's all."

"We stayed in touch," Tom motioned to Rudy, "me and Rudy and Carl and Ricky, we all stayed in touch over the years. We even got together once in a while, didn't we Rudy."

"We did," Rudy laughed, "fishing trips and ball games and such. My wife used to call them 'the boys' field trips'."

"Never thought to let me know huh?" Jimmy said, "That's nice, thanks guys."

"We were all here when we were kids Jimmy," Rudy said, "But once we were out in the world we had a lot more options, a lot more choices when it came to friends. You just weren't an option any longer because let's face it, you really are an insufferable jerk."

"So where are Carl and Ricky then, let's get them in here to piss on my head too."

"They're still alive," Tom told him. "Otherwise I'm sure they wouldn't have missed it." Rudy laughed at that.

"So what's the deal here, what do you want, an apology?"

"Way too late for that," Linda said from the other side of the bar. "We're just here to give you a proper send off."

"Kind of ease you on to the next stage," Rudy said, "I don't think you're going to like it."

"What, do I get to haunt this place for eternity?" Jimmy asked.

"They're tearing it down in a few days," Linda told him, "before it falls down."

"Then what?" Jimmy asked, "Come on, you must know."

"Maybe we do," Janey said from the stool next to Linda, "maybe it's reincarnation. Remember we used to talk about that all the time?"

"Yeah," Linda laughed, "you'll probably come back as a garden slug Jimmy."

"The world just isn't that balanced," Janey mused.

"Or you'll have to live this life over and over again," Ricky said, "Saw that in a movie once."

They all turned and looked at Ricky, Tom raised his eyebrows at him.

"Massive coronary," Ricky explained, "just this morning. Glad I could make it." They all laughed at that one, except for Jimmy, and Tom slapped Ricky on the back.

"None of you are here," Jimmy said, "this is all in my head because I made the mistake of coming back to this shithole just one goddamned time too many."

"Well you're right about that," Linda said and they all laughed again, except for Jimmy.

"So there is no redemption," Jimmy said to himself.

"There is," Tom replied, "For some, in time, but the debit sheet on you is a long one pal, and a man's character is his fate."

"But we're all here, one way or another, one more time," Janey said, "so let's have a few drinks, enjoy being young again and catch up a little before we move on. Not you Jimmy, we all know what you've been doing for the past fifty odd years. And stop looking at my boobs too, pig." Another big laugh from the group.

"Have a drink Jimmy," Linda said, "and try apologizing to us some more. It may do some good, who knows. It's a start anyway. Besides, we're not who you really have to worry about; Nora might just decide to put in an appearance tonight. Won't that be fun?"

Jimmy looked across the bar at her and she smiled sweetly at him. His eyes shifted to the door and he filled his glass again.

Five

The front entrance was completely overgrown by shrubs that had gone to riot so they walked around to the back of the building.

"Hey, there's an old car back here," the first guy said.

"Somebody probably abandoned it," the second guy said. "Come on, the dozer is going to be here any minute, let's do a walkthrough and see if there's anything inside worth liberating."

The kitchen door wasn't locked but that didn't surprise them, the place had gone out of business years ago so kids had probably gotten in at some point. They were halfway through the kitchen when the smell hit them.

"That is not good," guy number two said, "That's something dead."

"Just be careful," guy number one said, "could be a dead raccoon, those things carry rabies you know." They both put on their gloves.

They pushed through the kitchen door into the bar area and the raccoon theory went right out the window.

"Holy shit," first guy said, "there's a dead guy in here!"

"Really?" second guy looked at him, "you sure?"

"Screw you," first guy said. They both walked around to the side of the bar for a closer look.

"He's been dead a few days at least, maybe a week," second guy said.

"How can he still be sitting on that stool like that, he should've fallen off shouldn't he?"

Second guy motioned to the glass in front of the old man, and the bottle next to it. "Must have been his last drink," he said.

"Great," first guy said then pointed to the half dozen other glasses scattered around the rest of the bar, "So who do all those belong to then?"

THE GRASS IS ALWAYS GREENER

One

"If we run out of gas out here I will kill you," Sherrie said from the passenger seat.

He ignored her.

"I told you we should have stopped at that last gas station. Now we're in the middle of nowhere, we haven't seen another car in forever, and it's going to be dark soon. So I just want you to know, if we get stuck out here I'm going to kill you…sincerely."

"There'll be a gas station right over that next rise up ahead."

"You said that about the last three rises," she replied. "We're in the middle of freaking nowhere Josh; I will hit you over the head with something heavy and drag your body out into the desert where no one will ever find you, think about it."

"What do you want me to do, turn around?"

"We probably don't have enough gas to get back to the last station," she replied, "Do you think we do?"

"No," he said quietly.

"What? Didn't get that."

"No, I don't think we have enough gas to get back to the last station."

"Neither do I. So let's see what's over this next rise and if nothing is over this next rise, I want you to pull the car over so I can kill you."

He ignored her some more.

"Also, we're out of Bugles," she said.

That brought the conversation to a halt and they drove on in silence through the high desert toward the next rise over which there may or may not be a gas station.

A few minutes later they topped that rise and saw a vast flat plain stretching ahead, the two-lane blacktop they were on coming to a point in the far distance. There was nothing on either side of it but scrub brush and sand... and a gas station on the right hand side of the road in the near distance. Josh gave Sherrie a smug look, but kept his mouth shut.

"It better be open," she said to him.

It wasn't. Ten minutes later they pulled into the dusty parking lot in front of a small cinderblock building with two pumps out front, one service bay to the right side, a tiny office with a cracked plate glass window to the left and peeling white paint that may have been applied when Eisenhower was occupying the White House. There was one decrepit old car parked at the back of a cracked and sun-baked macadam parking area: it was sitting on four flats and coated with sand. Beyond that, just a whole lot of nothing as far as the eye could see.

Josh got out of the car and looked into the office. From the layers of dust on everything he didn't think the place had been open in a very long time. He also didn't think it wise to voice this theory to Sherrie just then. If he was right it meant that there was probably nothing in the underground fuel storage tanks, and that meant they were well and truly screwed.

He tried the door... locked, then walked over to the big glass garage door for the service bay ... locked, then around to the back where he found an old propane tank, the afore mentioned parked car and that was it. He returned to the front to see Sherrie standing by the pumps.

"They're locked," she said to him and he saw that they were, a short piece of chain and padlock on each fueling nozzle. The pumps were very old versions, with rolling metal wheels showing price and gallons pumped, and they were pretty rusty. So were the chains and padlocks.

"This place hasn't been opened for years," Cherrie said, "has it Josh?"

"Doesn't look like it."

She kicked one of the pumps then walked over to the office window and peered through the glass. Josh looked around until he found the cap for the underground fuel storage tank, hunched down to study it then got up to pop the trunk of his car. He got the tire iron out then returned to the cap and used it to pry it open. The cap was rusty too and it took some doing. By the time he got it open Sherrie was standing beside him. He got down on his hands and knees and put his nose over the tank opening. There was just a ghost of an odor of gasoline, not nearly strong enough to indicate that there was anything left in the tank. He stood up and looked around but there were no more tank caps. He walked back to their car and threw the tire iron into the trunk then slammed it.

"We're spending the night here," Sherrie was standing behind him, "aren't we?"

"Looks that way," he replied, "unless a car comes by and offers to give us a lift." He turned around to face her and sat back against the trunk lid.

"Ok, good," she said. "So let's sum up, shall we? We didn't get gas when we should have so we're almost out, leaving us with the option of spending the night in the middle of nowhere in an abandoned gas station or accepting a ride from a total stranger on a deserted road which is how at least half the slasher movies I've ever seen have started. I miss anything?"

"No, no I think that pretty much sums it up." Josh said. "Except that we're also out of Bugles."

She turned on her heel and walked over to the station's garage bay door and put her foot through the glass pane at bottom center. After clearing the glass shards out of the frame she stooped down, reached inside and flipped up the door's locking lever. She stood back up, grasped the doors outside handle and pulled. After pulling a second time she looked back over her shoulder.

"Could you come over here and help me please?"

Josh walked over and grabbed the handle with her. They both pulled and the door finally opened with a long torturous screech of metal against metal. A hot musty smell of oil and dust hit them as they entered the empty work bay. There were several rust colored stains on the floor that had once been oil and an empty metal tool rack against the back wall and that was about it. Josh walked over to the entry into the office and flipped the two light switches on the wall...nothing. The furnishings in the office consisted of a battered metal desk with a matching and equally battered metal chair, two molded plastic chairs facing the desk, a two drawer file cabinet, also metal and also battered but a different color than the desk and chair, three wooden shelves on the wall behind the desk holding absolutely nothing, a metal oil can display rack also holding nothing, and a calendar taped to the wall with a photo of a scantily clad model standing in front of a classic car. The calendar was from twenty-four years ago, December.

Behind and to the right of the desk was a short hallway that led to a bathroom door on the left. The bathroom smelled bad enough for Sherrie to wonder what in God's name it had smelled like twenty-four years ago. Against the rear wall of the hallway was a Coca Cola vending machine.

"I'll bet that thing's worth some money," Josh said, "Anything old with Coke on it is worth good money."

"Great, why don't you drag it out and strap it to the roof of the car," Sherrie told him. She returned to the desk, brushed the chair off then sat down and began going through the drawers. Josh stayed with the vending machine to try to get it open. The locking mechanism popped out when he turned it and he swung the front open to check the inside of the machine. He reached in and took out two cans of Coke and a can of Fanta Orange and put them on top of the machine. He checked the change box ...empty, and then he went into the bathroom and shut the door.

When he came out Sherrie was still at the desk. "Did you actually use that bathroom?" she asked him. "That's disgusting."

"I opened the window to air it out," he said and put the soda cans on the desktop. "These were still in the vending machine," he said proudly.

"They've been in there for decades, they're flat."

He opened one of the cans of Coke and took a sip then spit it out. "They're flat," he announced.

Sherrie shook her head and continued through the drawers. She held up a set of keys and jingled it for Josh to see. "I guess this means we own this place now," she said drily.

"I'm going to check on the car out back," he replied. "It may still have some gas in its tank." He unlocked the office door and went out then around the side of the building. Sherrie got up from the desk and looked around again. Her attention went to the rear wall where the soda machine was and she realized that it wasn't as deep as the work bay. She stepped through the door into the bay, walked to the rear left corner and found a closed door there, locked. She tried the keys on the keychain she'd found and the fourth one opened the door, which swung inward with an ear-grating screech. She looked into a small storeroom crammed with metal shelves and a metal workbench. There were car parts (she assumed that's what they were anyway) stacked up or scattered everywhere along with a few tires and three more cases of soda for the vending machine. It looked as if quite a few of the cans had exploded over the years from the heat that probably built up in the closed storeroom in summer. She stepped in and looked around a bit but didn't see anything that she thought would be useful, like a full can of gas for instance.

She was just leaving the work bay headed for their car when Josh returned from the back of the lot. "Gas tank in the old beater is bone dry," he told her. "Looks like it's been sitting there for a hundred years."

"So I assume we are spending the night then," Sherrie said to him, it wasn't a question.

"We could drive a bit further on and see if there's anything up ahead. Kind of stupid to spend the night here then find out that there was an open gas station just over the n...."

"If you say 'just over the next rise' I am going to hit you with something heavy and I just found a whole room full of something heavy, so think it over. If we're destined to run out of gas, I'd rather be walking this road tomorrow morning than in the dead of night."

"Fine, then we stay here for the night; we can spread the sleeping bags out in the office, shove the desk out of the way, then we'll at least be able to stretch out instead of trying to sleep in the car."

"Ok, but I think we should put the car in the bay and close the door, that way if some homicidal maniac cruises by in the middle of the night this place will still look deserted."

By the time they'd backed the car into the bay and pulled the door back down, then moved the desk aside and swept out the office with a broom Josh found in the storeroom, it was starting to get dark. They sat on either side of the desk and had dinner - bottles of warm iced tea and a box of Lorna Doones. By the time they had finished, it was just about full dark and Josh lit the little LCD lantern he kept in the car for emergencies.

"How long will that thing last?" Sherrie asked him.

"Don't know, I've never had it on for more than a few minutes at a time. I think the batteries are pretty fresh though so we should be ok."

"Well when it goes out it's going to be pretty goddamned dark around here; I'll tell you that for nothing."

"We'll be asleep by then and when we wake up it'll be morning, no sweat." He placed the lantern on the desktop and they laid two space blankets on the floor, then their sleeping bags on top of them. "Want to zip them together?" Josh asked.

"You are not getting any tonight," Sherrie said, "So just let that thought go. I am not doing it on a hard, dirty linoleum floor in a deserted gas station."

"Good story to tell our grandchildren," Josh replied.

"Right now we have about as much chance of having grandchildren together as there being a gas station over the next rise."

"Nice, one little hiccup in our scenic country drive and you blow up our relationship! Besides, I was thinking about body heat, the desert can get cold at night."

"Like hell you were." She finished with her sleeping bag then sat down on it and looked out through the plate glass window. She could still see the road beyond the pump island but it was hazy and indistinct now. In a few minutes it would disappear entirely, swallowed up by the darkness. She shivered a little then got up and went out into the bay to get her jacket out of the car while she could still see where she was going. While she was out there she locked the bay door and put the metal oil rack they had removed from the office in front of the pane of glass she had broken to get in. When she returned to the office she locked the office door too.

Josh had gone back into the bathroom again. "Does that toilet flush," she yelled back to him.

"No!"

"Then you had better not be dropping a deuce back there, if you need to do that go outside and do it." Nothing for a long moment then Josh stomped out of the bathroom, unlocked the door and stomped outside and around the corner of the building. She smiled and lay back on her sleeping bag. After two years together she had his habits down cold.

He was back about five minutes later. He had taken the little lantern with him and by the time he came back it was just about full dark. Sherrie could still make out the shadows of the gas pumps out front, but everything beyond them had faded to black. When Josh came inside she had to squint against the light from the lantern, then he put it on the desk and the light reflected off the plate glass windows turning them opaque and she couldn't see anything outside.

He lay down next to her on his sleeping bag and they stared up at the ceiling. "You should probably turn off the lantern," she whispered to him, not exactly sure why she was whispering, "to save the battery."

He reached up and back over their heads to the desktop and turned off the lantern. He lay back down and they went back to staring at a ceiling that they could no longer see.

"Good night," Josh said.

"Not so far," Sherrie replied.

Two

She woke up a few hours later to the sound of rain beating down on the roof of the gas station and the metal awning over the pumps. Josh was snoring softly beside her. She rolled over onto her side and tried to look out through the plate glass window, but it was pitch black outside. She thought it was weird that it was raining because they were in the desert, but she supposed it had to rain at least a little bit once in a while, probably wouldn't last long. She rolled onto her back again because lying on her side was uncomfortable on the hard floor. She had just started to drift off to sleep again when a faint light flickered across the window. At first she wasn't sure she'd really seen it, but it came back a moment later and she rolled back up onto her side. There was somebody out there with a flashlight. A moment later she thought she heard voices outside toward the back of the building.

She grabbed Josh's shoulder and shook him; "Josh, wake up, there's someone outside!"

He mumbled something and started to snore again so she shook him harder, but she didn't want to raise her voice. He mumbled something else then rubbed his face. She thought the voices were closer now, just behind and along their side of the building.

"Josh, did you close the bathroom window?"

"There's a screen on it, it's ok to leave it open," Josh mumbled.

"Not your bathroom at home, you idiot!" she whispered fiercely into his ear.

He opened his eyes and tried to look at her then frowned at the darkness around them. At home they always slept with the bathroom light on and the door opened a crack.

"We're in an abandoned gas station, remember? And I need you to wake the fuck up because there is someone outside! Did you close the bathroom window?"

"I don't think so," he muttered and sat up. The light flashed across the windows again and she noticed that it was kind of faint, like it was a distance away from the building now. But she knew she'd heard someone talking out there in the darkness a moment ago.

"You need to wake up!" she hissed at him again, "I'm going to go check it, be nice if you came with me."

"There's someone outside? Did they pull up in a car?"

"No, they've got a flashlight and it sounds like they're out on the desert behind the building." She stood up hunched over, ready to drop if the flashlight returned. She started down the little hallway and was relieved when Josh got to his feet and followed her. She reached the bathroom door and peeked around the jamb into the room just as the light swept across the open window and moved on. And the voices were there again. They sounded as if they were coming over the desert from some distance away; she supposed she might not have even heard them at all if Josh hadn't left the window open.

She stepped carefully into the bathroom, Josh right behind her. It was a testament to how freaked out she was that she didn't even notice the smell in the room. She got against the wall on one side of the small window and Josh got on the other. Then they both leaned forward and peered out into the darkness. The rain had stopped.

Behind the building in the distance they both saw several lights bobbing along and maybe half dozen shadowy forms around them. With no moon or stars, the darkness beyond the window frame was almost stygian so it was hard to judge how far away the lights were but the indistinct voices they'd heard had now faded to almost nothing. It appeared that whoever was out there was moving away from them and the abandoned station.

Josh started to say something, but she shushed him because there was no guarantee that the figures they could see were the only ones out there. So they watched and listened as the lights got further away and the voices faded until suddenly they were simply gone.

"They must have gone over a rise and down the far side," Josh whispered. "I'm going to look around the other side of the building."

"Do not go outside or open the doors," Sherrie said to him.

"I won't," he said as he leaned forward and kissed her then left the bathroom. She stayed by the window looking out into the night. She stayed back a bit because she had this vision of some- one, or something, crouching just below the window, waiting for her to get close enough for it to reach up, grab her, and pull her out into the blackness. After what seemed like forever, Josh came back and told her that he hadn't seen or heard anything else out- side the building.

"Let's go back to the front room and lay down," he suggested. "I'll close this window, if anyone tries to get in we'll hear it and it'll be light soon anyway."

"Can you close it without making any noise?" Sherrie asked, "Because if not, then forget it."

He reached up with both hands and very slowly slid the window down until it was closed, then he locked it. She looked out at the desert behind the building one last time then they returned to the front room and sat down on their sleeping bags.

"Don't turn the light on," she said to him.

"I wasn't going to," he replied and lay down on his back on his sleeping bag.

"And don't go to sleep either," she said.

"I wasn't going to," he replied.

She lay down on her bag next to him and slid up against him. He put his arm around her and they lay side by side staring into the darkness.

"Who would be out walking around the desert in the middle of the night, in the middle of nowhere?" she asked finally.

"Don't know," he replied and then they lay there for a while listening.

"If they start coming into the building what do we do?" she asked finally.

"Don't know," he replied.

"That's reassuring, thanks."

"You're welcome."

"I'm slightly freaked out right now Josh, don't poke the bear."

"I'm not. I don't think they're going to try to get into the building because they walked off in the other direction, we watched them do it."

"Yeah, off into the middle of the frigging desert, what the hell. And how do you know they won't come back."

"We'll take turns checking," he said.

"Go check now."

He got up and disappeared down the hallway. She heard him in the bathroom then passing into the repair bay. She turned her head and looked out through the plate glass windows at nothing and waited for dawn.

Three

It was one of the longest nights of Sherrie's young life. Neither of them slept; they lay on their sleeping bags staring up at an invisible ceiling and whispered to each other. Every once in a while Josh would get up and check the rest of the building then return to report all quiet.

Finally, Sherrie realized that she could see the ceiling. She turned her head and looked out the plate glass window and watched the rusty gas pumps slowly materialize out of the gloom. And as they did, she felt the tension slowly leaving her body; she felt like laughing and yelling and getting up to dance around because day had finally come.

As soon as it was full light they went outside to check around the building and saw the footprints in the still wet sand. They ran along one side of the building passing right by the bathroom window and suddenly Sherrie didn't feel much like dancing any more.

"They knew we were here," she said to Josh. "They were listening to us."

"We were asleep," he pointed out and that really didn't make her feel better at all.

"They knew we were here though," she replied, "They knew someone had to have opened the window."

"Well they didn't try to get in, they could have climbed in through the window and they didn't."

"If you're trying to make me feel better you'd better try something else."

"My point is maybe they did know we were here and maybe they didn't. If they did, they didn't care because they didn't try to get into the building and if they didn't, if they just assumed someone stopped here and left the window open at some point, then it doesn't matter anyway."

"They would have seen our car in the bay through the door."

"There aren't any footprints out front."

"It's concrete, they wouldn't have left any," she pointed out to him.

"Well either way they're gone and someone is bound to come by and we'll be on our way."

"And I don't care if it's a guy in a scary clown mask with a hook instead of a hand," she told him, "we're taking the ride and getting the hell out of here."

An hour later they'd eaten the last of their food and drunk the last two bottles of iced tea. They were sitting in the shade by the pumps watching the road. They hadn't seen a soul.

"I'm going to take a look around again," Josh said getting up and dusting off his jeans.

"Not far," she told him, "don't go wandering off into the desert or anything."

"I won't. If a car comes just yell."

Sherrie sat scuffing her sneakers against the old cracked macadam, watching the road. When someone did come it wasn't a guy wearing a scary clown mask; it was a really nice old man named

Zeke Boniface driving an ancient beat up pickup truck he called Richard the Deep Breather. She yelled for Josh who appeared from behind the building and just like that they were out of there.

There wasn't a gas station over the next rise, or the one after that, or the one after that. Sherrie gave Josh several sidelong looks as they trundled along further and further in Richard the Deep Breather until finally they came to a little rest stop with a gas station, a souvenir stand and a snake exhibit. It turned out that Zeke and his wife Mabel ran the rest stop and lived in a doublewide out behind it. It turned out that Zeke and his wife really liked solitude... a lot.

Josh tried to buy a five-gallon metal gas can to carry gas back to their car but Zeke wouldn't hear of it. He loaned them the gas can and then drove them back to the old filling station to get their car. He hung around while Josh emptied the can into the Toyota's gas tank.

"Do you know who owns this place?" Sherrie asked him, wondering if maybe he owned it himself. "I had to break one of the glass panes in the door to get it open, I'll be happy to pay for it."

"No one owns this place," Zeke said, looking around, "been abandoned forever. You kids really spent the night here?"

"We did," Sherrie replied, "and the weirdest thing happened last night too, we..." she stopped because Josh had given her a look across the trunk of the car. Zeke turned back to face her, "What happened last night?"

"We thought we heard animals around the building," Josh replied.

"Like coyotes maybe," Sherrie added, "big ones."

"Coulda been," Zeke nodded and scratched at his beard, "little bastards are always out and about at night. Won't really do you any harm though, more afraid of you than you are of them."

"Wouldn't bet on that," Sherrie told him.

They followed Zeke and Richard back to the rest stop and Sherrie wasn't ever happier to put a place in the rearview mirror as she was the abandoned filling station. Mabel made them breakfast and they filled the gas tank and Zeke assured them that there was a real town not thirty miles down the road. They thanked him and Mabel and they were off and that was the end of it, or so Sherrie thought.

Four

There was indeed a real town thirty miles down the road and Sherrie wanted to keep on going right past it, but Josh suggested they stop for lunch. After lunch he suggested they see the sights and spend the night. After the amount of sleep she *hadn't* gotten the night before Sherrie was too tired to argue with him so they got a room at the best hotel they could find in town, which was also the only hotel they could find in town. It was actually pretty nice, rustic and dated but nice. She took a long hot shower then fell into the big four poster bed and was asleep before Josh even finished his own shower.

They were eating breakfast in the hotel dining room the following morning when Josh told her he wanted to drive back to the abandoned filling station.

"Did you leave something there?" Sherrie asked.

"No, I didn't."

"Then no. Actually, absolutely no."

"There's a reason I want to go back and look around a bit, during the day."

"Don't care," Sherrie said as she sipped her coffee.

"There's something funny about that place, something really wrong."

"No shit, which is why absolutely no."

"Ok, how about this, you stay here for the day, do some shopping, relax, read, whatever, and I'll shoot back by myself and just satisfy my curiosity. I'll be back before you know it."

"Shopping? There's one clothing store in town and all they sell is the latest ranch attire by Woolrich… about what?"

"What?"

"Curiosity about what? The freaks we saw wandering around in the desert in the middle of the night? That's the kind of curiosity you don't need. Nothing good will come of that."

"More than just that," Josh replied. He glanced around the little dining room to make sure no one was in ear shot then leaned forward over the table toward Sherrie. "That car that was parked out back, the one that looks like it's been there forever. Remember that?"

"Of course I do, it was an old beater, probably from the 40's by the look of it," Sherrie had dated enough gear heads to know her cars.

"Yeah, 1944 to be exact, a Plymouth sedan from 1944."

"So what, is it a collectable? Is it worth a lot of money?"

"Probably, considering that it shouldn't even exist. Plymouth didn't build any cars in 1944 babe; neither did any other American car companies. It was the middle of World War II and all the car companies were cranking out tanks and airplanes and such. There's no such thing as a 1944 Plymouth sedan."

"Then you just got it wrong, that's all. What makes you so sure it was built in 1944?"

"Because the manufacturer's plate on the door jamb said so, so did the dealer sticker that was still plastered inside the glove box. And the build date stamped on the engine block. Not to mention that I *know* my 40's cars, and I've never seen that one before. And that's not even all of it."

She'd forgotten her coffee now and was looking at him across the table. "What else?"

"Last night when those jokers just disappeared out there, we thought they'd gone behind a rise or something, right? Well I stood on the roof of that old car in the morning and looked and there aren't any rises out there, it's as flat as a board for as far as you can see out into the desert. So where'd they go?"

"They all just switched off their flashlights and it was too dark to see them anymore, that's all."

"No," Josh shook his head, "they all disappeared at exactly the same moment. What are the chances they all switched off their lights at the exact same moment? And even if they had, there was enough ambient light to still see something."

"Come on Josh, no there wasn't, it was blacker than hell out there, there was no ambient light at all."

"OK, maybe there wasn't, but I still say the way they were just gone like that is freaking weird. Why would they all switch off their lights at once in the middle of the desert? If it was as dark as you say they wouldn't have been able to see where they were going, would they?"

"OK," Sherrie said, "Maybe you're right about that, but so what. I'm pretty sure that a basic rule of survival in the desert is to not mess around with strange people you see wandering around *in* that desert."

"I just want to take a look around, walk out there and look around in broad daylight. And I want to get some photos of that car, check it out a little better. I'm telling you, there's something weird going on with that place. Just a walk around, that's all."

"You think there's something out there don't you?" she said, "That's why you didn't want to tell that nice old man Zeke about the people in the desert."

"He either already knows about them, is one of them himself, or he would have thought we were both nuts. Either way it was a lose lose."

"Not going to talk you out of this, am I?" Sherrie said and Josh smiled and shook his head. "All right," she said, "But I'm going with you. I'm not sitting around this place while you're out there wandering around a weirdo infested desert."

A half hour later they were headed back down the highway the way they'd come, this time with a full tank of gas.

"Do you think Zeke will see us go by and recognize the car?" Sherrie asked.

"A Toyota Camry is about as generic as it gets with cars," Josh replied. "He probably won't look twice."

Sometime later, when they passed the run down little rest stop, Zeke was out at the side of the snake exhibit working on the enclosures. He stopped what he was doing and straightened up to watch as the Camry passed by.

"Before we left we should have asked the desk guy where we could get a gun," Sherrie said, looking out her side window at the desert. "It's the old west, there's probably a place to rent them."

"We don't need a gun, it's the middle of the day," Josh said.

"Yeah, and we're going to the middle of nowhere," she replied.

Thirty minutes later they swung into the abandoned gas station and Sherrie couldn't believe they were back there; it gave her the willies all over again. Josh pulled the car around to the side and parked near the old derelict car. When they got out of their car the heat hit them like a wall, more so because Josh had had the AC cranked on the drive out.

"Ok, so show me the dates," Sherrie said.

Josh pulled open the driver's door which produced a squeal of rusted metal that made them both wince and showed her the build plate that had the date on it. Around to the other side of the car he opened that door and popped the glove box open. She leaned in and could see a yellowed and tattered sticker still clinging to the cardboard back of the boxes interior. It had a dealership name, manufacturers date and sold date on it. Then around to the front and the engine, the hood made an even more tortuous sound than the doors had when Josh pulled it up. The engine was a rusted lump sprouting hoses and wires from several directions. Josh had wiped off the manufacture plate on the engine block on his first inspection so it was easy to read the date stamped into it. All of them, the door, the glove box, and engine, had the year 1944 on them.

"What about the tail light lenses," Sherrie asked, "Don't they show the date too?"

"I looked," Josh replied, "but they're too worn to be readable. Besides, that's just the date that the tail light was made; a car this old, the tail light lenses could have been replaced two or three times."

"Ok, so what now?"

"Take a walk out into the desert, see what's what."

"Fine, let's get it over with, and keep your eyes open for critters, I don't care what Zeke told us about coyotes."

"Coyotes are nocturnal; we won't even see any."

"How about rattlesnakes or scorpions or really big hairy spiders, are they all nocturnal too?"

"Let's hope so," Josh replied and started out into the desert behind the filling station. Sherrie fell in beside him. They crossed to the other side of the building and lined up with the bathroom window then started walking directly away from it. The surface was hard packed sand and scattered scrub growth that didn't reach much higher than their knees. They'd gone roughly thirty yards when they came across several sets of footprints indented into the surface.

"Could these be from the other night?" Josh said.

"It rained that night," Sherrie reminded him, "they could have made the prints in the wet sand and then it dried and preserved them."

"We saw a half dozen people though," Josh reminded her, "at least that's what it looked like. This looks like maybe two people, or three tops. If we look around, we may find more."

"Let's just follow these," Sherrie said, "they're going in the right direction." The sooner she was out of the desert the happier she was going to be.

Josh started out walking off to the side of the footprints, looking back every few minutes to stay orientated with the filling station's bathroom window. They were several hundred yards out into the desert when he stopped and looked around.

"Pretty sure this is about how far out they were when they disappeared."

"How can you possibly be sure," Sherrie asked, looking around too.

"When we first saw them they were close to the filling station, to us. We watched them walk out this way for about six minutes before they were gone. We just walked for six minutes." He looked down at the ground then swept one foot across the sandy surface. Then suddenly he jumped straight up into the air and came back down onto the ground with a thud.

"What the hell are you doing?" Sherrie said.

Josh started walking in an expanding circle out from where she was standing, pushing it further out into the desert as he went. Every few moments he would jump up and down again. "I'm looking for something," he told Sherrie, "know when I find it."

"Is it your mind?" Sherrie asked, "Because if it is, we may be out here for a really long time."

He kept going and a few moments later he jumped and when he came down instead of a dull thud there was a hollow sound. He jumped again, same thing, and again, same thing, a hollow sound. He swept a foot across the sand to see what was under it but most of the sand didn't move. He got down onto his hands and knees and tried and the sand still didn't move because it wasn't real sand, it was fake sand glued to a smooth surface to camouflage the spot. He stood back up and began stomping on whatever it was under the sand.

"Josh, stop! You don't know what that is, or who put it out here!"

"Going to find out," he replied and took a big jump. Sherrie rushed forward and grabbed him by the arm and suddenly they both felt like they were falling. They grabbed each other and tried to stay on their feet and then suddenly, as quickly as it had started, it stopped and they were standing in the middle of the desert holding on to each other.

They looked around for a moment then Josh said; "What the fuck was that?"

"I just got dizzy for a minute," Sherrie said, "that's all it was, probably the heat. Now can we please get the hell out of here? I've had enough of this desert to last me the rest of my life."

"Don't you want to know what this is?" Josh asked her as he pointed at their feet.

"No," she replied and started walking back toward the filling station. He watched her walk away for a moment then swore and started after her. After a few steps he stopped and looked around until he found a decent size rock which he placed over the spot where the fake sand was. Then he trotted away to catch up with Sherrie.

Five

When they reached the filling station the Camry was gone. They both stood there stupidly for a moment, staring at the spot where it had been parked.

"I don't believe this," Sherrie said finally, "someone stole our frigging car! In the middle of nowhere and someone just came along and took our car!"

Josh started to look around, as if maybe the Camry had moved to another spot on its own. He stopped once he was facing back toward the desert and he touched Sherrie on the arm.

"The old Plymouth is gone too; it was right there." He pointed, as if Sherrie wouldn't remember where the old wreck had been parked.

"Who gives a shit," Sherrie said and walked around the front of the building. It was still deserted and there was still no one in sight in either direction on the highway. She stopped at the pumps under the shade of the awning and shook her head. Josh came up next to her and put his hand on her shoulder.

"All our stuff was in that car Josh," she said, "our luggage, our clothes, my computer." She stopped and looked at him, "you didn't leave the keys in it, did you?'

Josh took the car keys out of his pocket and held them up for her to see. She turned and looked off down the highway again.

"Apology accepted," Josh said and started walking west.

"Where are you going?"

"I'm going to walk to Zeke's place. Maybe someone will come along and give me a ride, if not then it shouldn't take me more than two or three hours"

"Well I'm coming with you," Sherrie hurried after him. "And I'm sorry," she said as she fell in next to him.

It was high desert and it wasn't summer so they did OK. Water would have been good, but even without it they were OK and even made pretty good time. Sherrie was worried about snakes and kept checking the scrub growth along the shoulder as they walked. No cars passed them and for a few hours it was just a huge empty sky and a featureless desert with a narrow strip of undulating black asphalt running down its middle. Sherrie spent a good part of the walk staring down at the pavement and silently cataloguing everything that had been in the Camry.

They finally topped the last rise before Zeke and Mabel's place and could see right away that something wasn't right. For one thing the array of cages that had made up the snake exhibit and had occupied one entire side of the property was not there. For another the souvenir shop looked like it had been totally rehabbed since they'd driven past it a few hours earlier, and instead of a trailer out back there was a cute little white clapboard cottage. Lastly, there were two classic cars parked out front in place of Richard the Deep Breather and Mabel's beat up Taurus that had been there before. They looked at each other then started down the rise.

"That car on the left looks kind of like a 70's Chevy," Josh said as they got closer, "but there's something off about it, someone customized the crap out of it."

"The other one reminds me of the car my grandmother had when I was little," Sherrie replied, "kind of."

"So we're going to totally ignore the fact that the place looks completely different," Josh said.

"We'll ask Zeke when we get there," Sherrie told him.

Except that when they did get there it wasn't Zeke who came out to meet them, but a much younger man with blond hair and glasses.

"Afternoon," he said, holding a hand up to shade the sun. "You folks have car trouble out on the road?"

"You could say that," Sherrie said. "We parked at that old gas station to take a walk in the desert and when we came back someone had stolen our car."

"That's terrible," the man said, "don't know what the world's coming to these days."

"It's a Toyota Camry," Josh told him, "You didn't see one go by this way, did you?"

The man frowned a bit, "Afraid I don't know that model," he said, "but no one's driven past here all morning so they must have gone east. Why don't you folks come on inside and have a nice cool drink and we can call the Sherriff."

Once they were inside things graduated from just not right to pretty strange. The inside of the shop was structurally the same as the room they'd been in with Zeke and Mabel, but that was where the similarities ended. The man led them over to a soda fountain, an honest to God soda fountain, that took up one side of what was a very nicely appointed gift shop right out of a Norman Rockwell painting.

They sat on the stools he waved them to while he went around behind the counter, opened a metal ice chest and produced two Cokes in real long necked glass bottles. Then he took a church key out of his pocket and used it to pop the tops off each bottle, which he then put in front of them. "No charge," he told them, "couldn't charge you after your car's just been stolen."

Sherrie was pretty thirsty; she picked up her Coke and took a sip. She usually drank diet Coke or Pepsi (she'd never been able to tell the difference between the two), when she drank soda at all so it had been a while since she's had a regular Coke, but she didn't remember it being as sugary as this one was; it almost puckered her mouth every time she took a sip.

The man held his hand out over the counter to shake, "Tom Whitmore," he told them, "half owner and proprietor of this establishment." They all shook and Josh asked him who the other owner was. "That'd be my wife," Tom replied. "She's out in the back tending her garden; we take turns watching the shop you know. You two just relax and I'll get the Sheriff on the line." He turned to a wall phone behind the counter, took the receiver off and started to dial. Sherrie and Josh had never seen a rotary phone, except on TV, so they watched with interest as Tom dialed. His conversation with the Sheriff's office was short and when he hung up he caught them looking at the phone.

"I know," he laughed, "the wife keeps telling me we should upgrade to one of those new push button phones, but Ma Bell is already charging us dearly for this one and besides, it works just fine. Sheriff's office will have someone here quick as they can, by the way. Either of you hungry? Be happy to put together a couple of sandwiches for you."

"Thank you," Sherrie said, 'but I think we're fine, just needed something to drink, that's all."

"OK well, you two just sit and relax and wait for the Sheriff. If you don't mind I'm going to go out back for a minute and check on the wife."

As soon as he was gone Sherrie turned to Josh, "What is going on here? How did Zeke's dumpy roadside stop change into this in the four hours since we drove past it? And what's up with that phone, and these Cokes?"

"I have another one," Josh replied, "how is it that he's never heard of a frigging Toyota Camry? It's only the best-selling car in the US, after the cozy coup anyway."

"And where are Zeke and Mabel? Should we ask him about that? I think we should."

"Sure, and what if he doesn't have a wife, what if he's out back hiding their bodies or something."

"Yeah," Sherrie said. "He killed them both then completely renovated their roadside tourist trap, complete with retro cars and phones and soft drinks, and he did it all since we drove by here at ten o'clock this morning."

"So you tell me what's going on," Josh said. "You explain all of this."

"I can't," she said softly, "but it's seriously creeping me out. And I'm starting to feel nauseous too, you don't think he put something in the Cokes, do you?" She pushed her bottle away across the counter.

"We watched him open them," Josh reminded her. "With a bottle opener no less."

"I think we should get out of here," Sherrie said suddenly. "I think we should just get up and leave, right now."

"And do what? Walk to town? We'd get there sometime tomorrow. That is of course if the sheriff doesn't get here, find us gone and drive along the highway until he finds us. Our car's gone, remember?"

"I'm not sure I care anymore," Sherrie said. "I don't like any of this, it's not right." She took her phone out of her pocket and checked it, "And still no frigging signal. Where in America isn't there a frigging cell phone signal?"

"We are in the middle of the desert Sher; maybe we've found the last place in the entire country without service."

"I want to leave Josh; I have a bad feeling about this."

A white and green police cruiser swung into the parking lot out in front of the shop and they both noticed that it was at least thirty years old, but neither commented on the fact because they didn't see the point.

A man wearing a tan sheriff's uniform with dark brown trim got out of the car, put on a Smokey Bear hat and walked into the shop. Josh knew something about handguns and noted that he was wearing a large frame revolver on his belt. He hadn't thought any cops anywhere were still carrying wheel guns. Like the cruiser, he noticed it, then let it go because he didn't see the point in doing anything else.

"You the couple had your car stolen?" he asked when he reached the counter.

"Yes," Sherrie said, "it was parked at that old abandoned gas station up the road."

"What were you doing there?"

"We were driving west and we decided to stop to take a walk in the desert," Sherrie replied. "It seemed safer to park it there than out on the highway."

The Deputy nodded as if to say that made sense. He took a note pad and pen out of his shirt pocket and sat down on one of the counter stools. "I'm Deputy Tomlin by the way, and you are?" They gave him their names and addresses, told him that they'd taken a week's vacation to see some of the country and were just driving wherever they decided to go."

"Sounds like fun," Deputy Tomlin commented. "Could you give me a description of your car?"

"It's a 2014 Toyota Camry, its dark green." Josh replied.

Deputy Tomlin frowned, "I'm not familiar with that model. What make is Toyota, is that one of those Jap cars?"

"Ah, yeah, it's a Japanese car, Toyota; they've been selling them..." Sherrie pinched the back of his arm and he stopped talking. "It's a four door sedan," she told the deputy, "its dark green with California plates on it."

"What's the number on the plate?" Tomlin asked.

Before he could say anything Sherrie pinched Josh's arm again, "I'm afraid we don't remember the license plate numbers, we just got the car recently," she said. Josh had owned the Toyota for over a year. She gave Deputy Tomlin one of her 'sorry but I'm just a dumb chick' smiles and shrugged her shoulders.

"OK," Tomlin lowered his notebook, "shouldn't be hard to spot anyway, doubt there are many Japan cars driving around. I'll radio it in and we'll see what we can do. You folks need a lift into town?"

"We don't," Sherrie said quickly, "we're going to call someone to come and pick us up so we're all set, but thanks."

"That's fine, the only other thing I need is a number to reach you at if we find your car."

Without thinking about it Josh reeled off his cell phone number, the deputy wrote it down then flipped his notebook closed and got off the stool. He actually tipped his hat to Sherrie then headed for the door. "We'll be in touch," he said over his shoulder and was gone.

As soon as the door closed Josh turned to Sherrie, "We kinda do need a ride," he said, "unless you want to walk to town."

"I don't think we should go to town," she replied, "I think we should get the hell out of here and think about what we're going to do next. I'm actually thinking that it might be a good idea to head back to the filling station."

"What for, there's nothing back there," Josh said. "I think we should go into town and wait in our room for the cops to call us, hopefully to tell us they found our car."

"They're not going to find our car," Sherrie replied.

"I can give you a ride into town," Tom said and they both jumped and he laughed. "Sorry, didn't mean to startle you, was just coming in the back door when I heard you talking about a ride into town. I have to take a run in to pick up a few things."

"That would be great, "Josh replied before Sherrie could say anything.

Six

The town was at least three times the size it had been when they'd left that morning. There were whole streets, whole neighborhoods, that hadn't been there that morning. Josh was in the back seat and he kept his mouth shut. Sherrie was riding shotgun and he waited for her to freak, but she was just sitting very still and staring straight ahead through the windshield. When Tim pulled up in front of their hotel, which looked pretty much the same as it had that morning except that that morning it was a free standing building and now it was flanked by two six story brick office buildings, she all but flew out of the car. Josh thanked Tim for the ride then climbed out too.

"What odds do you want that we no longer have a room at this hotel," Sherrie said as they watched Tim's old imitation Chevy drive away.

"What is going on," Josh replied, "I mean what the fuck is going on?"

"He had an eight track tape player in his car," Sherrie said, "and the only reason I know what one of those is is because I dated a classic car nut once. I'm not going into the hotel, Josh. If you want to check on our room you go ahead, I'll wait right here."

"You look really pale," Josh said, looking at her. "Are you ok?"

"You mean other than the fact that I'm in the Twilight Zone? No, I don't feel ok, I told you back there that I felt nauseous and it's getting worse."

Josh spotted a bench in front of one of the buildings that hadn't been there that morning and led her over to it; the building was shading it from the afternoon sun. "I'll be right back, you just sit and rest for a few minutes."

"We don't have a room," she told him.

"I have to check; I'll only be a minute." He was back in a bit less than five minutes and sat down on the bench next to her. "We don't have a room," he told her. "They've never heard of us."

"So what do we do now?"

"Well, I think we should rent a room, another room, and get some rest, then we'll get something to eat and figure this out."

"Don't try to use your credit card in there," Sherrie said, "I don't think it will work."

"I have cash; I always carry cash on vacation, just in case."

"Just in case you end up in bizzarro world," Sherrie laughed and Josh didn't like how it sounded, it was a shrill humorless laugh. He got her up and into the hotel, the lobby was pretty much the same so that was OK. He paid for a room for one night and they went upstairs. The room wasn't the same one they'd had the previous night, but it looked pretty much the same and that was OK too. Because right at that moment what they needed was a little frigging continuity in their lives.

Sherrie immediately got in the shower and while he waited Josh stood at the window and looked out at the town, almost a small city now. Sherrie finally emerged from the bathroom with a towel wrapped around her and lay down on the bed. Her eyes had kind of a crazy vacant look that Josh didn't like at all. He thought she might be going into shock.

"How about I go out and get us some clean clothes," he said to her, "and maybe something to eat? I don't know about you, but I'm starving."

"I don't want to be here alone," Sherrie said.

"Sher, you'll be fine, I think you need to rest a bit, maybe take a nap. You'll be perfectly safe here."

"What if you don't come back?"

He walked over, sat down on the bed next to her and leaned over to kiss her. "Of course I'll come back, and then we'll try to figure out what's going on, ok?"

"If you leave me here alone I'll kill you," Sherrie told him then closed her eyes. Josh rolled her over, pulled the bedcovers down and got her under them then tucked her in. He leaned over and kissed her again then left the room.

He turned right out the front door of the hotel and walked along the sidewalk noticing things. He noticed that all the cars were old like Tim's had been, but most of them looked new and they were quiet, he could barely hear them running. He noticed that there were telephone booths scattered about and that they contained honest to God payphones. Josh hadn't seen a payphone in quite a while and he had never seen a real, functioning phone booth, not in the US anyway. He noticed that no one on the street was texting, or talking on a cell phone, or wearing ear buds; in fact, he didn't see a single person with a cell phone. He noticed that, while some of the car names were familiar to him, just as many weren't. And when he spotted a clothing store and went inside he noticed that he didn't recognize many of the brand names; Levis was there, as was Woolrich and Champion, but there was no North Face, or Ralph Lauren, or Polo, or Izod. Instead, there were a bunch of brands that he'd never seen before. Twenty or thirty years ago that might have been OK, different regions of the country had different brands, like that you never saw a Piggly Wiggly supermarket outside of the south. But now everything had pretty much become standardized, you saw mostly the same stores at a mall in Arizona as you did at one in Massachusetts. So he found it just a bit odd to be looking at Greenvalley jeans now, because he'd never heard of them before.

He ended up buying a couple of changes of clothes for both of them then he left the store. He'd gotten a few blocks back toward the hotel when he spotted a bookstore and went inside. It was the same thing with author's names as it had been with the clothes, some he knew but many he didn't. He found the history section and picked out a book on world history put out by National Geographic because he did know them. He made one final stop at a burger place called Sizzle Burger to get them some food. He'd never heard of Sizzle Burger either, even though they claimed to be a national chain.

When he got back to the room Sherrie was still asleep so he put her food on the bureau then sat down in a chair by the window and ate his burger and fries while he thumbed through the history book. After an hour or so of reading he'd seen more than enough. He put the book on the bureau and went into the bathroom to take a shower.

When he emerged some time later Sherrie was awake. She was sitting in the chair by the window reading the history book. The empty wrapper from her burger was crumpled up on the window-sill beside her.

"Feel better?" Josh asked her.

"I did," she replied, "until I started reading this. Where did you get this?"

"At a bookstore down the street, in the history section." He was pulling the labels off the clothes he'd bought for himself and getting dressed.

"Have you looked at it?"

"For over an hour while you were sleeping, before I went in to shower."

She put the book down on the floor next to the chair; she did it gingerly, as if it may bite. The vacant expression was gone from her face and her eyes no longer had that glassy shocked look, but she still didn't look good. Josh thought she looked like she may be starting to unravel a bit at the corners.

"So what the fuck is going on Josh?" she said.

"I don't know."

She suddenly got out of the chair, went into the bathroom and threw up the burger and fries into the toilet. He moved to the doorway to help her, but she waved him away so he sat on the edge of the bed and waited. After a few minutes she came out with a glass of water, which she placed gingerly on the windowsill as she sat back down in the chair. She reached down, picked up the book again and opened it to a place that she had marked earlier by folding over the top corner of the page. She looked at the page for a few moments then looked up at him.

"According to this book, according to National freaking Geographic, World War I and World War II never happened," she flipped to another marked page, "the moon landings never happened," another page, "John F Kennedy wasn't assassinated in Dallas because he was never the president," another page, "The Viet Nam War, didn't happen," another page, "more than half the presidents listed here are people I've never even heard of." She closed the book and looked at him.

"What do you want me to say Sherrie?"

"I don't want you to say anything; I want to get the hell out of here right now because I've had enough. I want to go home."

"And how do we do that exactly?"

"We take a bus or a train, we hitchhike, I don't know, I don't care. I just want to get out of here." She paused to take a drink of water then stared out the window for a moment. "Or," she said finally, "or we go back out to the desert behind the gas station and we stand on that spot again and click our heels three times and see what happens."

"You think that will work?"

"How the hell do I know? But it all started there, didn't it? You remember when we jumped up and down, I felt dizzy for a minute, you did too."

"So what, it was for a split second and nothing changed. The desert didn't spin around, there was no jump through a tunnel or anything, and we didn't budge from that spot. We probably got dizzy because we were jumping up and down in the desert, in the heat, with the sun beating down on us."

"Maybe," she said, "but maybe not. I think we should go back out there and try it again and see what happens. No one knows anything Josh, let's just try it and see what happens."

"Ok, what the hell, I've got nothing else. The only question is how do we get back out there."

"We'll get a cab, or a bus, or we'll hitchhike, I don't know. But I think we need to do it and I think it needs to be soon, the longer we're here the worse I feel."

"I feel fine," he said.

"That's great, I'm happy for you,"

"What I mean is that maybe you're just coming down with a bug or something. I've been here as long as you have and I'm OK. That's all I meant."

"I don't know what it is, I just know I want it to stop, so let's go back out there and try."

"And what if nothing happens."

"Something will," she replied quietly.

Seven

They looked in the phone book, there was an actual phone book in the room, and found a bus terminal not far from the hotel. They decided to go there first and see if a bus was running out past the old filling station. If that didn't work out they'd try a cab company. Sherrie was stuffing their dirty clothes into one of the shopping bags the new clothes had come in when someone knocked on their hotel room door. They both froze and looked at each other.

"Mr. Everett? I'm with the Sheriff's office, I'm here about your report of a stolen vehicle."

"How did they know we'd be here?" Sherrie whispered at him.

"We told the deputy we were staying here," Josh reminded her, "because we still thought we had a room at that point." He walked over and opened the door.

The man in the hallway wasn't wearing a deputy's uniform; he was wearing a suit and tie. He didn't look like a cop to Josh. He did have a little notebook though, like the deputy had had. Josh wondered if anyone there used mobile devices for anything. He wondered if any of them knew what a mobile device was.

"Mr. Everett," he nodded to Josh then turned to Sherrie and glanced down at his notebook again though Josh had the feeling it was just for show. "Ms. Sherilynn DeWitt I presume?" He stepped into the room.

"Did you find our car?" Sherrie asked him.

"Not exactly," he said. "We don't have possession of your car at the moment, but we do know where it is."

"And where is that?" Josh asked him.

"At the abandoned filling station, just where you parked it this morning."

"So the thief was kind enough to bring it back," Josh asked, a hint of sarcasm in his voice.

"Not at all, there was no thief; the car has been parked there all day, right where you left it."

"May I see some ID, "Josh asked and the man produced a thin leather folder from his jacket pocket and handed it to him. Josh opened it and looked at the ID then back up at the man. "This says you're with something called the Federal Office of Compliance, not the Sheriff's Department."

"It does indeed," the man said. "Do you mind if I sit down?" he asked and then crossed the room and sat down in the chair by the window without waiting for a response. He smiled at both of them. "Why don't you two sit as well, on the bed? I just need to speak to you about a few things; you're not in any trouble or anything like that."

"Speak to us about what?" Sherrie said, "And what did you mean about the car."

"About there being no mobile phones here," the man replied, "and about the two world wars that never happened, little things like that." He smiled again and motioned to the bed and they both sat down on the edge of it.

"You've noticed that things are a bit different from what they were this morning when you woke up," the man said. "I'm here to help you with that. As Josh saw from my ID my name is Hugh Bryce, please call me Hugh."

"OK Hugh, why *are* there no mobile phones," Sherrie said, "and why doesn't that book mention either world war, or President Kennedy, or the Apollo missions?"

"Simple answers to all of those questions," Hugh replied. "There are no cell phones because they haven't been invented yet, not here anyway. The book doesn't mention any of those historical events because here they didn't happen."

"Where is 'here'?" she asked.

"Here is the very same town you woke up in this morning, just a different version of it." He leaned forward in the chair and rested his elbows on his knees. Sherrie and Josh leaned forward too, without even realizing that they were doing it. "When you were out there in the desert this morning," Hugh said, "you found a spot that was a bit different and you jumped up and down on it. What made you do that?"

"It sounded hollow," Josh said. "I wanted to test it to see if it really was. The sand and rocks were fake too."

"Weren't you worried that, if it really were hollow, you'd fall in?"

Josh frowned for a moment, "I never thought of that," he said.

"I did," Sherrie said.

"And when you did that," Hugh went on, "did you feel anything?"

"I felt dizzy," Sherrie replied, "just for a second or two, but I definitely felt it."

"I did too," Josh said. "Are you going to tell us what happened out there Hugh, because it does all come back to that, doesn't it?"

"It most definitely does," Hugh said. "When you jumped up and down on that spot, on that hollow thing, you opened a doorway into a parallel dimension, very small doorway, but a doorway all the same. I'm going to assume here that you've both heard of the theory of parallel dimensions?"

"I have," Josh told him, "A little bit anyway."

"They're supposed to be worlds just like ours that are right next to ours, but just a little different," Sherrie said. She looked around the room as if for the first time.

"No offense," Josh said, "but that's a little hard to believe. It sounds more like an episode of The Twilight Zone than real life."

"Well we're definitely not in the Twilight Zone, "Hugh laughed. "We're just in a place that's a little different, a plane of reality that shadows yours and is in some respects almost identical but in many other respects is very different."

"So if that's true then how do you know about cell phones and the wars and all that?" Josh asked him.

"I've been over to your side," Hugh replied, "numerous times actually, so have a small, select group of others. At first, when the portal was discovered we were curious. Now we just like to keep tabs of what's going on over there."

"Does what we do over there affect what happens over here?" Sherrie asked him.

"Thankfully it does not." He didn't elaborate because Sherrie seemed to understand what he meant.

"You were the guys we saw out in the desert in the middle of the night," She said.

"Not me personally but yes, some of my compatriots. They were returning from a short fact finding trip and didn't realize you were there until it was too late. That filling station has been the guardian of the gate between our worlds for decades. We use it as a landmark, as you saw, one patch of desert looks very much like another."

"So you just bop back and forth into our world whenever you want?" Sherrie asked. "Does our government know about that?"

"They don't, and only a very small, very select group of people know about it in ours. And we don't go over very often. To be brutally honest we don't see much to recommend your dimension and not much we can learn from it. We're more concerned with anything from there coming over here."

"You don't even have cell phones, or the internet, from what I've seen," Sherrie said. "I would think you'd have a lot to learn from our dimension."

"You would be wrong," Hugh replied. "We get along just fine without those things. What we also don't have over here is war; the last major war in this world was the American Civil War which produced such horrific carnage that the people of this world vowed never to have another, and so far we haven't. And because we've had no wars we've benefited in ways you couldn't dream of, beginning with the fact that we've not experienced the Spanish Flu, Influenza, and a host of other diseases that often originate and find rich breeding grounds in such events.

"You don't have cell phones or the internet because you didn't have the wars," Josh realized. "Wars accelerate technological advances, and medical ones as well. I'm not saying I'm a fan but you have to admit, wars do move a lot of things forward very quickly."

"You are right about that," Hugh said, "and because we didn't suffer through the wars and the resulting pandemics I'll admit that our world suffers from a serious problem with overcrowding. Our planet wide population is much larger than yours, but that gate swings both ways. There was a man named Walter Martindale who existed in both of our dimensions. Which is a common occurrence by the way, individuals existing on both sides. In your world he was killed at the age of 29 when his field hospital was overrun by the Vietcong in 1969. In our world he was never there because there was no Viet Nam War and in 1981 he developed a cure for cancer. Francois Bonne was another significant resident of both dimensions; in yours he died in France fighting the Nazis in World War II at the age of 19, in ours he developed a viable and renewable alternative to fossil fuels that's used everywhere here. That means no oil embargos, no western interference in the Middle East over control of oil fields and all the resultant issues that brought about in your world. The Middle East is a quiet backwater in our world. And of course without the burning of fossil fuels our atmosphere is much cleaner than yours is."

"Is that why your cars are so quiet?" Josh asked.

"It is. There are no internal combustion engines here; our engines run on a plant based fuel, mostly corn, that burns cleanly and is, as I said, totally renewable."

"And you know all of this about our dimension from quick little trips through the gate?" Sherrie asked him.

"More than just quick little trips as I'm sure you suspect from the tone of your voice. We've done enough research to know that we are better off here and want no part of your dimension. We may be evolving more slowly technologically and yes Mr. Everett, much of that is due to the lack of wars, but we're doing just fine and cell phones and the internet and all the rest will come in its own good time, if it comes at all. Who knows, maybe we'll end up with something better. I can't say I'd look forward to a future here of everyone walking around staring at their cell phone and wearing headphones to block out the rest of the world."

"So are we the first people from our world to find the gate?" Josh asked.

"By accident yes, well, almost. There was one other before you. But there are others from your side here, people we've asked to come over and who have decided to stay. It's a small number of people."

"Don't want us infecting your utopia, huh?" Josh said.

"Something like that," Hugh replied drily.

"So now that we know about the gate, what happens to us?" Josh asked, "Are you going to make us stay here?"

"On the contrary, I'm going to drive you back to the filling station and you're going to get your butts back through it and out of here. And your car will be waiting for you right where you left it."

"You're not afraid we'll tell people about it, show it to them?"

"Who would believe you? And even if you convinced someone to drive out into the middle of the desert to look for it we'll be watching and would take steps to stop you."

"You'd get rid of us," Josh said.

Hugh laughed, "Have you heard nothing of what I've been telling you? This world isn't like yours; violence isn't the answer for everything here. We have other ways to deal with it. But I trust that if you give me your word not to do that, then the issue will be settled."

"Just like that."

"Yes, just like that. Here, a person's word means something, it has weight. It's just one more aspect of our civilization that yours is in dire need of."

"You have my word," Sherrie said, "And you don't have to worry about me trying to come back here, I've felt terrible ever since we got here and it's getting worse. You may not have fossil fuels, but something here is making me sick."

"You're making yourself sick," Hugh told her.

"What does that mean?"

"These are parallel worlds as I said, and there are as many similarities as there are differences. There are also a great many people who exist in both worlds and you must be one of them. If your exact double, your mirror image, exists in this dimension then there can't be two of you here, it seems to violate some law of nature. You're feeling the other you, you're sensing her presence here, and because she belongs in this world and you don't it's making you ill."

"So if I stayed here I'd die?"

"I don't know, you may, or you may lose your mind. No one's ever taken it that far, why would they?"

"So if I feel fine, which I do," Josh said, "then that must mean that there's no other *me* in this dimension."

"That is correct. For some reason your mother never met your father in this world, or their mothers never met their fathers, or so on. It would take just a single break in a very long chain of events for you to never have been born in this dimension."

"That's kind of depressing," Josh said, "not to mention making me feel extremely small and very insignificant."

"Zeke knows about all of this doesn't he?" Sherrie asked abruptly and Hugh gave her a somewhat impressed look. "He does," he replied, "What made you put that together?"

"I don't know," Sherrie said, "it just clicked. Why else would he live there like he does? Why doesn't he just come live over here?"

"He can't," Hugh replied. "He's already here and we can't have two Zeke's running around, can we? He keeps an eye on the gate for us; he's become a good friend over the years. We were watching for you because he warned us that you might find the gate."

"So when are you taking us back?" Sherrie asked. "I don't mean to be rude and this is all very mind blowing, but I really do feel awful, and it is getting worse."

"We can go right now," Hugh said and he reached down to pick up the history book as he got out of the chair. "I'm sure you'll understand if I keep this here with me," he said and gave them a smile.

Eight

The ride out to the filling station seemed to Josh to take no time at all. He was in the front seat with Hugh peppering him with questions. To Sherrie it seemed to take forever, she was in the back seat trying not to throw up again. She had the chills now too and that was a fun new wrinkle.

"So no moon landings either," Josh was saying to Hugh, "I have to say that is disappointing to me; when I was a kid I built every model of the Apollo capsules and rockets that I could find. I had a three-foot high model of the Saturn V rocket in my room."

"No, no moon landings," Hugh said, "sorry to disappoint you. We will be colonizing Mars within the next decade or so though, if that makes you feel any better."

"What? How is that possible when you guys don't even have cell phones?"

"Were there cell phones in your 1960's when the Apollo program was going on?"

"He's got you there," Sherrie said from the back seat.

"OK," Josh said, "but how is that possible? We haven't even done that yet."

"It's pretty much a question of necessity," Hugh replied, "We need the living space. And we went down a different road than you did. Your space program depends on solid fuel rockets that were pioneered by the Germans during your second world war. After that war everyone grabbed the German's rocket technology and ran with it since it had already been started and was workable. No one really thought of other options, not really, so you were tied to solid fuel rockets. Here there was no second world war, no German rocket program and no strong push down that path. The result was other technologies that not only worked, but also ended up working better than rockets. We have pulse engines that are smaller, more powerful, more fuel efficient, and permanently attached. That's what will take us to Mars."

"That's amazing," Josh told him, "I would love to be around to see that."

"What do you do for work over on your side?" Hugh asked him.

"I'm an electrical systems manager, I repair stuff mostly. But I'm just finishing up my masters in electrical engineering and plan on moving on to bigger and better things."

"How about you?" Hugh looked over his shoulder at Sherrie.

"Doesn't matter," Sherrie replied, "I'll be dead soon."

"You'll feel better as soon as you're back on your own side," Hugh assured her.

"She works in internet marketing," Josh told him.

"Have a little trouble finding work over here," Hugh laughed.

"People could live without smart phones and the net," Josh said. "They did it for centuries, doesn't really matter to me."

"It does to me," Sherrie said from the back seat.

They came up on the tourist stop that, in their world, belonged to Zeke and Mabel Boniface and in this world belonged to Tom Whitmore and his wife, whose name they never got. Tom's alternative dimension Chevy was parked out front.

"Tom seems like a nice guy," Josh observed as they passed by, "actually everyone we've met seems overly pleasant."

"Like the Stepford Wives," Sherrie opined from the back seat.

"Having spent time in your world I could see how you would see it that way," Hugh said. "As much as everything looks the same here, pretty much, there are fundamental differences that to both of you would seem like unusual behavior."

"You've lost me," Josh told him.

"Certain events change people, certain very large events change a lot of people which then results in a change of a societies psyche, and in the manner in which a species may perceive the world."

"Now you've really lost me," Josh said.

"Me too," Sherrie said from the back seat.

"War, especially war on a global scale, will cause a shift in the societal views of that world. The results include a deep-seated distrust in authority, in those in charge, and also a fatalistic view of the world, an inability to really rely on anyone or anything, including the sanctity and security of civilization itself. War on a global scale damages people's beliefs in what is good and just, in what they can believe in or depend on. Your world has had two such wars in one century, and a lot of smaller ones before and after. This world hasn't. There's an old saying, war is a total suspension of rational thought...we're big on rational thought here."

"So it's a kinder gentler place, is that it?" Josh asked.

"If you choose to phrase it in that way then yes, it is. People here haven't had their faith in humanity shaken over and over again the way those in your world have. And no one here has ever lived with the fear of being nuked into oblivion...it makes a difference."

"Yeah," Josh said, "I guess I could see how it would."

"Hey," Sherrie said from the back seat, 'if our ETA is more than three minutes I think we need to pull over because I'm going to heave again."

"Two minutes," Hugh told her and in fact, a minute and 40 seconds later he pulled into the cracked and dusty parking area next to the filling station. Sherrie was out of the car as soon as it stopped and off behind the building. They could hear her as they got out as well.

"Should you go see if she's OK?" Hugh asked Josh.

"She doesn't like anyone to be around her when she's sick," Josh told him, "believe me, it's safer to wait right here."

Sherrie finally emerged wiping her mouth and looking miserable. Josh took one arm and Hugh the other.

"I can walk out to the spot," Sherrie told them. "Just move fast if I start to make funny noises so I don't barf on your shoes."

They made their way back to the spot and the rock Josh had placed over it was still there. Hugh picked it up and tossed it away.

"How many spots are there like this?" Josh asked.

"Including this one?"

"Yeah."

"One, so it's easy to keep an eye on."

"So this is it?" Josh said, "We just go back?"

"Yes," Hugh replied, "You just go back, and we trust you to leave it at that. I can ask you to swear on your mother's life or something like that if it makes you feel any better."

"I'm good with it this way," Sherrie said. "I'd like to say it's been fun but, it really hasn't." She stepped onto the spot, jumped, and she was gone. Josh just stood there and looked at the spot for a moment then turned back to Hugh. "Don't suppose you'd like to look me up next time you're over on my side," he said, "let me know how that Mars thing is going?"

"Who knows," Hugh said, "anything's possible." He held out his hand and they shook, then Josh stepped onto the spot.

"You really don't have to jump," Hugh told him, "Just stamping your foot on it is sufficient."

Josh smiled and nodded, and stamped his foot.

Sherrie was sitting in the sand waiting for him and she already looked better. She stood up and they walked slowly back to the abandoned filling station and the Camry was parked right where they'd left it that morning.

Epilog

Sherrie had a key to Josh's apartment so she let herself in. She found him sitting on the balcony watching the sun set behind Wasson Peak. She sat down beside him and for a few minutes they both watched.

"So," Sherrie said finally, "when one person in a relationship tells the other person in the relationship that they want to talk, it's not good."

"Always?"

"Usually, pretty sure you didn't ask me over to propose to me."

"You don't think so, huh?"

"I hope to God not, because I'd say no." She turned to look at him, "I care a lot about you Josh, really do. But I'd still say no and

I'm pretty sure you already know that. Just like I'm pretty sure if I asked you you'd say no."

"I didn't ask you over here to propose, or to dump you, not really."

"Not really? You either are or you aren't, there's no 'not really'."

He didn't say anything for a moment then he turned his chair to face her. "I've been out to see Zeke a few times in the last couple of months. Hugh's been here to visit me too and we've done a lot of talking. I've given it a lot of thought and I want to go back, and not to visit again, to stay this time."

She turned back to the mountains and shook her head then she smiled a tight little smile.

"You knew," Josh said.

"I had a feeling," she replied, "a really strong feeling. Since we've been back you've been different, kind of absent I guess is a good way to put it. They're going to let you do that?"

"Yeah, set me up with a job and everything. I can just keep being me since I don't exist over there. They think my background and my education would make me useful working on their Mars mission. It would be my dream job Sherrie, and something that I'd never get to do here. And there's something else, it's saner over there, more livable I guess, at least I think it is. It's the kind of a world I'd like to live in. My parents are gone, I've got no close family, there's really just you."

"I do exist over there," Sherrie said, "you know I can't go back."

"I know."

"And I wouldn't want to if I could."

"I know that too."

She looked at him, "So I'm all that's holding you here, Josh?"

"Yeah, pretty much."

It was her turn to be silent for a moment and when she finally spoke her voice was soft, "I guess it's time for truth here then, huh?" She stood up abruptly, "I think I need a beer, do you want one?"

Josh said that was a good idea and Sherrie disappeared into his apartment. It took longer than it should have, but she finally reappeared with two bottles of Coors. She handed one to him then sat back down in her chair. She took a couple of sips then put the bottle on the patio table that was between them.

"All right," she said, her voice still soft, "here's how I see it; you and I are good together, really good. I have a great time with you and there's nothing about you that I don't like. You're also pretty good in the sack which believe me, isn't that common. So we may go on like this for another year, maybe even two because we're still young and there's no rush. But I think that would be about it Josh, I really do. And maybe I'm wrong about that but I don't think I am, if you think I am, please tell me. You're a great guy, a really great guy...but, you're not *the* guy. And I'm pretty sure I'm not *the* girl either...am I?"

"No," Josh said, "I don't think you are. It's just kind of a cold way of looking at it. I do really care about you."

"And I care about you, but we're talking about a major life decision here. Like I said, it's time for truth between us. You're the one who's leaving but, it's probably easier this way than it would be a year from now, if one of us did meet *the* one while we were still together. We can look at it like that. That's the way I'm going to look at it anyway."

"I'm going to miss you a lot Sherilynn."

"I'm going to miss you too Joshua, and don't ever call me that again, you know I hate my name."

He smiled a little at that. "Ok, I'm going to go then."

Neither could think of anything else to say so they sat back and picked up their beers. The sun was almost gone behind the peak now so they both just sat and watched as it sank out of sight. Sherrie thought she could almost physically feel time passing. And then the sun was gone and the peak fell into shadows.

"When?" She asked finally.

"Soon, I just need to tie up a few loose ends, nothing important. *This* was the only important thing."

She smiled a little at that. "I am going to miss you. You can come for a visit once in a while, right?"

"Sure, I can do that," he said and they both knew it would never happen.

"OK. Well I want to see you again before you leave, but right now I have to go because I'm going to start crying a little and that wouldn't be fair to you." She stood up and he stood up and hugged her. She put the apartment key on the table next to her half full beer and started for the door, then stopped and turned back.

"One thing," she said, "don't look up the other me once you're over there, because that would just be so wrong in so many ways." She turned and was gone.

HIDDEN PLACES: FINDING THE NECRONOMICON

Chapter One

It was raining hard, damned hard, and the Green Line train was late as usual. Dan had lived in a lot of cities at one time or another and hadn't found many with worse public transit systems than Boston, not in the US anyway. The fact that he'd forgotten an umbrella didn't help either. When the train finally arrived he got on and dripped on the floor for six stops until he arrived at Haymarket Station then it was up the stairs and a long walk through a nasty night.

The apartment Phineas had rented was in Boston's North End and Dan had some trouble finding it. It was in Poe Court which was not much more than an alley really, off of Michelangelo Street which itself was so narrow that he walked right past it before realizing he'd done so. And all the while the rain came down. Finally, he arrived at a red brick building built sometime in the century before that last one, used the key Phineas had sent him and spent a moment in the vestibule shaking the water off of his rain slicker before heading up wooden stairs that were so dark with age that they looked as if they'd been painted black. There was no elevator.

The apartment was on the fourth floor - 4G, and he wondered what the G was for because there were only six apartments on each floor. One knock brought Dalton Land, who they all called Lannie, to the door.

"Oh, is it raining out there?" she asked sweetly.

"That's funny," Dan said entering the apartment, "you've been waiting for me to get here to use that one haven't you. Could you have found an apartment any further away from a T stop?"

"I didn't pick it," Lannie replied, "Phineas did." Phineas Gage was the leader of their little group, he'd founded it and then re-cruited the rest of them. He was also their resident elder because at forty-five he was the oldest member. He also knew many people and was the one who lined up the clients, on the jobs where they actually had clients, and most importantly, he came up with the money. He was currently sitting at a round dinette table by a set of double windows on the far side of the room. The table was covered with papers.

"For a very good reason," he said without looking up from the paper he was studying, "one that will become apparent shortly. We were lucky to get it too; apartments in the North End don't stay empty for very long."

"I'm afraid to ask what happened to the previous occupant," Dan replied. He draped his still dripping rain slicker over a chair and Lannie immediately picked it up and re-located it to the shower curtain rod in the bathroom where it could drip happily into the old claw foot tub. She came back into the main room and gave Dan a look.

"Nothing nefarious," Phineas told him, "I had someone keeping an eye out for an apartment in this neighborhood and someone finally moved out. They'd been keeping that eye out for the better part of a year."

Dan looked around for a moment. The apartment was fairly good size, two bedrooms, separate kitchen and a large center room that served as a living room and dining area. The age of the building showed once again with uneven plaster walls, high ceilings, high windows and steam radiators providing heat. It also showed in a bathroom that looked as if it had last been updated sometime in the 1940's. It was clean though and because if it's location he guessed it probably went for somewhere north of two grand a month...without utilities.

"Well it's a little hard to find," he told them. "Especially at night, in the rain; the streets around here are like a rabbit warren."

"I thought your people were supposed to be good trackers", Lannie said, "with amazing senses of direction."

"That is a racist statement that I will choose to ignore at this time." Dan replied. His last name was Birdsong and he was a full blooded Lakota Sioux Indian, almost; he had his suspicions that a white settler or two had managed to climb into the family tree back when they were taming the west and stealing his peoples land.

"Besides," he added, "where are Robert and Abbey? They're obviously having trouble finding it too."

"Robert had to pick up a few things on his way," Phineas said getting up from the table and stretching his back. "He'll be here any minute. Abbey on the other hand has probably wandered over the bridge into Charlestown by now."

Dan snorted at that and headed for the kitchen knowing that it would already be well stocked.

"I'd like some too," Lannie told him.

"Some what?"

"Whatever it is you're getting for yourself."

"Could you make some coffee?" Phineas said, "There's a tin of Kona in the cupboard. We're probably going to need it."

Lannie followed him into the kitchen because from past experience she didn't trust him in there alone. "That sounded ominous," he said to her as she made coffee and he watched.

"Oh it's on," she replied, "why else do you think we're here?"

"So what is it that's on?"

"I have absolutely no idea," she said. "But I'm sure it's going to be good, it always is, isn't it?"

"Some better than others," Dan said under his breath to be sure Phineas didn't hear him. "I'm still sore from the last one; running around the Sahara looking for a crashed airplane. And I still have a sunburn too."

"How can you possibly tell?" Lannie said as she turned the coffee maker on and stepped back to smile at him.

"And yet another racist statement related to my proud heritage, my aren't you on a roll tonight! I'm beginning to consider this a hostile work environment."

"You already knew that," she laughed and headed back out into the living room. He waited in the kitchen for the coffee to brew and he'd been right, it was fully stocked which meant that whatever project they were kicking off Phineas planned on using the apartment as a base of operations which meant that at least one of them would probably be taking up residence here, probably him.

When the coffee was ready he took full cups along with cream and sugar into the living room. While he was putting everything on the table Robert Cornelius entered the apartment, using his own key. He was dripping wet and Lannie started toward him, but he waved her away.

"Take it easy mom," he told her, "I've got it." He kicked off his sneakers and took his saturated jacket into the bathroom. Robert Cornelius was their unofficial second in command, seven years younger than Phineas, and their imaging expert specializing in still photography and video, both authentic and not.

Robert had just returned from the bathroom and poured himself a cup of coffee when Abbey Simons made her own rain-soaked entrance.

"I got lost," she announced to the room. "I almost ended up walking over the goddamned bridge into Charlestown." Abbey was their computer person and was a walking, talking cliché of a computer geek to the point that sometimes the others suspected that she affected the image on purpose and wasn't nearly as absented minded and socially inept as she seemed.

Abbey's arrival made them five and that was a quorum within their little organization so they began...

Chapter Two

With coffee in hand and rain drumming against the windows, they sat around the scarred old oak table that had come with the apartment and began.

Phineas handed around a manila folder to each of them, which was the way most of their meetings began when they were starting something new. They opened them and the first sheet of paper was a street map of the North End of Boston. An electronic pushpin marked the building in which they currently sat.

"Right," Phineas said, "we begin." He slid the map out of his folder and closed it, putting the map on top. "This is the North End, one of the oldest sections of Boston which is of course one of the oldest cities in North America. I've rented this particular apartment solely due to its proximity to this landmark." He put his finger down on a large oddly shaped patch of green on the map. "Copps Hill Burying Ground," he said, "located just on the other side of the building across the court from us. It is one of the oldest cemeteries in North America, a historic landmark and a national treasure. It is also the reason we're sitting here in this lovely turn of the century apartment tonight." He reached down into the leather legal bag that was on the floor next to his chair and took out a thick hardcover book that he placed next to the map. They all leaned forward to look at it.

"The collected works of H.P. Lovecraft" Dan said aloud on the off chance that some of the others at the table may have suddenly lost their ability to read.

"Anyone ever read him?" Phineas asked.

"In high school I think," Robert said. "I went through a short classic horror stage when I was sixteen, I don't really recall any of his stories though, except that they were bizarre to the nth degree."

"I'm actually still *in* my horror stage," Abbey told them, "but I haven't read much of Lovecraft, *The Dunwich Horror* and maybe one or two others. Robert is right, his fiction is very strange."

"Well we are going to have a crash course on him tonight, not his work so much as the man himself, and one particular story of his." He pushed the book aside and took an 8x10 black and white photo out of the leather bag. It showed a man probably in his 30's, short black hair, lantern jaw, tall and gaunt and gazing back at the camera with a world-weary look on his face.

"H.P. himself," Phineas told them, "age about 32 here, Howard Philips Lovecraft, born in Providence, Rhode and died there at age 46 from cancer. He wrote for pulp magazines of the era mostly and wasn't terribly successful during his lifetime. As is sometimes the case with artists, his work only became famous in the years after his death. For a short time about when this picture was taken he resided in Boston, very possibly here in the North End. He wrote a story called *Pickmans Model* during that time that takes place right in this neighborhood."

"Ok, that one I remember," Abbey said. "It was about an artist, with a studio around here, who painted pictures of hideous creatures roaming the city at night eating people and digging up graves and such. The hook of the story was that it turned out the monsters weren't products of the artist's twisted imagination but were real, they lived in ancient tunnels under the city and came out at night. Oh, I remember that story all right, because it creeped the bejesus out of me when I read it!"

Phineas pulled the book back over and opened it to a marked page at the beginning of a story. "*Pickmans Model*," he tapped the page, you're all free to read it when you have time. It's a bit dated and formulaic, not much like his more famous stories, but it's still pretty good. So, H.P. lived here for a short time, maybe, and wrote a story about monsters living in a labyrinth of ancient passageways under the North End. No one's ever been able to pin down the house that he had in mind as the artist's studio, but there's reason to believe that it was pulled down not long after the story was published. Anyway, that's not our concern."

"We're not going to be roaming around in colonial era sewers looking for monsters, are we?" Dan asked him, "Because that sort of thing doesn't do much for me, really. I could keep the home fires burning here whilst the rest of you carry on."

"Thanks a lot," Robert said.

"Whilst", Lannie looked at him, "you actually just used the word whilst in a sentence?"

"No one is going into any tunnels," Phineas told them, "although that does sound interesting. Lannie has been doing some research on Mr. Lovecraft for us because it's germane to what we *will* be doing, so listen and learn, there will be a quiz later."

Lannie opened her tablet. "OK," she said, "I've put everything I'm going to tell you guys into a PDF so you don't need to take notes, it's in all of your email folders now." She looked up from her computer at them and spoke from memory.

"Howard Phillips Lovecraft, H.P. Lovecraft to you, born in Providence, Rhode Island on August 20, 1890 and died in Providence, Rhode Island on March 15, 1937, age 46."

"He was born, he lived, and he died, the end. Good story Lannie, thanks." Dan said.

She gave him a look then continued; "As Phineas just said, Mr. Lovecraft was never successful as a writer during his lifetime. He never made a living at it but subsisted off of a small inheritance along with what little money he did make. His stories were published in pulp genre magazines of the era, one in particular that was called Weird Tales. He was reclusive with the exception of family and a small group of close friends. He was married for a short time, but he didn't seem to care for sex or love or even human contact and so his marriage was kind of a farce; he and his wife spent more time apart than together. A friend said of him once that 'he seemed to view humanity from a distance'. He may have suffered from Asperger's Syndrome, but there's no hard proof of that. He lived in New York City for a period of time, but spent the majority of his life in Providence, a city that he seemed to love. He also came to Boston a lot along with New Hampshire and other parts of New England." She paused to take a sip of coffee then continued.

"His fiction, for those of you who haven't read any of it, can be pretty bizarre. He created this entire fictional dimension or universe complete with its own history. After his death; it became known as the Cthulhu Mythos, but he himself referred to it as Yog-Sothothery. It's basically a separate dimension from ours where 'The Old One's' live, 'The Old Ones' once ruled over the earth, but were somehow banished. Lovecraft said that someday, when the time was right, 'The Old One's' would return to rule the world again and destroy or enslave humanity." Another quick sip of coffee.

"The 'Old Ones' knowledge, their history was, according to Lovecraft, contained in a Grimoire entitled The Necronomicon. This book also contained spells for summoning the 'Old Ones'... and any other creatures or demons that you wanted to say hi to. Lovecraft described the Necronomicon as the most dangerous book ever written. He said that it contained ancient knowledge from the 'Old Ones' that allowed the reader to cast spells, raise demons and allow these 'Old Ones' to re-enter our world. It first appeared in a Sumerian city, possibly UR, millennia ago. Then, in the 8th century a copy entitled Al Azif surfaced in Damascus where it was translated from Arabic to Greek by Abdul Alhazred, also known as the 'Mad Arab'. According to Mr. Lovecraft only a very few copies of the book exist and these are kept hidden away to prevent anyone from using the spells contained inside.

"So this is all supposed to be true?" Dan asked her.

"It's not," Lannie replied. "Lovecraft invented the book to fit in with the world he'd created for his stories, he said as much any number of times in interviews and in correspondence with friends."

"We'll get back to that part later," Phineas said. "Is that all Lannie?"

"Pretty much," Lannie said, "except that there are real grimoires out there, and new ones are still written from time to time. There are also copies of books claiming to be the actual Necronomicon, you can buy them on Amazon; they're just not the real thing because there is no real thing. That's it," she looked at Phineas.

"OK," Phineas said glancing at his watch, "we'll take a dinner break then continue."

"Is Lovecraft buried in Copps Hill?" Abbey asked. "Is that why we're here?"

"He's buried in Swan Point Cemetery in Providence," Lannie replied.

"Are we cooking or ordering out?" Dan asked.

"Ordering out," Phineas said. "Already done, it should be here any minute."

"Chinese food?"

"We're in the North End," Phineas said to him, "the Italian enclave of Boston so that's blasphemous. We're having veal scaloppini, pasta primavera and antipasto and you'll like it."

Chapter Three

Dinner arrived a few minutes later and after they'd stuffed themselves with excellent Italian food they all pitched in to clean up. When they sat down at the table again to continue their conversation the rain was still drumming incessantly against the glass panes next to them.

"Not looking forward to walking back to Haymarket in that," Dan commented.

"Actually the weather this evening suits our purposes wonderfully," Phineas replied then continued on before anyone could respond. "All right, Lannie gave us a little background on Mr. Lovecraft and now I'm going to give you the rest, including the reason that we're all here. It's true that conventional wisdom states the Necronomicon was purely a figment of the man's very fertile imagination. As Lannie told us, he stated as much himself on numerous occasions over the course of his lifetime. The thing is, I think he was lying, I think that the Necronomicon was and is very real and is pretty much what H.P. Lovecraft depicted it to be in his writing, or nearly so. I'll tell you why I, and others, believe this to be true.

"Howard Lovecraft's father died when he was young and prior to his death he'd been a traveling salesman so he hadn't been around much. Lovecraft's father figure during his youth became his grandfather, Whipple Phillips Lovecraft."

"You're kidding," Robert said. "That's an actual name?"

"It is, Whipple, and I doubt he went by that name but who knows, became a central figure in Lovecraft's life. The man was fairly successful, very intelligent and, he had a huge collection of old books. Whipple collected old books his entire life and he traveled to Europe quite often in the late 1800's on business where I suspect he regularly found new additions to his collection.

At some point, in his helping to raise young Lovecraft, the grandfather gave him free reign of all the books in his collection;

Lovecraft mentioned this many times later in life. He also said that a lot of very old books were tucked away in the attic of their house and he loved to root them out and read them. I believe the Necronomicon was one of those old books that Lovecraft rooted out; the old man had probably stumbled across it during one of his book hunts on the continent. Maybe he actually gave it to Lovecraft to read or maybe he didn't even know what it was and Lovecraft just stumbled across it. In any event, H.P. had it and he read it.

From 1908 to sometime in 1913 H.P. Lovecraft's movements and activities are lost to history; researchers aren't sure where he was or what he was doing. After that lost period ended he became reclusive and maintained a distance from the rest of humanity. He would have been between the ages of 18 and 23 during the lost period and I believe it was then that he actually read the Necronomicon and tried to come to grips with its contents. His behavior for the remainder of his life may strongly indicate that he was only partially successful in doing so." Phineas swirled the coffee around in his mug for a moment, realized it was cold then put it down.

"Later in his life, the last ten years or so, he began traveling a lot, all over the country or at least the eastern part of it. This is a bit odd when you consider that he had very little money and typically lived a hand to mouth existence. I think what he was doing was looking for more examples of the Necronomicon, chasing down rumors he'd heard about additional copies, all the while hoping that he wouldn't find any. Lovecraft always told people that the book was a figment of his imagination, that the name and the idea for it came to him in a dream and that's pretty much all he would say. The Necronomicon is supposed to be at least 750 pages long, a pretty complicated dream if you ask me." He picked up his coffee cup again and started to rise out of his chair.

"I'll make another pot," Lannie jumped up and took his cup, "you keep talking, I can hear you from the kitchen."

"Thank you," Phineas said to her then continued. "So, Lovecraft has this book, this Grimoire, full of awful spells and ways to summon demons, that portends ways to bring about the end of civilization, that may even predict it. I believe that book, what he read in it, affected him for his entire life and that he spends much of his later life trying to find any additional copies to keep them from being used by someone who either doesn't realize the consequences or doesn't care. At some point he wrote a short history of the book in which he states that there are five known copies in existence; one is in the library of Miskatonic University which doesn't exist, Lovecraft invented it for use in his stories so I think we can discount that one. The others were reportedly at The British Museum, The Bibliotheque nationale de France, The Widener Library at Harvard University and the University of Buenos Aires. None of these institutions have copies, or at least none will admit that they do. Other than that Lovecraft's short history of the book contains very few real details concerning the work itself. He does however state in this history that it was rumored that the artist R.U. Pickman, from our story *Pickman's Model*, owned a Greek translation of the book but that it disappeared when he died in 1926."

"Is that mentioned in the short story itself?" Abbey asked.

"It is not, he only mentions it later in the history and that's a bit odd because *Pickman's Model* was a minor work of his that, as said, is a pretty conventional story overall; it doesn't involve the mythos at all, it couldn't have taken him very long to write, and it isn't considered one of his better efforts.

"But you think it's significant," Abbey replied.

"I do."

"So I see the connection between all of this and where we're currently sitting," she said. "But what makes you so sure the book is real, and anywhere near here?"

"I'll answer your first question first," Phineas said. "Lovecraft had a longtime friend by the name of Frank Belknap Long, a fellow writer. H.P. met him while he was living in New York City and they became lifelong friends. They saw one another often and corresponded faithfully right up until Lovecraft's death in 1937. Frank Long died in 1994 at the age of 92. He died a pauper in New York City and was buried in a pauper's grave. When his friends learned of this they arranged to have his body exhumed, put into a proper casket, and buried in his family plot in Woodlawn Cemetery, also in New York. One of those friends was a woman named Barbara Jackson whose grandmother, Winifred Jackson, had collaborated with Lovecraft on a couple of stories in 1918 and had known a lot of the same people he knew. When Frank Long was moved to the family plot Barbara Jackson took custody of his worldly possessions. Wasn't much there, but included in what was there was a last will and testament of sorts by Mr. Long in which he admits to knowledge of the Necronomicon, that H.P. possessed it, that it almost destroyed his mind, and that at some point H.P. hid it were it would never be found. I've seen the document myself, though Ms. Jackson did not allow me to borrow it nor make a copy of it.

"If this book is so terrible why didn't Lovecraft just destroy it?" Lannie asked from the kitchen.

"I don't think he could bring himself to do that," Phineas replied. "I think it terrified him and he wanted to be sure that no one ever got possession of it and used the knowledge it contained, but I don't think he could bring himself to destroy it. Maybe he was afraid to try, maybe the book scared him that much. So he did the next best thing, he hid it where he thought it would never see the light of day again."

"In Copps Hill Burial Ground?" Lannie asked as she returned to the table and put a cup of coffee in front of Phineas.

"I'd like one too thanks," Dan told her.

"Kitchen counter," she told him as she sat down at the table. The others smiled.

"Yes," Phineas said, "in Copps Hill Burial Ground, for the following reasons: Lovecraft was up here from Providence regularly. He was nocturnal, he rarely went out during the day, but would wander the city all night, be it here or Providence or New York City. He loved the North End, something that he mentioned to friends regularly, because it was such an old part of the city. He wrote *Pickman's Model* in the fall of 1926, not long after he'd separated from his wife for good and moved back to Providence from New York City. He was at loose ends and psychologically not in great shape, even for him. This may have made him careless about keeping the secret of the book, a secret that until then he'd kept for years.

I believe he chose the North End as the setting for the story for a reason, not just because he was fond of it. The main character, the artist Pickman, had a studio in the North End, Copps Hill is significantly mentioned multiple times in the story and H.P. describes hideous creatures digging things up there. Later in his brief history of the Necronomicon he goes out of his way to say that Pickman reportedly owned a copy of the book. At the end of the story Pickman disappears and so does his copy of the book. *Pickman's Model* was written at the beginning of what turned out to be Lovecraft's peak period as a writer and yet, it's just a simple tale with a classic horror story ending, it's not like most of his other work at all really. Lastly, Frank Long's written statement says that he doesn't know where the book was hidden but he thinks, from comments made to him by Lovecraft, that it's in a historically relevant place where no one will ever find it because it's a place where no one would, or could ever look. What better place than the sacrosanct ground of a historical cemetery? Copps Hill is the only one of those in this part of the city and it's fairly secluded, the other two cemeteries' in the city that fit the bill are downtown and about as un-isolated as you can get."

"I don't think that's a word," Abbey told him.

"Cemeteries?" Dan said.

"Un-isolated, halfwit," Abbey replied.

"You do realize that the Mad Arab's name doesn't make sense, right?" Robert asked Phineas. "Abdul is a generic term that has no significance because Alhazred isn't a surname; it's just a reference of a person's place of birth."

"I did notice that," Phineas replied. "I just think it's another blind that H.P. threw up there to keep people away from the truth."

"Your evidence is a bit flimsy," Abbey pointed out to him, "I mean, other than the dying declaration of an old man all you have is conjecture and theories."

"We've moved on less with other cases we've worked," Dan said.

"That's true," Lannie agreed.

"So you think the Necronomicon is buried somewhere in Copps Hill then?" Robert asked.

"I do."

"Any idea where? It's a big cemetery."

"I have a few thoughts on that," Phineas smiled.

"Hold on," Dan said, "please don't tell me we're going to be out there in the rain tonight digging holes in a graveyard..."

"Digging holes? No, not digging holes," Phineas said...still smiling.

Chapter Four

Robert got a big canvass bag that he'd brought with him and put it on the sofa. All the furniture had come with the apartment and it really wasn't half bad. Dan was standing next to the not-half-bad sofa trying to find a rain slicker that fit among the pile Cornelius had provided. The one he'd worn coming in was still soaked and happily dripping away in the bathroom.

Robert zipped open the bag and took out what looked like a hunk of wood. It was curved on one side and had bark on the other and was roughly the size of a softball. He took two more from the bag then held one up so they could get a good look.

"We're going to attach these to the trees on Copps Hill, high enough up that they don't attract attention, but low enough to have unimpeded views of the grounds. As you can see, they're made to look like tree bark and shouldn't arouse suspicion unless someone gets a really close look at one. They have brackets on the back that fit into fasteners that we'll attach to the tree trunks. They're motion activated, have low light capability, are wireless and the batteries should be good for longer than we're going to need them."

"What are we looking for?" Dan asked.

"Patterns of activity," Phineas replied. "Before we go rooting around in a historic burial ground in the middle of the night I want to know what goes on there in the middle of the night, kids necking, ghost hunters, homeless people, a security guard or the police making rounds, anything. So we let the cameras run for a few nights, maybe a week, see what we see then go from there."

"So we have to install these tonight?" Dan asked. "Are they waterproof?"

"There are over twenty trees on Copps Hill so we have plenty of places to fix the cameras, you can attach them on larger branches as well as tree trunks," Robert said. "We have a big area to cover and it's hilly but we're going to focus on the perimeter to see if anyone comes or goes so that will make it a bit easier. Be sure to place them well above eye level; the people visiting the cemetery are going to be looking down at the stones not up at the trees. The back end of the burial ground borders Charter Street with one gate that's usually locked, but the fence there is low enough along a good length of it that someone could jump it, so we have to cover that area well. The same with Hull Street, that's where the main entrance is and it's where most people enter the space. Fortunately, there are a couple of big old trees along there so we should be good. There are apartment buildings around the entire

burial ground so no flashlights; we have lowlight goggles for everyone. I'll show you how to mount the cameras and once you've done
a couple you'll be able to put one up in two minutes' tops. If law
enforcement shows up, we'll deal with it."

"We've got thirty cameras which should be enough to cover the
grounds, or at least enough of it to suit our purposes," Phineas told
them. "We're going to cut across Michelangelo Street to the parking area which abuts the burial ground, that's where we'll make
entry so we won't have to go out onto the street at all. There are
two trees right there so we'll use them for Robert to demonstrate
installation of the cameras then we'll spread out and put them in
place. I want them all placed as quickly as possible. When you're
finished look for the rest of us and help out then return here by
the same route. Any adjustments that may be needed we can do
tomorrow night, got it?"

"We all going?" Lannie asked,

"We are, except for Abbey, she's going to be setting up the
hardware here to monitor the cameras."

"Lucky her," Dan said drily.

"If you knew anything beyond on, off and control/alt/delete
you could stay and do it," Abbey told him.

"Abbey wanted to come along, but I need her back here setting
things up. I want the cameras all live tonight." Phineas said. "The
rest of the equipment is down in Robert's car, let's get it and move."

Three hours later Abbey had everything set up on the table and
already had live camera feeds going when they all trooped back
into the apartment tired, muddy and soaked to the skin. They'd
all been there before and knew the drill when Phineas called so
they'd all brought what they referred to as 'go bags' for use in case
a project required an extended absence from home; they were all

prepared. Lannie took the bathroom while the men used the bedrooms to dry off and change into dry clothes.

Robert was the first one out at the table with Abbey, going over the camera feeds. They were close enough to the burial ground that the wireless signals were coming through well, even with all the interference generated from being in the middle of a city. The cameras all looked well placed and Robert began marking them on an on-screen diagram and numbering them so they'd know which camera was which and what it was showing them. He would have liked to have had scanning ability, but it hadn't been possible using the equipment they had at hand so each camera just showed a static view. From what he could see though they had the perimeter completely covered and quite a bit of the interior of the cemetery as well. If someone came or went they wouldn't miss them. And even on such a shitty night the low light pictures they were getting were good enough to see what was going on, which at the moment was absolutely nothing.

As always, Robert had done his homework on the ground that he'd been asked to put cameras on. Copps Hill Burying Ground covered 86,110 square feet of slightly hilly terrain surrounded by multiple story apartment buildings. Several brick walkways intersected the grounds with no rhyme or reason to their direction and while some sections were crammed with grave markers standing haphazardly in low rows, other sections were noticeably free of markers and looked more like grassy meadow. This by no means meant that these areas were bereft of graves, only that they were unmarked graves. Some had never had a marker, the last resting place of slaves or the poor possibly. Others may have once been marked by loved ones, the markers lost over the centuries as families died out or moved away or simply forgot, leaving no one to tend the spot or remember those resting there.

So present day there were 1,200 marked graves, 272 tombs, and many thousands more unmarked graves on Copps Hill, some famous: Increase Mather and his son Cotton Mather, the father famous as a minister and public speaker, the son infamous, deserved or not, for the Salem Witch trials. Edmund Hartt, builder of the heavy frigate USS Constitution that still sits moored just across the harbor, in sight of his grave if not for the buildings blocking the view. And Captain Daniel Malcolm, solider, hero, his grave marker still bearing the scars of musket balls fired at it for sport by British Soldiers during the Revolution. But for every one of these there were hundreds of markers remembering the final resting place of ordinary people who had lived in and known a world very different from the present day, many of who died young of maladies easily remedied today with a single trip to a doctor's office.

Within a few minutes they were all back around the table studying the images on the large computer monitors that Abbey had set up. Phineas was happy with what he saw and announced that they were done for the night.

"Everything is set up to run on its own," Robert told them. "As said, the cameras are motion activated, when they come on they'll immediately start recording to the hard drive. We'll be able to check the log each morning and see if we've caught anything. There's also an audio cue when one of the cameras kicks on, but I'll turn that down so it doesn't bother whoever is staying here."

"Which brings me to the final point of the evening," Phineas said, "someone has to stay here to monitor and safeguard the equipment. At some point we may all be staying here for a few nights, but at the moment I just need one person."

"I'll take the first shift," Lannie said, "brought everything I need and it'll mean not going back out into the rain."

"Excellent," Phineas said, "kitchen is fully stocked, fresh linens in both bedrooms. I will see you sometime late a.m. tomorrow." He went to retrieve his jacket, Robert and Abbey trailing behind him.

"I'm starving," Dan told them, and since it's 3 a.m. I think I'll grab something here before I head home."

"Well I'm going to jump in the shower," Lannie said, "make sure you lock the door behind you when you leave."

Phineas, Robert and Abbey left, Dan went into the kitchen and Lannie headed for the bathroom. She had just stepped into the claw foot tub under a scalding hot stream of water when Dan, naked as she was, climbed in with her.

"Wash your back babe, or your front?" he smiled sweetly at her.

She looked at him for a moment then handed him the soap and turned around for him to start on her back.

"Do you think Phineas knows about us?" he asked her.

"Phineas knows everything," Lannie replied. She turned around so he could do her front.

Chapter Five

They were both up fairly early the following morning and Dan left to run some errands so it wouldn't appear that he'd spent the night. Lannie may be right about Phineas, but they didn't want everyone else knowing they were an item. She sat down in front of the monitors with a cup of coffee, checked out the live feeds then went back through the previous night. It didn't take long because none of the cameras had tripped during the night.

Boston was a big tourist city thanks mostly to its history and during the summer it would be inundated with travelers, mostly from other parts of the country and from Europe, although the city got its fair share of Asian tourists as well. Tourist season typically ran from June to the end of August and it was currently the middle of May so while there were early birds and some locals out seeing the sites the real crowds wouldn't start arriving for weeks yet.

So as Lannie sat at the monitors she began to see people filtering into the burying ground. They wandered the paths taking pictures and leaning down to try to read the weather worn stones. Some began doing rubbings on the stones although signage throughout the cemetery clearly stated that it was not allowed. Lannie had the urge to walk up there and slap a few of them around. Instead, she turned her attention to the book Phineas had brought and began reading *Pickman's Model*. She had considered turning the system off. They were only interested in what went on in the burying ground at night, after all, and the cameras were constantly being tripped by the people roaming the grounds. Phineas hadn't said anything about doing that though, so she left the system running.

Pickman's Model wasn't a very long story and she was just finishing it when Robert and Abbey entered the apartment. It occurred to Lannie for a moment that maybe they were fooling around too, like she and Dan were. They seemed to be together a lot. She dismissed the thought just ask quickly, she didn't think Abbey even thought about stuff like that.

"Reading up on our guy?" Robert asked as he dropped his backpack onto the sofa.

"*Pickman's Model*," Lannie told him, "compared to most of the other stories in here it's extremely brief."

"I liked it," Abbey told her as she went into the kitchen and got a soda out of the fridge them came back to the table. "There was a made-for-TV version of it back in the 70's too," she said as she sat down, "an episode of *Night Gallery* I believe."

"Great show," Robert said. "Rod Serling hosted it and wrote some of the stories."

"*Twilight Zone* Rod Serling?" Lannie asked. "Cool."

"Anything interesting happen overnight?" Robert asked and for a moment Lannie thought he knew and was yanking her chain.

"Nothing," she said, "it was quiet as a graveyard all night."

"Ouch," Abbey said, "really bad Lannie."

"There are a good number of people in there now," Lannie continued. "The cameras are tripping on almost continuously, but Phineas didn't say anything about shutting it down so I've left them running."

"You can turn them off," Robert replied. "No point in running down the camera batteries looking at a bunch of tourists. We'll fire it back up when it gets dark."

A while later Lannie left and Abbey and Robert took over the watch. Robert was there through the night with Dan scheduled to relieve him the following day. And that's the way it went for a week, keeping tabs on the burying ground at night to see what, if anything, went on there. After a few days they starting keeping the system on during the day, watching the tourists wander around, guessing at where they were from, what they did for a living, just to stay occupied. At the end of seven days they still hadn't seen anything going on at night with the exception of pedestrians passing by on the streets from time to time, but even that petered out by one a.m. or so when the bars in the city closed.

At the end of the week Phineas had seen enough to decide to move on to the next step in his plan, but they left the system running...just in case.

Chapter Six

They all met for dinner at a small, but excellent restaurant on Hanover Street then walked to the apartment on Poe Court. The table was covered with the computer drives and monitors for the cameras so they sat around the small living room area. Phineas produced yet another file folder and placed it on the coffee table.

"So it appears that our burying ground is a very quiet place at night; in the past week we haven't seen any activity at all once the gates are closed. Which leads me to believe that we're safe to move on to stage two of this little exercise." He flipped the folder open and the top sheet was a map of the cemetery that included the abutting streets and buildings. He placed the tip of his pen on a spot at the rear left corner of the grounds, not very far from the gate in the rear wall that bordered Charter Street. On the diagram there was a small square depicted right next to the brick walkway leading into the grounds from the gate. There was writing next to the square, but it was too small for any of them to read.

"This is the area we're interested in," Phineas said. "Unfortunately, as you can see, it's not very far inside the perimeter wall and hence very close to Charter Street. In our favor are the facts that there is some vegetation in the area to shield our movements, it is the rear corner of the grounds, and Charter Street is much less heavily traveled than is Hull Street at the front of the cemetery. We will be there late at night and will have cover should we need it."

"I know I mentioned this before," Dan said, "but please tell us again that we're not going to be digging up any two hundred year old corpses."

"We will hopefully be digging up something," Phineas replied, "but it won't be a corpse. Besides, after so much time having passed I doubt if we would find much in the way of corpses anywhere within the grounds; earth to earth, dust to dust you know."

"You are aware that there are hundreds, maybe even thousands of unmarked graves in there," Lannie said to him. "So even if we're not digging at a marker we're very likely still going to be disturbing someone's grave."

"Yes, which is why we first go in with ground penetrating radar to try to identify our target. We're certainly not going to be able to just dig up the place willy nilly so we're going to try to target a small area where we're reasonably sure the item we're looking for is buried."

"And I assume the item we're looking for is Lovecraft's copy of the Necronomicon," Abbey said.

"It is."

"So you're sure it's real, we're not going to go to all this trouble to find a piece of fiction that Lovecraft put together himself? We're looking for the real grimoire that he describes in his writing?" Bob asked.

"We are," Phineas replied. "I think it's real and that this is where he hid it. The only way to know for sure is to find it."

"Remind us again why you think he hid it in Copps Hill," Robert asked, "and why this particular spot."

"I believe it's in Copps Hill for several reasons. Firstly, because it fits what Frank Belknap described in his dying declaration. Secondly, because Lovecraft was very familiar with this area, he walked the streets here late at night on many occasions, and he liked old cemeteries. Third, what safer place to bury it than in a historical burying ground that he knew no one would ever disturb. And finally, this particular spot because this," he put the tip of his pen on the little square on the map again, "is the Mather family tomb. Cotton Mather is in it, as is his father and assorted other Mathers. H.P. knew a lot about the Mather's; he mentioned them on numerous occasions. In their time the Mathers were into the occult almost as much as H.P. was in his. Increase and Cotton Mather both wrote extensively on the occult during their lifetimes and in fact, Lovecraft owned several very old editions of their works and he actually used one, Cotton Mather's *Magnalia Christi Americana* in his story *The Unnamable.* Mather's work dealt with beast demons, and "bringing forth a great creature", sound familiar to anyone? So if one believes, as I do, that Lovecraft hid his copy of the Necronomicon in this burying ground it would only make sense that he would bury it as near the Mather tomb as possible."

"Why not *in* the Mather tomb?" Dan asked.

"No," Phineas shook his head, "Lovecraft had great respect for the Mather's and he would never desecrate their tomb."

"So you believe it's somewhere in that little corner of the cemetery?" Lannie said.

"Yes, likely very near the tomb, and protected from the elements as much as possible, which would probably involve a metal container of some kind."

"Which will show up on ground penetrating radar," Robert said.

"And would be of a size just big enough to hold a large book," Lannie added.

"Exactly," Phineas smiled, "that will be our target. Now, there's no reason for all of us to risk exposure in searching for it, three of us are sufficient to operate the radar, Robert, Abbey and myself. Which will leave Lannie and Dan to monitor the cameras and warn us should anyone approach our position. Once we've located a promising object Dan or Lannie will join us to assist in retrieving the item, leaving one person here to monitor the cameras."

"I'll help dig," Lannie said, "Dan doesn't like to get his hands dirty, he's delicate."

"I'll let you," Dan told her, "as appealing as the thought of digging in a graveyard in the middle of the night is, I'd hate to deprive you of that experience. And yes, I am delicate."

"All right then," Robert said, slapping his hands on his knees and standing up. "There's only one thing left to do to kick off this little project."

"Oh God," Abbey said, "I really hate this part! Do we have to do this every time?"

"We do, it's a tradition," Robert said. He went into the kitchen and returned a moment later with a bottle of Bushmills Irish Whiskey and five glasses. He put a glass on the coffee table in front of each of them, cracked the bottle open and poured each a finger of whiskey. He placed the bottle in the center of the table, sat back down on the sofa and picked up his glass. "Who did the toast last time?" he asked.

"I did," Dan said, "it was incredibly moving and insightful."

"It was stupid," Abbey said. "I don't remember what it was, but I do remember that it was stupid."

"Do you think that perhaps your opinion is jaded by the fact that you hate whiskey?" Dan asked her. "And if that is in fact the case then your comment is incredibly unfair...and hurtful."

"I don't care to have my throat and my stomach lining horribly abused every time we start a new project, sue me," Abbey said. "But it was still stupid."

"All right," Robert said, "I'll do the toast this time." He held up his glass and they all did the same. "And don't toss it over your shoulder onto the floor again," he said to Abbey, "it's a waste of good Whiskey."

"That's a contradiction in terms," Abbey replied but she held up her glass and closed her eyes.

Robert held his glass higher, "Eat life," he said, "or it will surely eat you." He tossed back the shot of Bushmills and the others did the same, followed by a coughing fit from Abbey.

"Man, that will put hair on your butt," Dan said.

"Must you say that every time?" Lannie asked him.

"Well I'd say it will put hair on a different albeit nearby part of my body, but that would exclude two of the people here and that would just be wrong."

Lannie shook her head and put her glass on the table.

They had several hours to kill before they could begin; Dan and Robert played around with the ground penetrating unit for a while to be sure it was working then sat down in the living room area and watched TV. Abbey and Lannie left to run some errands and when they returned Abbey went straight to the system set-up on the table while Lannie got the Lovecraft book, sat down on the sofa next to Robert and leafed through it while she watched TV. Phineas had left the apartment after the meeting and didn't return until just before they were scheduled to head out.

Chapter Seven

The Mather family tomb was tucked away in a very out-of-the-way corner at the back of the burying ground. Considering how important a family they'd once been in New England it was odd that the tomb was in such a secluded area. It was also very fortunate for the little group as they reached the area and began to set up the radar. The tomb was actually just a dozen yards of so from the rear boundary of the grounds and Charter street. The low red brick wall that ran the length of the boundary and separated the grounds from the sidewalk was very low, but it was topped by a black wrought iron fence with pickets that came to wicked points so while the wall didn't really obscure the view into the cemetery it was an effective determent to anyone entering the grounds from the street. There was a single gate in the fence, locked at night, which opened onto a brick path that ran straight up the hill toward the main part of the grounds. Less than a dozen yards on from the gate a smaller path branched off to the left leading into a lower and less significant area of the grounds. The Mather tomb was located immediately next to this smaller path just after it branched off from the main one so the tomb was only roughly 30 or 35 feet from the boundary wall…and Charter Street.

The team had several factors working in their favor, however. There were several large trees in that corner of the grounds that partially blocked a view of the tomb from the street and completely blocked the view from the apartment building that abutted that corner of the cemetery. Additionally, directly across Charter Street and running almost the entire length of the cemetery was a park that was obviously deserted at night and which had still more large trees that further blocked the view from several apartment buildings on that side of the street. Unless someone came bebopping up the sidewalk on Charter Street in the middle of the night, chances were they would be OK.

Copps Hill consisted of dry sandy soil down well past the depth they were interested in. They were using a unit with a 250MHz antenna, which typically would penetrate to as deep as 40 feet in that type of soil so Phineas was confident that they would be able to see everything they needed to see. He and Robert both had extensive experience with ground penetrating radar, as did another member of their team, Verity Quinn. Verity wasn't with them on this project, but she was available if Phineas and Robert needed her expertise in reading the data they collected.

Phineas and Robert got the unit set up while Abbey connected the small notebook laptop they were using, being careful to turn the screen toward the interior of the cemetery. She also draped a towel over it to keep the light from the screen from traveling. It was just past two a.m. by then and very quiet. With a few exceptions the windows in the apartment buildings that bordered the burying ground were dark and there hadn't been any traffic on Charter Street since they'd arrived. Abbey had set up the laptop on top of another tomb nearby and was sitting on a little campstool she'd brought along. It was still only May so she was wearing a fleece pullover against the chill night air.

The Mather tomb was a low red brick structure not much larger than a small casket capped by a stone lid with a broken corner. It was situated with one long side facing the street and the lower end right up against the edge of the brick walkway that passed by it. It was surrounded by an uneven group of partially buried granite blocks that long ago had been the base of a fence surrounding the tomb. Four of the blocks still showed rusted holes at their centers where iron fence posts had once been anchored.

Phineas started the radar scan on the side of the tomb away from the street assuming that Lovecraft would have chosen that side as well, for obvious reasons. He placed the unit as close to the granite blocks as he could and started moving it slowly across the grass with Robert's assistance.

"I'm getting all kinds of soil disturbance," Abbey told them as she peered at the screen.

"That's to be expected," Phineas said, "lots of burials took place here so the ground's been dug up who knows how many times."

"You'd think it would have settled a bit after more than a century though," Abbey replied.

"On the surface probably, not deeper down though."

"I've got a solid hit," Abbey said suddenly, "It's to the left edge of the scan, probably just under one of the granite blocks. It looks too big to be our target though, think it's a coffin, or what's left of one."

Phineas and Robert left the unit and moved over to either side of Abbey, peering at the screen. "I think it may be the lead liner from a coffin," Robert said. "The outer wooden shell probably disappeared long ago, but a lead liner would last a lot longer. It's maintained the shape of the coffin fairly well though."

"Think you're right," Phineas said. "Much too large to be our target in any event." They returned to the radar and continued moving it slowly across the grass.

They reached a spot roughly ten feet past the tomb and turned to come back along another line; Phineas didn't think Lovecraft would have strayed any further from the tomb than that to bury the book. At the end of that line, up to the edge of the brick path, they turned and went back the other way. Twice more they did that and now they were getting further away from the Mather tomb than Phineas would have liked.

"Still getting lots of return," Abbey told them, "and I'm not sure what some of it is. How about I switch places with one of you guys? You're both a lot more experienced at reading this stuff than I am. I'd hate for us to miss something."

"You're doing fine," Phineas told her. "We're looking for a small square return, in a relatively shallow depression, that's all. You'll know it when you see it."

"Ok," Abbey replied, "Then in that case...I see it."

They both stopped and turned to look at her.

"No really guys, I think I see it. Just as you said that Phineas, this reading came up that looks like a small square at the bottom of a not very deep soil disturbance."

They both straightened up, still looking at her.

"I am not shitting you, get you asses over here!"

That worked and they walked over to where she was set up and leaned down to look at the screen.

"You know," Robert said after a few moments, "that could actually be it. It's the right size, and it's not down that deep, not as deep as a burial would be." He turned to Phineas who was leaning down beside him to peer at the screen. "What do you think?"

"I think it's a promising target and we need to dig it up to be sure," Phineas replied. "Good work, Abbey." He straightened up and arched his back to stretch out the kinks from dragging the radar unit across the grass. Then he took out his phone and activated it, turning away from the street to shield the light from its screen. He sent a text then dropped the phone back into his pocket.

"Want to take bets on who shows up, Dan or Lannie?" he asked the other two.

Eight minutes later Lannie appeared at their spot from the depths of the burying ground. She was carrying several military style folding camp shovels and a canvass satchel that, from the way she was carrying it, was obviously heavy.

"Dan's been asleep since you guys left and I didn't want to wake him," she told them as Phineas and Robert relieved her of her load.

"Right," Abbey said, "Did you at least flip for it or did he just ask you to come?"

"I volunteered," she replied, "digging in an ancient cemetery in the middle of the night, are you kidding me? Besides, Dan's afraid of ghosts, the dark, bugs, trees, and manual labor, all of which I'm assuming will be present here tonight."

"You got that right," Robert told her. "Did you bring the tarp?"

Lannie produced a folded blue plastic tarp from the satchel and handed it Robert. It opened to a three-foot by three-foot square and Robert spread it out on the grass next to the spot he'd marked for them to dig. All four of them grabbed shovels and went to work side by side. The idea was to get down to the object and identify it as quickly as possible, but they also needed to leave the ground looking undisturbed for the tourists and park rangers who would show up again the next morning.

They started by neatly cutting out the sod and placing it off to the side. Then they began slowly clearing away the dirt and depositing it on the tarp. Abbey assumed the job of going through it looking for possible artifacts. There was sufficient light from the stars and the not too distant streetlights for her to see fairly well. When she came across something that she thought might be interesting, she turned on a small flashlight and shielded the beam while she checked the object. She tried not to do this often because each time she turned on the flashlight her night vision went to hell and she would have to wait while it re-adjusted to the low light conditions. Finally, she just started putting anything that seemed interesting in a little pile at the edge of the tarp; she'd look at it all at once when she was done sifting through the dirt.

Meanwhile, the other three dug down into the soil with the shovels, afraid to go too quickly and maybe damage whatever may be down there, but also aware of where they were and that the less time they spent there the better. The radar reading had showed the object at around four feet in depth and just as they reached that depth Lannie's shovel blade hit something hollow and they all stopped, then began again more slowly and cautiously. Finally, they put their shovels down and Phineas reached into the hole.

"It does feel like a metal box," he said, "let's keep going."

"I just hope it's not an infant burial," Lannie said as they all worked to clear around the object, "because that would suck."

"Not deep enough," Robert told her, "probably."

"Thanks," Lannie replied, "that's re-assuring."

They got the dirt cleared around the edges of the object and used a shovel to free it from the ground and bring it up.

"Been down there a long time," Robert grunted as they got it out of the hole and onto the tarp. Phineas produced a small hooded light and they all closed in to block the light.

The object was indeed a metal box, roughly 12x10 inches and 5 inches deep. Lannie produced a brush from the satchel and cleaned it off as best she could, they saw that it was made of dark green metal and the lid was sealed on somehow.

"Well that's definitely not colonial period," Robert said, "way more modern than that."

Phineas gently shook it… nothing, then he hefted it to feel the weight. "Something in there," he told the others. "Ok," he said, "let's fill in the hole and replace the sod then pack it up and get out of here; we've been lucky so far and I don't want to push our luck any further. If this isn't it, we'll put it back and try again tomorrow night."

Lannie and Robert filled in the hole then carefully replaced the sod and tamped it down. When they were done it looked like there had never been a hole there. While they were doing that Abbey was packing up the equipment and Phineas the radar unit. They were done and on the way back to the apartment with their find in thirty minutes.

Chapter Eight

They all sat around the table while Robert and Dan worked on the lid to the box. It was stamped metal, definitely modern era although it looked like it had been in the ground long enough to be their box. The lid had been sealed with an epoxy material of some kind and then further sealed with what looked and smelled like roofing tar. It took the better part of forty minutes for them to carefully cut through the layers and free the lid. When they finally did everyone stood up and leaned over the box. The inside was almost wholly taken up by a black rubber sheet that had been wrapped around something. Phineas reached in, lifted the bundle out of the box and placed it on the table. Whatever was inside the rubber shroud was square and the right size for a book, a large book. The rubber was cemented together at its seams; Ben produced a folding knife from his pocket and carefully sliced the seams open. When they removed the rubber they had a large leather bag sealed at one end. They got that open and finally Phineas reached in and slowly pulled out a book.

It was just a bit smaller than the box, 11x9x4, and it was bound in very old dark brown hide of some sort that was covered with engravings that they really couldn't make out very well because the binding was blackened with age. Two wide straps held the volume closed, secured with tarnished brass clasps. Phineas put on a pair of medical gloves, unfastened each clasp and slowly opened the book to its title page.

The paper was a creamy white color that almost looked wet and wasn't nearly as aged as the binding. The title page was covered with images that they only got a quick glimpse of before Phineas closed the book again and returned it to the leather case.

"That's it isn't it," Lannie said.

"Aren't we going to look at it?" Bob asked.

"I'm fairly certain that this is the book Mr. Lovecraft buried," Phineas said. "But whether or not it is real, or just another product of his very vivid imagination is the real question. Before we started looking through it and possibly damaging it I want to have it examined by experts. If it is truly a copy of the Necronomicon, then it needs to be preserved. If it's not, then you can all read it to your hearts content."

"Even if it's not," Robert said, "it would still be a hitherto unknown work by H.P. Lovecraft which would make it a pretty significant find."

"I'll have it checked out," Phineas said. "I know some people who can be trusted to keep a secret, no matter which it turns out to be. If it's real we'll need to deal with that, if it's by H.P. himself we can all read it then donate it somewhere. The tests are going to take a couple of days so why don't you all head home. We'll meet back here day after tomorrow for dinner and I'll tell you what we have, or what we don't have, and we'll go from there. Good job everyone; now get some rest because if this turns out to be real, you'll need it."

They packed up the equipment and their stuff and headed out. Phineas waited to be sure they were gone, that no one had forgotten anything. When he was sure he took the book out of its leather case again, sat down at the table and began to read.

Chapter Nine

Two nights later, they were all back at the scarred old table, eating yet another superb Italian meal from a restaurant a few blocks away. Phineas had refused to tell them anything until after dinner but they couldn't help but notice that the metal box, and the book, were nowhere in sight. So they talked about past jobs, and possible future jobs, and they waited. They all knew from past experience that Phineas did things only when Phineas was ready to do them.

After dinner with coffee and expresso and Italian pastries on the table Phineas was finally ready.

"The book's gone," he told them, "I've disposed of it."

They all just sat and looked at him for a moment.

"Mind telling us why?" Robert asked him finally.

"It was the real Necronomicon, wasn't it?" Lannie said.

Phineas gave her a little nod and a hint of a smile.

"Holy shit," Dan said, "it was? It was the real thing?"

"After you all left two day ago I began reading," Phineas told them. "And I continued reading until I'd read enough to know what it was. Lannie is correct, it wasn't something H.P. produced to fill out his mythos; it was real. And while it wasn't exactly what he'd represented it to be, it was close enough. I read enough to realize that the Sumerians had gotten it right; it was not meant to be found by man. No good could come from anyone ever laying eyes on that book again. So I made sure that no one ever would.

"That was the object of this exercise all along," Lannie said to him, "Wasn't it?"

"It was one possible one," Phineas replied.

"The likely one?" Robert said.

"I really had no idea," Phineas said. "I was fairly certain it was there, I just wasn't sure what *it* was. But it struck me as illogical that he would go to all that trouble if it weren't real."

"What did you do with it?" Abbey asked.

"Did you destroy it?" Lannie asked. "You didn't, did you?"

"I did not. I wasn't sure what trying to destroy it might lead to, or bring about I should say. I suspect that H.P. had to deal with that very same problem. Let's just say I put it somewhere where no one will ever find it."

"That's probably what Howard thought he'd done," Abbey pointed out.

"I have more resources at my disposal than Howard did," Phineas told her. "The book is gone, and I believe that none of us can realistically comprehend the magnitude of the service we've done mankind in bringing that about. Where it was someone else might have found it, just as we did, possibly with horrifying results. Now no one will."

"What about other copies?" Dan said, "Lovecraft always talked about there being several other copies of the book."

"That is an issue for another day," Phineas told him. "For now let us enjoy the satisfaction of a job well done, enjoy these exquisite pastries, and then prepare ourselves for one final nocturnal visit to Copps Hill."

"The cameras," Dan groaned.

"Yes, the cameras," Phineas said. "If we all attend to the chore together it should take no time at all. And at least it's not raining."

"Does that mean that Abbey has to go with us this time?" Dan asked.

"It does," Abbey said, "and thank you for thinking of me... schmuck."

They went as quickly as they could while at the same time being sure that they didn't draw any attention to themselves. They'd waited until well after midnight to start so, just as they'd been a few nights before, the neighboring buildings and streets were quiet.

Lannie and Dan were working together and one of the last cameras they had to retrieve was mounted on a tree near the Mather tomb. Lannie showed Dan the spot where they'd dug up the box. They got the last camera and where folding up their ladder when Dan suddenly stopped.

"Do you think he did the right thing?" he asked Lannie.

"Don't you?"

"Mostly yes but, there may have been something in that book that was useful, a cure for cancer or something. Something Phineas missed that a scientist wouldn't. Now we'll never know."

"I don't think it's worth the risk," Lannie replied, "not if the book was actually even close to what Lovecraft described, and Phineas said that it was. Doesn't sound to me like any part of it was meant to help anyone. And besides, how do you know that Phineas isn't a scientist."

"Is he?"

"I have no idea, he's not all that forthcoming about his background, you know that. But he does seem to know a great many things on a great many topics. I trust his judgment, always have."

"I guess I do too," Dan agreed grudgingly. "He at least could have let us have look at it though, before he got rid of it."

"Maybe he was protecting us," Lannie said.

"From what?"

"From the book," she picked up their bag of cameras, "come on, let's head back. This place is starting to creep me out a bit."

He hoisted the ladder onto his shoulder and followed her through the moonlit burying ground, back toward Poe Court.

Chapter Ten

They'd had to wait for hours after dinner for it to be sufficiently late to collect the cameras so by the time they returned to the apartment Ben and Robert were hungry again. They were in the kitchen cooking up a big batch of Eggs Florentine; Ben would have preferred Eggs Benedict because everything was better with bacon, but he'd been outvoted. They didn't have any Canadian bacon anyway.

Phineas and Lannie were cleaning the camera units and packing them away. Abbey had begun to break down the monitoring equipment. None of them noticed when she stopped doing that and began studying some of the stored video from several of the cameras.

When the eggs were done they all sat down around the table for their last meal in the apartment.

"What's going to happen with this place now?" Dan asked Phineas.

"The management company was good enough to allow me to rent it for just a month, with the proper monetary incentives of course. Next week it will be available for long term rental if you're interested."

"Right," Dan said, "as if I could afford a two bedroom in the North End."

"I don't know," Robert said, "you may want to think about it. The lead paint in that hovel you rent in Allston must be affecting you by now."

"That building was de-leaded years ago," Dan informed him.

"Was it de-roached," Lannie asked, "because the last time Verity and I were there I saw one that was big enough to ride."

"That was Henry, we're very close," Dan said and they laughed.

"Well I just want to thank everyone again," Phineas said, "for yet another job well done. I really believe we accomplished something of profound significance here, you should all be proud of it." They all acknowledged the compliment and they all meant it because there had been other instances where things hadn't gone nearly as smoothly and the results had been much less positive.

They finished their meal and began cleaning up. As they finished that chore Abbey spoke up. No one had noticed that she'd been unusually quiet while they'd been eating.

"Before we leave I think there's something you all should see," she said and they all turned to her. She sat back down and slid one of the video monitors to the center of the table then pulled the laptop over in front of her.

"If you could all gather round so you can see the monitor," she said and they did. She tapped a few keys and a view of the burying ground came up on the screen. It was one of the cameras that had been situated by the front of the cemetery looking south down Hull Street. The fence that ran along the front of the cemetery was mounted atop a six-foot-high stone wall and was much more of an obstacle than the fence that ran along Charter Street at the rear boundary.

The view on the screen showed the corner of the cemetery and a good portion of Hull Street both through and above the fence. There were street lamps located at regular intervals along the street so it was fairly well lit and they could all see that what had tripped the camera was a group of people approaching along the near side sidewalk.

"This was last Saturday night," Abbey told them, "just after one a.m., when the bars close in this provincial little city. Judging by their unsteady gate I'd say the group approaching the camera have just left one. We never looked very closely at it before because it's just some partygoers on their way home."

"Yeah, they do look kind of lit," Dan agreed. "So what?"

"So," Abbey said, "look to the left of the fence, just inside the cemetery, next to the tree."

They all turned their heads a bit and looked. Dan was the first one to see it even though he didn't realize what he was seeing.

"What is that?" he asked Abbey.

"Keep watching," Abbey said.

And then they all saw it; next to the trunk of the tree, which was very large and very old, was the faint figure of a woman. She was standing slightly behind the tree's trunk and she was watching the group of people coming up Hull Street toward her. There were two problems that they all saw immediately. The first was that she appeared to be wearing a head bonnet, a long bulky skirt that reached to her ankles and a high-necked blouse. She was dressed for the 18th century, not the 21st. Strange as that was, the second problem presented a much larger issue; they could all see the trunk of the tree through her body.

"Holy shit," Robert said, "We actually have this recorded?"

"Just keep watching," Abbey said again.

The group on the street passed by the spot where the woman was standing, none of them were looking into the cemetery so they were totally unaware that she was there. As they continued on down Hull Street the figure moved away from the tree and slowly moved along through the burying ground, keeping pace. Abbey switched to another camera to keep the woman in view.

"Jesus, she's following them," Lannie said softly.

"You can see the lights from that building in the background right through her," Robert added.

"She's not walking, she's just kind of gliding," Dan added. "Everyone see that?"

"She just passed right through that tomb," Robert said, "I saw that."

The figure continued pacing the group out on the street until it reached the edge of the burying grounds, then it stopped just inside the fence and stayed there watching them until they were out of sight down Hull Street. Then it turned back toward the interior of the burying grounds, traveled ten or twelve feet and just faded away.

They all just stood around the table looking at the monitor until Abbey said, "That's it, that's all there is."

Author's note

H.P. Lovecraft was of course a real person who wrote real and terrifying stories. I've tried to incorporate facts from his life and his work into this story whenever possible, but I have also taken artistic license when necessary to move the story forward.

And while real Grimoire's do exist, the Necronomicon was nothing more than a figment of Mr. Lovecraft's very vivid imagination... probably.

KING PHILIP WAS A RUNNER NOT A FIGHTER

Prologue

It has always been known as The Great Cedar Swamp by locals, but maps of the area label it the Burrage Pond Wildlife Management area. There is a small, but devoted group of people who include it in a larger area they call The Bridgewater Triangle and claim that all sorts of odd things go on within its boundaries and have gone on for centuries: ghost lights, disappearances, animals not known to science roaming about, spirits of the people who've died there. What it is in reality is a really big swamp that borders three towns and covers somewhere around 2,000 acres of wetland.

The area consists of numerous lakes, swamps, overgrown cranberry bogs, and miles of hiking trails that follow the narrow strips of dry land that haphazardly intersect the area. There are also a few small islands of dry land, some accessible on foot, some only with a boat. There are very few trees other than those on the islands, a few on the raised walking trails, and around the perimeter. So the overall effect is one of wide open space, a huge dome of sky or, at night, of stars, over an untamed world of water, swamp and low growing scrub. The hiking and walking trails are open to the public and used by hikers, hunters and bird watchers. They are accessed by several public entrances located in the different towns around the boundary. There is also an old abandoned railroad bed that is raised well above the swamp and runs through it in a straight line from northwest to southeast. Despite these features offering access to its interior, the Great Cedar Swamp is usually a deserted and desolate place. Even on warm days very few people are seen walking it's trails. No one goes there after dark.

The areas reputation for being a haunted place reaches back centuries. Some simply ascribe it to the fact that it's such a desolate place, especially at night. Others attribute it to the violence that happened there during the Indian wars that raged throughout the area for a few bloody years in the 17th century. Still others attribute it to the fact that on occasion people have gone into the swamp and simply vanished. And there was the case of a light aircraft that crashed into the swamp back in the 1970's, killing both occupants. The wreckage remained in place for years, doing its part in contributing to the creepy atmosphere.

The main source for the ghost stories though is King Philip's War. King Philip's War was a conflict between European settlers and several Indian tribes indigenous to New England. The war was led by Metacom, known to the settlers as King Philip, Chief of the Pokunoket tribe which included the Wampanoag, Nipmuck and Narraganset tribes. The war began in 1675 and while it lasted just fourteen months, it resulted in a great deal of bloodshed and loss of life on both sides.

During the war it was common for the Indians to set up camp in swamps because they knew that the European settlers disliked swamps and were unlikely to venture into them very far. Swamps also usually involved open land that made it easy to see an enemy force coming. The Indian forces under Metacom used several large swamps for this purpose during the course of the war including the two largest swamps in southeastern Massachusetts, Hobomock Swamp and Great Cedar Swamp. And while the largest 'swamp battle' of King Philip's war actually took place in Kingston, Rhode Island, several smaller actions were rumored to have occurred in the Great Cedar Swamp, resulting in heavy losses on both sides.

Typically, the Indians would make camp and fortify raised islands or hillocks that were surrounded by wetlands or water deep within the swamps. Legend had it that King Philip and his lieutenants would always have an escape route or back door established and would use it to flee when the settlers attacked. This may have been settler propaganda meant to degrade the Indians' reputation however, it is a fact that Metacom was shot and killed while doing this very thing, that in fact an ambush had been laid for him in anticipation of him fleeing in this manner.

One persistent legend of Great Cedar Swamp was that late at night, if one were brave enough to be in the swamp in the first place, you would be able to hear the sounds of battle and see the ghosts of Indian warriors running from one of the raised islands; no one was sure which one. One may even catch a glimpse of King Philip himself, running from yet another onslaught of European militia.

Three hundred and forty odd years later there were still some who were willing to brave the swamp at night for the chance of just such an encounter.

Chapter One

"If you're too afraid just say so," Dean said, "and you'll forever after be known to us as Suzy."

"That's not what I said," Mark replied.

"We'll call you Suzy every day, all the time, in front of girls."

"God you're an asshole," Mark said.

"Sometimes we'll break it up by calling you Suze instead. You know, just to add a little variety."

"Sally would be good too," Scott chimed in.

"Screw you," Mark told them.

"So just say you're afraid to go and we'll change your name right now."

"I didn't say I was afraid to go, all I said was that it's supposed to rain tonight."

"We've walked the swamp a million times Mark," Dean said.

"Not at night," Nicky pointed out.

"All...I...said...was...that...it's...going...to...rain!" Mark said, "Unlike you halfwits who spend your time playing video games or jacking off when you're home, I actually pay attention to the weather lady."

"Because she's hot," Scott pointed out.

"Which one?"

"Channel 10, the one that's on in the morning."

"She's ok, but the one on at night is way hotter."

"Yeah, I'd like to get to know her!"

"She's probably like thirty years old, and you're freaking fourteen."

"She's only twenty-six, I Googled her."

"Oh, only twenty-six, why didn't you say so! You should give her a call then! She can ride on the back of your bike...moron."

They were sitting on the grass island at the edge of the Dunkin Donuts parking lot on Main Street with their bikes sprawled around them. The commuter rail station was behind them, a feed and grain store to their left. And that was about it because Main Street hadn't been the center of town for decades. That distinction went to Liberty Street two miles away where the town hall was, and a supermarket, and a drug store, a McDonalds, and yet another

Dunkin Donuts because in New England you just can't have too many Dunkin Donuts.

It was high summer and they had nothing in particular to do and nowhere they had to go. A state of being they would look back on with wistful fondness not too many years down the road. The swamp that was currently under discussion was the Great Cedar Swamp, whose northern border could be found just down the street from where they were presently sitting. They had been exploring the swamp for years and they knew it pretty well, although it was so big that it would be hard to know every part of it and some areas were accessible only by boat and they didn't have a boat. They had recently been digging around on one of the small mounds of dry land that they called an island even though it was accessible by a narrow raised path and they'd found a half dozen arrowheads. That had brought up the subject of the Indian wars that they'd learned about in school, which had then led to the stories about the ghosts that roamed the swamp at night. And that had led to them talking about visiting the swamp after dark, something they'd never done before.

"We need to plan this out anyway," Scott said, "tents and camping equipment and shit. I'm not going to walk out there and just sit on my ass in the dark getting eaten alive by bugs. And we need a story for our parents, camping out is a good one."

"And not in the rain," Mark said.

"Why is camping out a good one?" Dean asked, "I haven't been camping since I was nine."

"I've never been camping," Nicky said.

"Because we are actually going to be camping," Scott said slowly, as if he were talking to a child.

"I don't have any camping stuff," Nicky told them.

"I do," Mark said, "and so does Scott; we'll bring a tent and some other stuff, just see if you can get a sleeping bag."

"Where am I going to get a sleeping bag?"

"Ask your sister," Dean said. "I think she uses one to cushion her ass when she's banging her boyfriend in the back seat of his Toyota."

"Just find one," Mark told him, "borrow one from somebody. And if you can't find one just bring a couple of blankets."

"Fine," Nicky said. "And I'm going to tell Samantha you said that about her," he said to Dean. "I wouldn't come over to my house for a while if I were you."

"So why don't we plan on tomorrow night then," Scott suggested.

"Is that ok with you?" Dean asked Mark, "what's your girlfriend on channel 10 have to say about tomorrow night?"

"You are such an asshole," Mark told him.

Chapter Two

Mark and Scott were in Hanson Hobby which was located in a converted barn about a mile down street from the Dunkin Donuts they'd been at the day before. They were checking out remote control airplanes that both had included on their Christmas lists for the past four years and that both their parents had passed on each and every time.

"You know," Scott was saying, "pretty soon we're going to be too old for this shit and then they'll be sorry they never got them for us."

"Yeah," Mark said, "I'm sure it will keep them up nights."

"My father said he was afraid I'd fly it through a window and into the house," Scott said. "What did your father say?"

"He said that he wasn't paying hundreds of dollars for something that I'd destroy the first time I tried to fly it. It was really a heartwarming moment."

They left the shop and walked their bikes south down Main Street past the police station on the right and the old Grange Hall on the left that neither could ever remember anyone using. Just after that the left side of the street opened up to a huge expanse of cranberry bogs that stretched back for more than a mile and ran for over a hundred yards along the road.

"My dad told me that when he was a kid some of his friends saw a UFO in there one night." Scott said. "There were four of them and they all saw it. They didn't tell anyone for a long time because they were scared and when they finally did the Air Force came down to talk to them and everything."

"Yeah, I've heard that story," Mark said. "We should sit here at night on watch instead of in the swamp, be a hell of a lot more comfortable."

"You afraid to be in the swamp at night?"

"Hell no! But there are things you need to think about if you're going in there at night, snakes for one, quicksand for another. And what if there are drug dealers in there at night shooting up or making deals or something and they see us, ever think about that?"

"What about ghosts?"

"Ghosts can't hurt you."

"And you know that, how?"

"I read it somewhere, but drug dealers can hurt you; drug dealers can slit your throat and sink your body in the swamp to keep you from talking."

"There aren't any drug dealers in this dinky little town. We just got a McDonalds four years ago for Christ sake!"

They walked for a while in silence pondering drug dealers and fast food franchises. Everyone was meeting at the Hanson AA bowling alley to hang out for a while before riding back toward Dunkin's then heading into the swamp for the night. Mark and Scott both had sleeping bags and other camping paraphernalia tied to their bikes in various places. The tent was rolled up and draped over Mark's seat which was one of the reasons they weren't riding.

When they reached the bowling alley Dean and Nicky were already there, sitting out front waiting for them.

"So what did your girlfriend, the weather girl, have to say this morning?" Dean asked Mark as soon as they joined up.

"She probably asked him if it was in yet," Nicky said and laughed at his own joke. Nicky always laughed at his own jokes which was good because usually no one else did.

"It's going to be warm and humid," Mark told them.

"Just like her crotch," Dean said.

"God you guys need to grow up," Mark said. "Seriously."

"Well she was wrong about last night; it didn't rain, did it?" Dean pointed out.

"They're wrong like half the time," Nicky said. "That's why they're all babes and dress like they do. It's to take your mind off the fact that they're wrong so much. Personally I'm happy with that arrangement, it works for me."

"Tell me someone remembered the bug spray," Scott said, "because if they didn't then I'm out."

"Why didn't you bring some then?" Dean asked.

"We brought the tent jerk off," Scott said, "we couldn't think of everything."

"I've got two spray bottles of it," Nicky told them, "and some kind of skin lotion that my mom says works really good too. She also said we should be careful of snakes in the swamp."

"You told her we were going into the swamp?" Dean said, "You really are a moron."

"She said it was ok if there was a bunch of us, and she has to know where I am in case she needs to come get me for something. I always tell her where I'm going to be, she's my mom." He said the last bit in a tone of voice that said he couldn't believe everyone didn't do the same thing.

"It's fine," Mark told him, "in fact the more I think about it the more I think someone should know where we're going, just in case."

"What about food?" Dean asked.

"We brought energy bars and some trial mix," Scott said.

"I have a bunch of beef jerky," Nicky told them. "If we see an Indian's ghost we can use it as a peace offering."

"What'd you bring," Mark asked Dean, "other than your dick, which is of no use to anyone."

"That's not what your mother said last night."

"Bwwwwaaaaahhhhhaaaaa," Mark leaned over holding his sides and pretending to laugh.

"What *did* you bring?" Scott asked Dean. "Other than the sleeping bag on your handlebars I don't see anything."

"I brought three flashlights, a hunting knife, and one of my dad's old film cameras that has high speed film in it because your iPhone's aren't worth shit taking pictures at night. It's all rolled up in my sleeping bag." None of them asked him why he'd thought he'd need a hunting knife; it was the swamp at night after all. Mark wished he'd brought a frigging gun!

"We can stop at the convenience store down the street for more stuff," Nicky said. "I wouldn't mind bringing along some more snacks and something to drink."

"My dad says that people that live along the edge of the swamp on Elm Street hear screams sometimes at night," Scott said to no one in particular and that pretty much brought the conversation to a halt for a moment.

"I heard that too," Nicky said finally, "and lights that flicker or just kind of float along above the ground."

"That could just be swamp gas," Mark said.

"I got your swamp gas right here!" Dean lifted his leg and farted. "Now if you ladies are done with the ghost stories I say we start out. By the time we stop at the store then get to the train tracks it'll be starting to get dark. We want to be in the swamp with our camp site set up before it gets all the way dark."

They all stood up and Scott and Mark got the tent positioned on Mark's bike so he could at least ride it, even if he couldn't use the seat.

Dean and Nicky pulled ahead a bit because Mark had to pedal standing up, but Scott hung back with him. They rode in silence for a few minutes.

"You think we're all going to stay friends," Scott asked finally, "once we graduate from high school and go to college?"

"Nicky's not going to college," Mark laughed, "he's running on maybe a few dozen brain cells now and once he gets a little older and starts drinking and smoking weed he'll kill off most of those."

"Yeah," Scott agreed, "but he's a good guy, he means well." He paused for a moment then; "I can't really see us staying friends with Dean, seems every year he's a bigger asshole than he was the year before."

"You ever meet his father?"

"No."

"His father is the king of the assholes; I think he has a crown and everything. And that's when he's sober. When he drinks, which is a lot, he's even worse, he's a mean drunk. Dean's starting to take after his dad."

"That sucks."

"Yeah, if I lived in that house I might be the same way."

They pedaled in silence for a few minutes. "You think we're actually going to see anything in the swamp tonight?" Scott finally said.

"Nah, it'll be fun and a little scary and we'll get eaten alive by bugs and won't sleep at all, but we'll be able to tell everyone that we did it and that'll be cool."

"But King Philip really did hide out there and there was fighting, we learned about it in class. And we found all those arrow heads."

"Yeah, but he actually got killed down in Rhode Island somewhere, so why would he haunt this swamp instead of the swamp he got killed in?"

"Maybe it's not him, maybe it's one of his men that *did* get killed here. Or maybe it's like this story I read about a beach in France where there was a battle during World War II. The beach is actually haunted by the whole battle, not anyone who got killed in it. So once in a while people hear the battle going on, usually at the same time it actually happened."

"Everything I've ever heard was about ghost lights floating over the water, or screams coming from deep in the swamp late at night; never heard anything about anyone hearing a whole battle going on."

"The screams were probably made by a bunch of kids who were stupid enough to spend the night out there and ended up scaring themselves shitless," Scott said drily.

"Works for me," Mark replied.

Dean and Nicky had reached the convenience store on Main Street and pulled in. They leaned their bikes against the side of the building and went inside. Mark and Scott got there a few moments later and followed. They bought drinks and more snacks. Nicky found some chemical light sticks and bought two packages of them with the last of his money, and they got more bug spray. They split everything up into two triple strength plastic shopping bags that they could hang from their handlebars and grabbed ice creams for the road. Mark sprung for Nicky's because he'd blown his cash on the light sticks, and they were off again.

Of the several ways to gain access to the swamp their entrance of choice had always been the railroad tracks. Along the south side of that stretch of Main Street was an old falling down complex of wooden buildings that had once been a thriving cranberry business. The company had moved on to bigger and better digs decades ago and now the buildings were slowly falling to ruin. The train tracks crossed Main Street in front of the complex and then cut right through it before running along the edge of the swamp. It was an active track used by the commuter trains, but they could ride their bikes along the tracks and just after they'd enter the swamp an old abandoned track bed veered off to the right and they would take that. Besides, they knew the train schedule by heart. So they hit the train tracks and headed in.

Chapter Three

The old abandoned railroad embankment cut almost right through the middle of the swamp and still ran on for over half the distance to the far side before it had begun to collapse, its sides crumbling and falling into the black water until it finally disappeared into the muck altogether, about a half a mile shy of the far side of the swamp.

The tiny island where they'd found the arrowheads lay on the right side of it a couple of hundred yards out into the swamp. It wasn't a true island because it was connected to the embankment by a long narrow earthen dike that someone had constructed, who knew how long ago and for who knew what. They left their bikes on the flat top of the embankment; the tracks had been pulled up decades ago, and gained access to the island on foot by way of the dike.

Once they reached the island an argument ensued concerning the best place to camp, on the island itself or back on the flat top of the embankment.

"If we camp here and the island is haunted, the ghosts are going to show up right on top of us," Nicky finally pointed out. They decided on the embankment.

It had been coming on dusk when they'd reached the island, by the time they had the tent up and were settled in on the embankment it was really beginning to get dark. Dean strapped on the hunting knife then positioned himself at the edge of the embankment facing the island and announced that he wanted to be the first one to see a ghost. Nicky hung two of the chemical light sticks around his neck, sat right by the door of the tent and announced that at the first sign of a ghost he could be found inside the tent deep down inside his sleeping bag.

Mark and Scott slathered themselves with bug spray then sat on the edge of the embankment facing the island, five or six feet from Dean because he wanted to be the closest to the island and every time they moved closer to him he'd move further down the bank. They watched as night settled over the swamp like a blanket and stars began to appear above them. The closest trees were a handful of stunted oaks on the island so the bowl of the night sky above their heads seemed huge. Mark used the last of the quickly fading light to make sure he knew were his stuff was, how close the tent was and that his bike wasn't near the edge of the embankment.

There was no moon so once it was dark, it was really dark and it took their eyes some time to adjust. After a while they were able to see the dike around them, the reflection of the starlight off the water and a dark indistinct shape that was the island. Dean clicked on one of his flashlights; he'd brought three but had only given one to Scott, keeping the other two for himself. He played the beam over the island then clicked it off again.

"Thanks," Scott said, "you just screwed up our night vision. Now it's going to take another ten minutes for us to be able to see anything again."

"And you should save the batteries for when you really need them," Nicky said from over by the tent where he was still sitting in front of the door eating beef jerky. Dean clicked the flashlight back on, turned and shined it in Nicky's face then turned it off again.

"So," Scott said to no one in particular, "we're sitting in the middle of a swamp, at night, with an asshole. How great is this."

"You shouldn't talk about Mark like that," Dean said, "he's sitting right next to you, you'll hurt his feelings."

"Hey Dean?" Mark said, "Want to make a bet? I'll bet you fifty dollars that if a ghost does show up you'll be the first one to go, you'll run off down this rail bed screaming like a twelve-year-old girl."

"You don't have fifty dollars," Dean said.

"I sure as shit do," Mark replied, "it's my birthday money, been saving it for something special and I sure would like to double it tonight, what do you say?"

"It's a sucker bet," Scott told Mark.

"You don't think he'd do it?"

"Oh I know he'd do it, not only screaming like a twelve-year-old girl, but pissing himself while he did it. It's a sucker bet because *he* doesn't have fifty dollars."

"You're on," Dean said, still looking at the island.

"Do you have fifty dollars," Mark asked him.

"I don't need fifty dollars because you're going to lose because if a ghost shows up I'm going to be right here taking pictures of it. You won't see it though because you and Nicky will be hiding in the tent together, probably holding each other's dicks."

"Told you," Scott said.

"Your sister's the only person I let hold my dick," Nicky said to Dean from over by the tent. That bit of witticism shut them all up for a while and they sat swatting bugs and trying to make out the details of the swamp around them.

Two hours on the starlight seemed a bit brighter because their vision had completely adapted and the bugs had really found them. Scott and Mark had broken out some snacks and were in their spot eating away and sipping Cokes, covering the opening in the cans when they weren't drinking so no bugs crawled inside. Nicky had finally joined them partly because there was safety in numbers, but mostly because Scott had pointed out to him that a ghost could just as easily show up behind them on the other side of the embankment and sneak up on the tent. Dean was still sitting nearer to the island and staring intently at it through the darkness. The only sounds they heard were the insects having a convention all around them and once in a while a train whistle off in the distance as the last few commuter trains of the night hit the crossing on Main Street. Mark commented that a train whistle at night had to be one of the loneliest sounds on earth and got general agreement on it from the group.

They heard the last train a little after eleven, Scott had checked his wristwatch and informed them that the train they were hearing was the eleven-ten train and it was the last one for the night, there wouldn't be any more. Nobody said it, but it felt like they'd just lost a connection to the outside world.

It wasn't very long after the eleven-ten train that things started to go really wrong.

Chapter Four

"Guys?" Dean said quietly.

"Yeah," Scott answered, he wasn't sure why they were whispering. He and Mark were still in their spot, Nicky had gone back to the front of the tent and stated that he was going to go in and go to sleep soon. No one believed him.

"I think there's someone on the island," Dean said. "I can hear them moving around."

They all sat quiet and a moment later Mark and Scott both heard a twig snap on the island. "Holy shit," Mark whispered, "there is someone out there."

"It's probably just an animal," Scott said.

As if in response to that statement, they all thought they now heard muted voices from the direction of the island.

"That isn't English," Dean whispered

"You can't tell," Scott said, "we can't even understand what they're saying."

"Because it isn't English," Dean insisted.

"Maybe their hunters," Nicky had moved back over next to Scott and Mark.

"Shine your light over there," Scott said to Dean.

"The hell with that," Dean replied.

"If they're out here jacking deer they may shoot at us," Mark told them.

"There aren't any deer out here."

"Why don't you go tell them."

They heard a faint splash and then the sound of something moving through the water.

"I think it's time to go now guys," Nicky said and stood up.

"We haven't seen anything yet," Mark replied.

"Maybe it's an alligator," Scott said and grabbed Nicky's leg.

"I am telling you guys, that is not English," Dean repeated.

"Then what is it?"

"I don't know; I can't tell, but I can tell it's not English."

Another splash, louder this time, and then all hell broke loose. On the far side of the little island the night was lit up by flashes and the sound of gunshots echoed across the swamp. There was yelling now and it definitely was not English.

"What are they saying?" Scott asked.

"They're saying that the white man stole our land," Mark replied, "I think we should get the fuck out of here."

Something appeared out of the undergrowth on their side of the island and started running down the earthen dike toward them. It was dark and the figure on the dike looked filmy and kind of out of focus but Mark knew a goddamned Indian when he saw one and there was an Indian running across the dike toward them. It passed by and Mark noticed two things, he could see through it, and it was running knee deep in the railroad embankment. When it passed through their tent and kept on going without giving them a second glance they all stood there and watched. Then they turned back to the island because the noise level was rising.

"That's it for me," Scott announced, "I'm going with the Indian."

And then the screaming started and they all broke, running down the top of the embankment as more shadowy figures emerged from the underbrush and ran across the dyke toward them. Mark tripped over his bike then got up and kept running, Scott was next to him. At one point he had the image of a shadow passing him, running full tilt boogie and only coming up to his waist because whatever it was it was running through the railroad bed instead of on top of it.

After that he went into full panic mode and just ran, somehow staying on the top of the rail bed in the darkness and not being able to figure out later how he ever managed that. The sounds behind them began growing fainter and before they knew it they reached the point where the old rail bad intersected the active commuter rail line. They all stopped and put their hands on their knees gasping for breath. The spectral Indians seemed to be gone and they could no longer hear any sounds coming from the swamp. The quiet was almost as unsettling as the noises had been.

Mark got his breath and straightened up to look around and then said "Hey, where's Nicky?"

Scott and Dean straightened up and looked around too and Nicky still wasn't there.

"Nicky!" Dean yelled, "not funny Nicky, where are you!" There was no answer and after the third try Dean gave it up.

"Maybe he fell off the embankment or something," Scott said.

"Maybe he ran off the embankment," Dean said.

"We have to go back and look," Mark replied, "We've got to look for him." They all turned and looked back down the old embankment toward the island.

"Why don't we just call someone for help," Dean said.

"Who, the Ghostbusters?" Scott asked him.

"The cops shithead, they can go look for Nicky."

"*We're* going to look for Nicky," Mark told him. "He could be hurt, or drowning in the swamp or something."

"There's some seriously weird shit going on back there man," Dean said. "Are you sure you want to do that?"

"I am," Mark said then turned and started back up the embankment.

"So am I," Scott said and followed him. Dean hesitated for a moment then hurried after them.

Mark was out in front so he saw Nicky first. Or rather, he saw an indistinct lump lying on top of the embankment; he couldn't make out any details in the darkness, except that whatever it was, it wasn't moving."

As he got closer he could see that it was Nicky, lying face down on the path. He knelt down beside him and started to reach out then stopped because he wasn't all that sure he wanted to touch a dead body.

"Nicky, Nick? You ok?"

"Are they gone?" Nicky asked him.

"Yeah, I think so, you ok?"

Nicky rolled over and looked up at him. "they shot me in the ass," he said.

Chapter Five

Detective Franks, Massachusetts State Police, poured a cup of coffee then turned and sat down at the table across from the state medical examiner.

"So," he said, "according to your report the kid has a deep puncture wound to his left buttocks caused by an unknown object."

"Right," the examiner said, "but it's weird because there's nothing in the wound track,"

"Could it have been a long sharp object, say like a broken stick, that made the wound then pulled free...or was pulled out by someone."

The medical examiner was shaking his head. "Something like that would have left indicators, slivers of wood, something. Also the wound would have been much more jagged than it is. It's a very clean wound track. I just couldn't find any type of foreign material at all inside it."

"Well what do you *think* it was?" the detective asked.

"I'm not going to speculate, not officially. But between you and me, I've seen hundreds of bullet tracks in my time; they're always different but they're very distinctive and they're very unique. This looks like nothing else in this world but a bullet wound. But since there is no bullet present, nor any fragments of a bullet, my report is going to say 'puncture wound by an unknown object'".

"The kid claims he was shot in the butt," the detective said. "They all claimed that there was someone out in the swamp shooting guns and that's why they ran. I also spoke with people at the local gun club, which is less than two miles from the swamp by the way and *they* all claimed that they don't know anything about anyone messing around out in Great Cedar and firing off guns late at night. Kind of believed them. We also canvassed the neighborhoods that abut the swamp and no one heard any gunshots, or anything else for that matter, during the time in question, although some claimed to have heard some odd things out there at other times. So what we have is a bunch of teenagers who decided that it would be fun to camp out in a swamp. And then we maybe have one or more idiots going out into the swamp late at night to shoot off their guns, maybe trying to jack a few deer...maybe just for shits and giggles."

"And the kids didn't see anything at all?"

"Naw, according to them they were out there minding their own business when someone starts yelling and shooting guns on a little island nearby their camp site. They get scared and run because they think they're drug dealers or something, and that's when one of them gets shot. They carry him out and call the local police and that's about it."

"You find anything useful out on the island?"

"About a thousand mosquitos and some other bugs we haven't identified yet. Other than that nothing, just the kids' tent, sleeping bags, bikes and stuff on the embankment nearby. There was evidence that people have been hanging around out there though, hunting, birdwatching, partying, getting romantic, whatever. Maybe someone got pissed off that someone else was invading their territory or maybe they were drunk, who knows; they try to scare the kids off and end up shooting at them. Then they get scared and vacate the premises." He drained his coffee then got up and tossed the paper cup into the trash. "I don't suppose there's any chance a bullet could have fallen out of the wound track before the EMT's got to him, like while his buddies were carrying him out to the road?"

"Afraid not," the examiner told him, "it's a fairly deep track. The muscle tissue would have partially closed around it after penetration; no way it would have just fallen out."

"Yeah, figured as much," Detective Franks shrugged into his sports jacket and headed for the door. "I'll let you know if I need anything else," he said, "but don't wait by the phone."

"Sorry I couldn't have been of more help," the Medical Examiner said. "How is the kid doing?"

Franks stopped in the doorway and turned back. "He's fine, I think he's getting released tomorrow."

Nicky was propped up in his hospital bed and laying a bit to one side to avoid putting pressure on his wound. There were a couple of flower arrangements and some get well cards scattered around the room

"Oh and I saw Bonnie yesterday," Mark was saying, "She asked about you, she was very concerned, at one point I thought she might cry."

"You're full of shit," Nicky said, "she didn't ask about me. You probably didn't even see her."

"I did see her and she did ask about you, I think her exact words were 'how is that little jerkoff Nicky doing', or something to that effect."

"And who the hell sent you flowers?" Dean asked him. "Is there anything you'd like to tell us?"

"You guys are supposed to be here to cheer me up. So far you're doing a really piss poor job."

"Your mom's going to be back in a few minutes," Scott said to Nicky, "Let's go over it one more time, just to be sure you've got it."

"I got it," Nicky said, "I'm not stupid. We decided it would be spooky to camp in the swamp and then some guys showed up and started yelling and shooting around us to get us to leave, they sounded drunk. So we were leaving when I got hurt. We think it was an accident and that they were just trying to scare us and then they ran off."

"Good," Scott said, "the state cop believed us and our parents believed us so they'll buy it from you too."

"Yeah, now that you're well enough to receive guests," Dean said sarcastically.

"So we should wait a few weeks until it all dies down before we go back," Mark said.

"Go back where?" Nicky said.

"To the swamp halfwit," Scott said.

"And next time we'll camp on the other side of the island so we won't be directly in the path of any fleeing ghost Indians."

"I'm not going back in that swamp, are you frigging nuts?" Nicky said.

"We'll plan it better this time," Scott assured him, "now that we know what to expect."

"I got shot in the ass!"

"So what," Mark said. "What's the big deal, it was already cracked."

"Yeah, don't be such a baby," Dean told him. "They didn't even find a bullet."

"You guys ran like little girls, I saw you," Nicky replied, "right before I got shot in the ass by a ghost that is. And now you want to go back?"

"Hell yes," Mark said.

"Last night was way cooler than any video game we've *ever* played," Scott said.

"And it's not as if we have anything better to do," Mark pointed out.

"We'll just go without you," Dean told him.

"Fine," Nicky said, "but this time I'm going to have to lie to my mother about where I'm going, just so you all know that."

"Always a major milestone in a young man's life, lying to his mom," Mark told him, "We're all very proud of you."

Scott and Dean nodded in agreement.

BUT WE *WANT* TO BE ALONE

Prologue

Carl Ferguson came out his kitchen door into the crisp darkness of an October night in Nebraska and crossed his backyard to his observatory. It was actually a prefabricated metal storage building, but it had heat and power, a computer workstation, a really comfy office chair, a microwave, a hotplate and a mini-fridge. And it housed his telescope, so as far as he was concerned it was his observatory. He spent most of his evenings in it, often late into the night.

It had taken him eleven years to save enough money to buy the components to build his telescope and another three to be able to purchase the building, set it up, and run power to it. He, and a buddy from the machine shop he worked in, had spent a weekend turning half of the fixed roof into a sliding roof and then another month getting the motorized pad that the square building sat upon to rotate so Carl could point his telescope toward pretty much any part of the night sky he chose to. Beyond the edge of

Carl's property was open prairie, a whole lot of it, which gave him a big sky to look at.

His telescope was 34 feet tall, the primary mirror was 70 inches, the secondary mirror was 30, and to the best of his knowledge it was the most powerful telescope in private hands when he'd built it six years ago. That wasn't true any longer of course; some guy in Illinois had built a bigger one just a year or so ago, but Carl didn't care. His telescope was more than sufficient for his needs.

Carl had a two -year community college degree in electrical engineering, and for his day job that was fine. For the hobby that occupied his nights he had taught himself astronomy, he had taught himself how to build a telescope, he had taught himself how to program the computer that ran it. He had even figured out how to keep his wife from leaving him while still allowing himself as much time as possible out in the back yard at night. It was a very delicate balancing act.

He spent some of his time searching the night sky for NEO's, Near-Earth Objects, harboring faint dreams of saving the planet one day. But he spent much more time looking at and photographing deep space objects; nebulas and other galaxies. The list was endless and he was sure he'd never get through a fraction of what there was to see out there in his lifetime.

And then some nights he would just tool around the solar system, his real backyard as he liked to think of it. Compared to the objects he was usually looking at, the nine planets that made up the solar system were right next door. Pluto was still a planet to him and he didn't give a tin shit what anyone else said on the subject.

On this particular crisp October evening he was listening to an Avalanche game on the radio and looking at Jupiter when he saw something hit Jupiter's moon, Ganymede. At first he thought that, whatever it was, it was going to hit Jupiter itself, but then it seemed to swerve, trick of the light, and head straight for Ganymede. He immediately started a time- lapse video to record the event, thinking he'd have great footage of a comet or asteroid hitting the moon, very cool stuff. It was already long after midnight and he finally had to go to bed, but he left everything running. He'd look at the video the following night.

He was back in the observatory early the following evening, sitting in front of the computer terminal reviewing the video. He also had the telescope trained on Jupiter again just in case - sometimes comets broke up and the pieces would create impacts over several days.

He immediately saw several things on the video that made him forget all about comets. The first was that the movement he'd noticed the previous night didn't look like distortion or a trick of the light, as far as he could see the object *was* originally headed for Jupiter and then made an honest to God course change and went straight for Ganymede. It didn't swerve, it actually seemed to make an almost 90 degree turn. And something else - he couldn't be sure, but he would swear that it was slowing down as it approached the moon. Also, it didn't impact like an ordinary space body would have. When it reached the surface there was no flash, no nothing. It just seemed to reach the surface and stop. The final thing he saw was what really made him think he was seeing things; the stills he pulled from the video weren't as clear as he'd like them to be but, they were still pretty good because he had a great camera system. They were clear enough to show that the object sitting on Ganymede didn't look like a rock, or a hunk of ice. It had a lot of straight lines and right angles, things you didn't see in nature...it looked like some kind of spaceship.

That was when he decided to call the university in Lincoln and talk to someone in their science department.

One

"We've got another one", Major Reinman said as he hung up the phone, "another amateur astronomer, this one from Nebraska. He called Nebraska University's science department and told them he has time lapse video of the event."

"Well that only makes it three so far," Colonel Mantel replied, "could be a hell of a lot worse. Apparently not many people were looking at Jupiter the other night. That's a break for us."

"We've got people heading over there now," Reinman said. "We'll scoop him up by this afternoon."

"Good, let's hope he's the last. I'm not all that enthusiastic about holding citizens against their will." He picked up a leather portfolio and a couple of files. "Briefing time. You ready for this?"

"I am," Reinman replied, "It's going to be worth it just to see the looks on their faces." On their way down to the briefing room they picked up Emil Lorendo at the office that had been hastily set up for his use while he was at the base. In the briefing room they were met by a gaggle of generals, admiral's, presidential advisors, and the Secretary of State. Mantel was a bit miffed that the President wasn't there because at the moment he couldn't think of anything on the planet that could be more important than what they were about to discuss.

The SecState nodded to Mantel as he sat down and as if he'd read his mind said; "The President is tied up with something he couldn't get out of. I'll brief him within an hour of this meeting ending."

Mantel nodded and looked around the room. "Gentlemen, I think you all know Major Reinman. Also with me today is Emil Lorendo from JPL. I won't bother to list his credentials because that would take too long. Suffice to say that he's one of the best people in the country for us to have working on this." He looked around the room again briefly for comments, got none, and turned his attention to the computer in front of him.

"Gentlemen, if you'll all look at the big screen on the wall to your left I'll run the time lapse video for you." He hit a key and a video that Carl Ferguson would recognize ran on the wall monitor, except that Carl would have been amazed at how much clearer this video was compared to his.

"This is from Hubble," Mantel told them. "It was taken two nights ago".

"What are we looking at," one of the General's asked, "A meteor strike?"

'You know what you're looking at,' Mantel thought to himself, 'You just can't accept it.' He ran the video again, "As you can see, an object was approaching Jupiter in an unstable trajectory and at a fairly high rate of speed. At sixty-six seconds into the video it changes course by almost 90 degrees, which puts it on a collision course with Jupiter's largest moon, Ganymede. At the same time, it also begins to decelerate, slowly at first and then more and more quickly, until it comes into contact with the surface of the moon."

"How in the hell can an asteroid turn and slow down?" the same general as before.

"An asteroid can't," Mantel replied. "It's not an asteroid."

"Hold on," the SecState said, "Are you saying this thing was under intelligent control?"

"We are," Mantel replied, "It appears that whatever it is, it executed a controlled crash landing on Ganymede. Pretty slick one too."

"You'd better have more than this video to back that up," the general said. "I don't see how you can make that statement just from what we're seeing here."

Mantel glanced at Reinman for a moment. Reinman had a faint grin on his face. "We're not," Mantel told the General. He tapped another button on the computer and a still photo came up on the screen. "This is an enlargement of the object shortly before it touched down. With Ganymede providing a backdrop and with the image cleaned up as much as possible I think you can all see that this is definitely a ship of some kind." He tapped the button again, "Here it is just before touch down. There appears to be some kind of energy column being emitted from the underside of the craft and that's what we think it used to slow itself down." He looked at Lorendo who stood up and half turned to the screen.

"Good afternoon gentlemen. I understand that this is a momentous event and it will take some time to digest. I am here today to go over the details of what we've learned in the short time since this event occurred. I'm sure in coming days we will learn much more." He pointed up to the screen, "As Colonel Mantel has pointed out, the craft appears to have turned away from Jupiter with the intention of landing on Ganymede. It utilized some sort of propulsion system that we haven't yet identified to both turn the craft and to bring it down onto the surface of the moon. We believe that this was a controlled crash as opposed to a planned landing. I say that for several reasons. First the craft appears to be a bit unstable in flight, as if whoever is piloting it is fighting for control. Of course knowing very little about it to begin with this may be its normal mode of flight, but we don't believe that to be true. Also, while it did slow its descent to the surface of Ganymede it still impacted that surface with significant force – more force than one would likely find acceptable in a controlled landing."

"What did it do after that," one of the general's interrupted him.

"Nothing," Lorendo said, "It's still there. We believe that this was a forced landing and that this craft is unable to take off again."

"What do you base that on," the SecState asked.

"Several things; first, the landing, as I said, was rather hard and it appears that pieces of the craft actually detached from the main body upon impact. Several appear to be fairly substantial in size. Also, since the landing we've seen no surface movement. There's been no sign of exploratory activity, or any activity at all, around the craft. And finally, and certainly most significant, it's broadcasting a signal at regular intervals. We believe that this signal is a distress call of some sort."

"Is this signal pointed toward us?" the general asked.

"It's not, it's being directed toward deep space."

"What makes you think it's a distress call?" the SecState asked.

"Several things. The type of landing the craft made, with what appears to be substantial structural damage, the fact that it's still there. As far as we've been able to discern over the years the surface of Ganymede is mostly ice and rock, nothing of great interest and in any event, as said, we haven't noticed any activity around the craft. And lastly, the signal has all the earmarks of an SOS beacon. It's some sort of energy beam, similar to a laser and it never varies its pattern, it broadcasts the same signal each time, at set intervals, and it began broadcasting as soon as the craft landed."

"How many people know about this?" the General asked.

"Besides the people in this room, sixteen. Twelve people at NASA and JPL that are working on it, one staff person at SETI, and three amateur astronomers, all in this country, who we're putting on ice as we speak," Mantel told them.

"Is there any way to get clearer images of the ship," the SecState asked, "so we can study it more closely, and see what they're doing."

"Actually there is," Lorendo said. "NASA's Juno probe is in orbit around Jupiter right now; it's been there since last July. It's on the far side at the moment and as you may all remember from science class, Jupiter is a rather large planet, but it will swing back around in a few days and we'll be able to see this thing up close and personal."

"And it will be able to see us," the general commented.

"Well, yes," Lorendo replied, "We'll very likely have JUNO do a close flyby to obtain photographs but even if we don't, anyone on the ship won't be able to help but see her as she passes by."

"And we're all ok with that?" the general said.

"Yes," the SecState said, "I think that's a discussion for a different meeting. Colonel Mantel, how long do you think we can keep this thing under wraps?"

"Well sir, as far as we know we've got everyone who actually saw the event, unless this same conversation is going on right now in Beijing or Moscow, and now that the thing is down it would be pretty hard to spot unless you knew it was there and were looking for it."

"What are we planning to do with the three civilians who spotted this thing?"

"That decision is above my pay grade," Mantel replied. "With all due respect sir, I think that one is going to be your call."

"I suppose your right Colonel. Well, we'll work it out. A nice vacation at some remote resort, courtesy of the federal government, may be the ticket."

"One more thing," the general said, "This may just be my background talking, or good old paranoia, but that thing sure as hell looks military to me. Just something for us to think about."

Two

Two days later there was another meeting, this one in Washington at the SecState's office. Mantel, Reinman, Lorendo and the general traveled to D.C. together. They'd been pushed to the side a bit in the past two days and the general's nose was a tad out of joint about it. The number of people who knew about the craft, which was still parked on Ganymede, had grown to more than fifty. Colonel Mantel was reminded of the old saw about secrets; three people can keep one only if two of them are dead. He wondered how long fifty-three people would be able to keep this one.

This meeting consisted of the SecState, the president's science advisor, the head of NASA, several people from JPL, the head of NORAD, and the director of the FBI. Reinman had made the comment, on the way, that the more people with letters after their names you had at a meeting the more chance you had of really fucking things up. He'd made the comment out of earshot of the general.

Once they were all seated, the head of NORAD motioned to the minion he'd brought along and a still photo popped up on the wall screen. It was a shot of the craft sitting on the surface of Ganymede and it was a lot clearer than anything Mantel or Reinman had seen to date.

"This was taken early yesterday by Juno; there are a few others, but this is the best shot it got of the craft," the SecState told them. He looked across the table at the general, "After seeing this do you stand by your assessment that this is a military craft?"

The general stood up and walked to the screen. He looked at the photo for a few moments then pointed to several long narrow objects protruding from the sides and top of the craft. "I thought the other day that these looked like weapons of some sort," he told them, "And now seeing them up close like this I believe that's exactly what they are. Their placement on the craft, their shape, the fact that they appear to be mounted on turrets of some sort ...you can see that they're all pointed in different directions, all tells me that they're weaponry."

"Can we expect an alien craft to follow all the same structural rules that we do?" Lorendo asked. "This ship is from another world; how can we have any idea what those structures are?"

"Look here," the general pointed, "this top one is mounted on a circular base and is turned backward but not straight backward, the ones on the side are similarly mounted and facing in different directions. The only reason to take the trouble to mount them like that is to obtain a 360-degree turning radius and the most common reason for that is to enable you to fire in any direction. We saw the video of this thing landing. The energy beams that allowed it to control its decent and land didn't come from these structures. In my opinion they are weapons of some sort."

Lorendo started to speak and the SecState stopped him, "I'm sorry Mr. Lorendo but I'm afraid the President and his science advisor, and I, are of the same opinion. Add to that the fact that the craft has the appearance of being armored and I think the majority opinion is that we're looking at a military vessel."

"Another view of it may show us something totally different," Lorendo replied. "Do you all recall the famous 'face on Mars' photo that Viking One took back in the 70's? It looked to all the world like a human face and it created a sensation. Then when other images were taken of the same site under different lighting conditions, at different angles, it looked like what it really is - a rock formation. We could have something like that here."

"There aren't going to be any further close-ups of the craft from any angle," The SecState told him. "We've shut Juno down and sent her off into space, directly away from Ganymede."

"Why on earth would you do that?"

"It was a joint decision," the head of NORAD said. "We had it take a few photos from what we hope was far enough away to remain undetected. Remember, when this thing came in Juno was on the other side of the planet so there's no reason to believe it was detected then. After these photos were obtained we turned her off and got her out of there."

"1.1 Billion dollars heading off into space," one of the JPL people muttered.

"She was our best chance to study this thing, or possibly make contact." Lorendo said to them.

"She was our best chance of being detected as well," NORAD said, "And there's not going to be any contact."

"This has been discussed at length and a decision has been reached," the SecState told them. "You gentlemen are being asked to help us move forward from here."

"What is that decision," Mantel asked though he thought he already knew.

"We believe this ship did in fact crash land on Ganymede," the President's science advisor told them, "and that it has been sending out a distress call. We assume that if it's bothering to do that it must have some hope of a rescue. So we've had JPL listening very closely to its transmissions and in the past 18 hours they've changed. They are no longer sending out a repetitive distress call, they seem to be having a conversation with someone whom we can't hear, someone outside the solar system."

"Can we decipher the signals?" someone asked.

"We can't," the President's science advisor said. "It appears to be some sort of energy beam, almost like a laser. Our theory is that it's a method of communication consisting of beams of subatomic particles traveling faster than the speed of light, similar to a cosmic neutrino phone."

"I thought that nothing could travel faster than light," The Reinman said."

"Well it appears that this beam is," the science advisor replied, "Einstein's theory or no Einstein's theory."

"On their planet Einstein would probably have been assigned to remedial math," one of the generals commented.

"In any event," the science advisor continued, "they appear to be talking to someone out beyond the Kuiper Belt. Our assumption is that a rescue mission could be, and probably is inbound to them right now."

"And we don't want any part of contact," The SecState said. "Putting aside the massive upheaval it would cause worldwide, the fact that this thing looks like a military vessel has convinced the President, and other world leaders as well, that it would be better if we're not involved with it."

"Not involved," Lorendo said, "this is our first alien contact. We've been striving for this for decades, written books about it, made movies. Now that it's here we're going to bury our heads in the sand and hope they go away?"

"Would you agree, Doctor, that the ship up there on that screen is more advanced than anything we have, or will have for decades, maybe even centuries?"

"I do. All the more reason to try to make contact."

"Don't remember your history that well, do you doctor?" the general said, "The Spanish Conquistadors were that much more advanced than the indigenous people of the New World. So you tell me, how'd that work out for the locals? And we could ask the same for Christopher Columbus and the island populations of the Caribbean, or the Plains Indians when the Europeans showed up.

"This is a species that's obviously mastered deep space travel; it's doubtful they'd be on the same cultural or intellectual level as sixteenth century Spanish soldiers." Lorendo said to the general.

"You may be right," SecState said, "then again, you may be wrong. We're not willing to roll those dice."

"In every instance in history that a drastically more advanced civilization came into contact with a primitive one, the primitives took it in the shorts," the general said.

"And we're the primitives here," Lorendo said.

"We are, glaringly so."

"So what are you planning to do?"

"Go dark." NORAD said.

"Do you think that's even possible?" Mantel asked.

"What does that mean, go dark?" Lorendo asked.

"They're going to basically try to turn off the planet, make it appear that there's no one home," Mantel said. He turned and looked at the General, "I'm assuming that there are a lot more than fifty-three people who know about this now."

"We've already held a meeting with UNOOSA at the UN," SecState said. "SETI was there along with the heads of the space agencies of Russia, China, and the European Space Agency, pretty much anyone who actually has a space program. Things are already being turned off, starting with SETI and non-essential satellites. JPL is working with its contacts around the world to shut down the 17 space probes we have wandering around the solar system at the moment. Hopefully when this is over they'll fire back up. We intend to hold a full UN council meeting in the morning and we're including representatives from the countries that don't have members on the council. The President has been making calls all day to his counterparts around the world. We are going to do this."

"It's not a new concept," NORAD said, "the world's major powers and the UN have been talking about this for some time now. There are a lot of people who think it's foolhardy, even dangerous, to broadcast our existence to potentially hostile civilizations out there. There's even been talk about setting a time line to get it done, I believe it was ten years."

"Which we don't have," SecState reminded them. "We need to get this done as quickly as possible. That ship," he motioned at the screen, "is damaged and down on Ganymede's surface, but the ship that may be coming to its aid will be fully functional and have a clear field to detect anything coming from earth. We have no idea how soon a rescue ship might arrive so we're going to have to convince the world's population, at least a large portion of it, to go along with our plan. And we're going to have to do it quickly".

"The motivator is going to be fear I assume," Lorendo said.

"Bet your ass it is," the general replied. "We're going to tell the people on this planet that there's a space ship up there that doesn't look like it was built to deliver a welcome basket, that it looks like a warship, a warship with technology so far ahead of ours that we wouldn't stand a chance against it. Is there anything in that statement that isn't true?"

"Except that we don't know if they're warlike at all do we?"

"Once again, we're not willing to take the chance," NORAD said. "The decision's been made Doctor, you're in or you're out."

"I'm in," Lorendo replied, "I'll do what I can, but I want it on record that I think it's a mistake."

"Duly noted," SecState said and stood up. "All right ladies and gentlemen, let's make this happen."

Three

That evening Colonel Mantel, Major Reinman, Doctor Lorendo and an astrophysicist from JPL named Alison Chapel were in a conference room on the top floor of the Harry S. Truman building. They were still in the same building the SecState's offices were in, but the décor was decidedly less plush. There were multiple laptops and papers strewn around the table along with the remnants of a takeout dinner. They were putting together a to-do list for the next few days…it was a hell of a long list.

"Did Juno really cost 1.1 billion dollars," Mantel asked Alison. She'd been the one who'd made the comment in the meeting early that day.

"It did, and it was on station for less than a year, hadn't even started to collect the data we were hoping for."

"Well, when this is all over maybe they'll let you send up another one," Reinman said which elicited a snort from Alison.

"They couldn't just let you shut it down like the others?" Lorendo asked.

"It was too close to Ganymede," she replied. "It wasn't very big. The biggest things on it were its solar panels, nine feet by twenty feet, but it was right there, I'm surprised the ship on Ganymede didn't spot it."

"Maybe it did," Mantel said and that shut them up for a moment.

"What does UNOOSA stand for anyway?" Reinman finally asked, to break the silence as much as anything else.

"United Nations Office for Outer Space Affairs," Mantel and Alison said at the same time and laughed. "Not many people have ever heard of it," Alison told him, "Its mandate is to promote the peaceful use and exploration of outer space."

"Sounds like a group that would have pushed for first contact," Lorendo said.

"Not from what I heard," Mantel told him. "Apparently they jumped right on board. I guess the United Nations isn't quite ready to hand over the reins to the United Federation of Planets."

"Ok," Reinman said picking up a folder and looking at Alison, "So everyone who currently has a probe out there zipping around the solar system has agreed to turn them off. What about Voyager 1 and Voyager 2? I seem to recall reading that they're still ticking away and sending data back to earth."

"They are," Alison said, "which is amazing in itself considering they were launched in the mid-70's, before I was born. Voyager 1 left our solar system in 2012 and is heading out into interstellar space. Voyager 2 is currently in the Heliosheath, the outer most layer of the Heliosphere, which is the very edge of the solar system. It'll transition into interstellar space soon as well. They are both still sending data back, but the signals are extremely weak; unless you were really looking for it I think it would be lost in the clutter of space noise that's out there. Also, if you plot a direct path into our system and then to Ganymede along the line of the alien crafts transmissions a rescue ship probably won't pass anywhere near them."

"In a way that's too bad," Reinman said, "Getting a photo of the rescue ship as it passed by would be very cool."

"Sorry," Alison said, "the cameras on both Voyagers where turned off in 1990 to save power. Their heaters were turned off as well. And the computers and software that were used to receive their data no longer exist. Even if we could build a 1990's era computer and re-create the software they probably wouldn't turn back on anyway. They've been exposed to the cold of deep space for too long."

"Yeah well, I'm sure no one at NASA thought either probe would still be working at all by this point. My money would be on the cameras firing right up; they knew how to build things back then." Mantel said. "But it's just as well I suppose. If one of the Voyagers was close enough to get an image, it would be close enough for the rescue ship to detect it."

"Yeah, then we might have a whole V'ger scenario on our hands." Reinman said and Mantel smiled.

"I don't get it," Lorendo said, "I've never heard of V'ger."

"It's a Star Trek reference," Alison told him. "Apparently Major Reinman is a Trekker."

"And so are you," Reinman responded. "Otherwise you would have said Trekkie."

"Watching reruns of Star Trek and the original Battlestar Galactica is what got me interested in space," Alison said. "Probably why I ended up becoming an astrophysicist."

"How come you two don't know each other?" Reinman asked Alison and Lorendo. "You both work at JPL."

"JPL is a big place," Lorendo replied. "Do you know everyone in Air Force Space Command?"

"We work in different departments and on different campuses," Alison said. "Although Emil did hit on me at the Christmas party a few years ago."

"I have absolutely no memory of that," Lorendo said.

"Not surprised, you were pretty well loaded at the time." Alison picked up a folder in front of her and held it up. "So everything SETI was doing has been shut down; they weren't at all happy about it but they did it. The probes have been dealt with. So now we move on to satellites. Since we can't crash them all into the ocean we're going to have to be content to shut them down and hope the rescue ship doesn't detect them."

"That's being worked on by a group in Space Command," Mantel said, "The military satellites are first, everyone that has them has agreed to power down."

"If we can believe them all," Reinman added.

"We'll be able to tell," Mantel replied. "Once that's done and the commercial birds are off line it's going to get very quiet up there. If anything is still operating, it will definitely be detectable."

"It's going to play hell with Comms," Reinman told them, "But there's no helping that."

"What about cell phones?" Alison asked.

"Cell phones are encrypted and fairly short ranged, same thing with Wi-Fi. We are going to have to encrypt all radio transmissions though." Mantel said. "I'm following up on that myself tomorrow, as well as ham radio traffic, what there is of it still out there."

"Radars are going to be an issue," Reinman said, "They throw out a lot of power, especially military radars. They'll all have to be shut down.'

"On my list for tomorrow too, a lot of them already have been," Mantel said. "Also working on UHF transmissions, even if they're encrypted, they are very detectable."

"You know how we could solve all of this," Reinman said, "with an EMP pulse in the D-Layer. It would be like throwing a blanket over the entire planet, probably last for days too."

"You want to pop a nuke in the ionosphere?" Alison asked him.

"Pretty sure they'd detect *that*," Mantel said.

"Didn't say it was a perfect plan," Reinman replied dryly, "it's got its drawbacks."

"Just a few," Mantel agreed.

"Getting back to SETI for a moment," Lorendo said, "does anyone here think we're going to have trouble with them. I mean I know people there. This situation is what they've spent their life's work striving for, do we think they're just going to let it pass then start listening for radio signals again?"

"They've agreed to it, and they've been made aware that any deviation from that agreement would bring about some serious repercussions." Mantel said.

"We may already have trouble with SETI," Alison told them. "They've been sending out focused beams of energy for years in an attempt to make contact. I checked on those earlier today and one of them reached the Altair system in 1999, that's only 16 light years away by the way. Could very well be that our friends up there on Ganymede are from Altair."

"What's done is done," Mantel said, "Nothing we can do about that now. We'll just have to hope that no one on Altair was listening and that ship is from somewhere else."

"I'm more worried about the rest of the world," Reinman said. "What if someone out there decides they want to meet ET and aren't going to be pushed around by us or China or anyone else?"

"From what I've been able to pick up everyone is buying the high risk element of this," Mantel replied, "The major powers are pretty much scaring the living shit out of everyone, maybe for good reason, maybe not, but everyone seems to believe that instead of ET this is probably ID4."

"You said maybe," Lorendo said. "Do *you* think we should reach out to them instead of playing dead?"

"Not my call," Mantel replied. "It might all be for naught anyway; they may already know we're here. We've been sending out radio and TV signals since the middle of the last century; they could have come here because they're hooked on Mr. Ed or F Troop."

"Did you actually just use 'all for naught' in a sentence?" Reinman asked him.

"What's Mr. Ed?" Alison asked.

"It does bring up the question of why they were here in the first place," Mantel said, ignoring both of them. "They may have been headed here all along."

"No, I don't think so," Alison told him, "A bunch of people at NORAD and JPL looked at images of Jupiter prior to the crash and while they didn't have much to go on, it appears that the ship's trajectory was in through the Kuiper Belt and directly toward Jupiter which, because of where it was in its course past our solar system at the time, was the closest readily noticeable planet to the ships point of entry into our system. It appears that it was in interstellar space, got into trouble, and headed in here to look for a place to put down. I think we were just a convenient pit stop."

"Well let's hope so," Reinman said.

"Is there a contingency in place if they do conduct a rescue and then head straight here?" Lorendo asked.

"Everyone hide?" Alison suggested.

"I've been told there is a plan in place but I've not been made privy to it," Mantel said.

"Well, if they're coming from another galaxy we may have a long wait," she replied. "The nearest one is about twenty-five thousand light years away."

"You're accepting Canis Major as legitimate?" Lorendo asked her.

"I am," Alison replied, "aren't you?"

"I suppose; I haven't given it much thought though."

"Is this the astrophysicist version of Bigfoot?" Reinman asked.

"Sort of," Alison said. "It's a new dwarf galaxy that was discovered in 2003; not everyone accepts it as a legitimate galaxy yet."

"Doesn't really matter," Lorendo said, "if they're from there, or further away. It's going to take them a while to get here no matter what kind of propulsion system they're using. Then again, if they are from Altair, or someplace almost as close, someplace else inside our galaxy, and were already out cruising the neighborhood then they could be here tomorrow."

"Well let's hope not," Mantel said, "because we're not going to be ready by tomorrow."

Four

The following day they were all flat out, slowly working through what it took to turn the Earth off, as much as it could be turned off. It helped that mankind had already been steadily decreasing the amount of power that was radiated into space; TV and radio stations had been moving more and more to the internet, and the TV and Radio stations that were still broadcasting over the air were few enough in number that they could easily be shut down.

Another issue that was raised was the fact that since the beginning of the industrial age the amount of emissions produced had changed the spectroscopic profile of the earth, which was something that could possibly be detected by the aliens. But even if there was a solution for that, it certainly wasn't going to happen in a few days.

And they were all beginning to think that a few days might be what they had left before the ship sitting on Ganymede had company. The intervals between its transmissions, which no one on earth had been able to decipher yet, had been growing shorter. That probably indicated that whomever they were talking to was getting closer.

"What about space junk?" Major Reinman asked. He and Alison were tucked away in a basement room in the Pentagon compiling lists of who was on schedule with the 'going dark' timetable and who wasn't. It was almost lunchtime; they'd been there since 8:00 am that morning.

"Not really detectable from that far out," Alison said, "though as we've already discussed, any analysis of our atmosphere is going to peg us right away as an industrial society, there's no hiding that."

"If it's a straight rescue mission they're not going to care about stuff like that though."

"Let's hope," she said.

"Are you curious at all?" Reinman asked her. "I mean this may be our only chance to meet beings from another world. Do you think about that? You must."

Alison spent a moment looking at her computer screen before answering. Finally, she looked up at Reinman and smiled a little. "I do. I've spent my life studying space and from every measurable indicator those beings up there are generations, probably centuries, ahead of us with their technology, with they're knowledge. It boggles my mind to think about what we could learn from them, the leaps forward we could make. I've been thinking about it day and night since that ship appeared."

"But?"

"But the general was right. Whenever an advanced society interacts with a primitive one the primitive society vanishes one way or another, either through assimilation or annihilation or sickness or...something. I don't want any of that to happen to us. Also I don't think that, as a species, we're ready yet for something like this. And I believe that knowledge, the pursuit of knowledge, needs to be hard fought. It's not respected, it's not treasured, if it's simply handed to you." She hesitated again then said; "and there's something about that ship up there that frightens me, something about the way it looks, that makes me wary of those who built it. It does look like a warship; it looks like it was purposely built to intimidate." She looked at Reinman and shrugged. "What about you?" she asked him.

"I'm just following orders," he replied.

"You're a jerk, tell me."

"I'm not sure about respecting knowledge based on how it's gained," he said, "but I'm with you on the other three. We're not ready. We are the primitives here and that's not a good thing to be. It makes you extremely vulnerable. And that thing is definitely a military ship, you're right about that. It's got aggression oozing from every angle of its hull."

"Ok," Alison said, "so do you think this," she motioned to the stuff on the table they'd been working on, "is going to work?"

"If they're looking for us, no. But if they're looking for us then they probably already had a good idea that we're here so it doesn't

matter. If they're not looking for us, if this is a straight up rescue mission and they just come in, pick up their brethren off of
Ganymede and head back out, then we'll probably be all right."

"And what if we're not all right, what if they come this way?"

"Guess we'll deal with that if it happens. My guess is that planning for that is going on as we speak in some other part of this
very building." He threw the file folder he'd been holding onto the
tabletop. "What do you say we hit The Concourse Food Court and
get some lunch."

"God yes, I'm starving! How far is it?"

"In this building nothing is very far from wherever you happen
to be."

They had no sooner gotten to the elevators when Reinman's
cell phone rang. He slowed down to answer it while Alison continued on to give him some privacy. She was waiting by the elevators when he caught up with her and punched the button. "I'm
afraid lunch is on hold," he told her. "That was the Colonel and
he wants us back at the Truman building now. It seems that an
object just emerged from the Kuiper Belt and is headed straight
for Ganymede."

Alison just looked at him and when the elevator doors opened
he had to nudge her into the car.

When they got to the SecState's office the usual players were
there. There was a hush in the room, as if even with one alien ship
already sitting on a moon out there no one had actually believed
that another one would show up. Colonel Mantle was in a corner
talking to Lorendo, when he saw Alison and Reinman come in he
motioned them over.

"It emerged from the Kuiper Belt a little over an hour ago and
it's moving straight toward Ganymede." He punched a key on his
laptop and a blurry image appeared. "This isn't that great, Hubble
took it, but it's clear enough to indicate that this ship looks very
much like the ship that's sitting on the surface of Ganymede right
now. Obviously we'll get clearer shots as it gets closer."

"Colonel," Alison said, "with all due respect, Hubble didn't take that photo. I've worked with Hubble for years and it's not capable of an image that good, of something that small, that far away."

"I agree," Lorendo said. "Is there anything you'd like to share?"

"I suppose there's no harm at this point," Mantel said. "It's called Archangel and it's been up for about a year now. It was a black project between the Air Force and NASA. One of its assumed uses was a situation exactly like this."

"How good is it?" Alison said.

"It's a hundred times more powerful than Hubble, Hubble is twentieth century technology and this is twenty-first century all the way. We'll be able to see everything this ship does just about when it does it. And right now it's definitely coming this way."

"Are we ready?" Reinman asked.

"We're going to have to be," Mantel replied. "Everything is turned off that can be turned off. The UN is going to send out a blanket statement shortly announcing the ships appearance and asking every country on the globe to power down everything, as much as possible, including electrical power as night falls. If they don't get any closer than that moon, we should be fine."

"Turning off the lights could cause some panic," Alison said. "Everything's scarier in the dark."

"It could and it might, but it's the only way to do it at this point."

"Were do you want us?" Alison asked.

"I'm glad you asked. The two of you are on a flight to California in an hour. Emil will be going with you. JPL's Mission Control Center is up and running so you'll be able to stay on top of things from there and keep in touch with me. Major Reinman will act as liaison. I'm either going to be at NASA Houston or the Pentagon, not sure yet."

"Is there a contingent in place if they stop at Ganymede and then head straight for us?" Reinman asked him.

"There is and you don't need to concern yourself with it right now. Let's just hope they get their guys and leave. Your flight is out of Andrews. We requested something fast and I'm not sure what it's going to be so you'd better grab some takeout first and then get out there."

They backtracked to G Street and grabbed sandwiches at Potbelly's before heading for Andrews. It turned out to be fortuitous that they did because when they arrived at Andrews they were told that the SecState had stressed the need for them to be in California as soon as humanly possible so the Air Force had lined up three two seat F-15E's for them. After a brief orientation, much too brief in Alison's opinion, they were fitted for their flight gear and herded out to the three Eagles sitting on the tarmac. To Alison they looked large and deadly. They met their pilots and were airborne in minutes, flying formation and heading west. After they'd climbed to altitude Alison's pilot, Major James, call me Jim, Tuck, keyed his mike.

"Ok back there, Alison?"

"Yeah." She was looking out of the extremely small cockpit at the extremely large sky around them and then over at the two Eagles flying with them. The person in the rear seat of closest one waved to her and she waved back. She couldn't tell if it was Reinman or Emil because they were wearing a flight helmet with a full-face black visor that made them look like a big bug. She was wearing one too.

"Sure?"

"Yeah, I'm ok."

"Great. So here's the thing Alison, we gave the Secretary of State's office two options for your flight with us today. We could load external tanks and fly subsonic non-stop to California or we could go supersonic, push the speed, tank up a few times on the way, and get there a lot faster. They said you guys needed to be there as soon as possible so, in a few seconds we're going to go supersonic here."

"You're not supposed to do that over land, are you?"

"No, we're not. The sonic boom tends to piss people off but I'd say this was a unique situation, wouldn't you? Anyway, the people at State didn't seem at all concerned with that so that's what we're doing."

She looked outside again and the other two F-15's weren't there anymore. "Ok," she said, "what's going to happen?'

"You're going to feel a bump and then it's going to get really quiet and…that's it, ready?"

"Ready, one thing."

"What's that?"

"What does tank up mean?"

"Aerial refueling. At Mach we're going to be burning too much fuel to go non-stop."

"Oh, ok, that sounds like it will be interesting, one more thing."

"Shoot."

"For the rest of the flight can I call you Hans Solo?"

"Yes you can," Jim replied and then punched it.

Five

A erial refueling was one of the most amazing things Alison had ever seen. They had tucked up under the tanker until she thought sure they were going to touch; she could see the refueling guys face well enough that she would have recognized him if she knew him. Then the refueling boom had come down and connected into a port to her left and just behind her. Each time she kept turning her head back and forth to watch the boom and the aircraft looming right above their heads. She forgot for a while that she was in a tiny cockpit forty thousand feet above the earth with nothing but the canopy between her and an environment with no oxygen and killing cold. It was funny to her that when she did think about it the thought actually made the cockpit feel safe and almost cozy.

After they were done the boom would retract, the tanker would slide silently away to the left or right and they would accelerate away again. The bump would come and then that eerie quiet would return and envelope the cockpit.

They were wheels up to wheels down, a term she learned from Jim/Hans, in two hours and twenty-seven minutes. They were the second of the three F-15's to land, which seemed to irk Jim a bit. A car was waiting for them and as soon as they'd all arrived they thanked their pilots and were driven to Pasadena.

When they entered JPL's Mission Control Center it was humming. Alison and Emil had both been in the room before but Reinman hadn't and he was impressed. It looked exactly like what one would imagine a mission control center to look like. There was a long row of very large screens on the curved wall at the front of the room and facing them were several semi-circular rows of workstations crammed with computers, monitors and various other electronics. The center screen on the wall displayed the NASA logo and the screens on either side were currently showing different views of Ganymede and Jupiter. They were a lot clearer than anything Alison and Emil were accustomed to.

They approached the man who ran the Center, Chris Knight, introduced Major Reinman and got settled toward the back of the large room where they had a good view of everything.

One of the first things Knight asked them about was Archangel. The two monitors on either side of the NASA logo were obviously displaying images from the orbiting telescope.

"Did you guys know about this thing before this?" Knight asked.

Alison and Lorendo both said no and then they all looked at Reinman who just shrugged his shoulders and looked innocently around the room.

"Doesn't matter," Knight said. "I guess the important thing is we have it now." He motioned toward the screens. "And as it's showing us, this thing is on an intercept course with Ganymede and it's slowing down."

"How long before it gets there," Lorendo asked.

"Three hours, give or take."

"We're also monitoring energy emissions from Earth, correct?" Reinman asked.

"Not actually from here but we're receiving that data from multiple outside sources. I think we're about as quiet as we're ever going to be. If that ship just makes the stop at Ganymede, does the pick-up, then heads back out we should be all right."

"Do you know anything about the contingencies in place in case it keeps on coming," Alison asked Knight.

"Not a single thing. They didn't bother to tell us about Archangel and apparently it's been up for a year. Why would they tell us about their contingency plan?" With that they all turned and looked at Major Reinman again.

"Not a clue," he told them, "that is way above my pay grade."

They all kept looking at him for a long moment then turned back to the monitor wall.

"You may as well get comfortable," Knight told them, "it's going to be a while before they reach Ganymede." With that he headed down into the pit area directly below the monitor wall. Alison and Reinman sat down while Lorendo went to get them all coffee.

"So just tell me that the contingency plan doesn't involve nukes," Alison said to Reinman after Lorendo had left.

"It doesn't involve nukes," Reinman said.

"Asshole." Alison said.

—⟨+ +⟩—

Two hours and many cups of coffee later the room began to buzz as the ship approached Ganymede. Despite the coffee Alison was asleep in her chair. Reinman nudged her awake and they sat and watched as the alien ship approached the moon. The image from Archangel was clear enough now to see that the two ships were almost identical in appearance though the rescue ship appeared to be slightly larger. They stood in the back of the room with their eyes on the wall screens and despite the size of the room you could have heard a pin drop. It had finally sunk in to everyone there that very shortly their world was going to change forever, no matter what happened.

The ship circled Ganymede and then stopped directly over its stranded twin, establishing a stationary orbit above the moon's surface.

"It will be interesting to see if they go down to the ship or the ship tries to come up to them," Major Reinman said.

It turned out that they did neither. The rescue ship had only been on station for a few minutes when an object detached from the ship on the surface and rose quickly to the rescue ship. It docked with the rescue ship and remained there for several minutes. Finally, the object, which they took to be an escape pod of some kind, detached from the rescue ship and fell back to the surface of Ganymede, landing softly just next to the stranded ship. A second later a large energy pulse erupted from the pod, instantly enveloping it and the crashed ship in a roiling cloud of debris. The rescue ship remained on station until the cloud dissipated. Once it had, all that what was left of the stranded ship and the pod was wreckage, only a very small amount of which was large enough for them to see.

"Son of a bitch," Reinman said, "they're not leaving anything useful behind for us, or someone else to find."

"I do see some debris," Lorendo replied, "even that would very likely advance our knowledge tenfold."

"They're pulling away," Alison said.

The ship was turning away from the surface of Ganymede and circling back the way it had come. They all held their breath as it disappeared behind the moon for a moment then emerged on the same course it had come in on, back toward the Kuiper Belt.

"I think they're leaving," Lorendo said. "It really looks like they're leaving."

"They are," Alison replied. "They're on a reverse course of the one that brought them in. They are definitely leaving."

"We did it," Reinman said, "We actually did it."

"They're accelerating," Lorendo said.

"I think it's over," Alison said, "I think that's it."

"Yeah, they're heading away from us," Lorendo agreed, "not so much as a look this way."

There was a flurry of activity in the pit at the front of the room. A moment later Knight turned and motioned them to come down. They hurried down into the pit area directly below the big screens.

"What's wrong," Reinman asked, "What's going on?"

"Someone is sending a focused beam of energy at the alien ship from Earth. We think it's a message, possibly in a binary format. We're trying to decipher it now."

"Son of a bitch," Reinman said, "Someone is signaling them!"

"Where is the signal coming from?" Alison asked.

"One minute…" Knight was studying a computer screen, he said something under his breath and looked up at them, "Baikonur Kazakhstan."

"Fucking Russians," Reinman said. "I knew it would be them!"

"How long for the signal to reach the ship?" Alison asked.

Knight was working at his computer terminal again then said, "It's a very strong signal, maybe forty-five minutes give or take."

"Is there a contingency for this?" Lorendo asked and they all looked at Reinman.

"I don't know," he told them, "but even if there were, I don't think it's possible to get something to Baikonur to stop the signal before the signal reaches the ship."

"You mean a missile?" Lorendo said, "You think they're going to take out Russia's Cosmodrome?"

"It's too late, it doesn't matter," Alison said, "the signal's already been sent, it's on its way. Even if you stop the source of the transmission the signal is still going to reach the ship."

"She's right," Reinman said, "this is done and done."

"Have you deciphered it?" Lorendo asked Knight.

"Yeah, they're using an algorithmic format that CETI developed a while ago. Then it alternates to the 'Lone Signal' format, a binary encoding system that SETI's been using. We'll have it in a minute."

"Fucking Russians," Reinman said again, "they're probably asking the aliens to destroy North America."

"It's a basic 'hello message'" Knight told them a moment later, "greetings from Earth kind of stuff."

"Well originality has never been the Russian's strong suit," Reinman said dryly. His cell phone chirped and he stepped away from the group to answer it.

The rest of them stood and watched the screens even though they knew it would be a while before the signal reached the alien ship. Meanwhile that ship was continuing on its course away from Jupiter and toward the Kuiper Belt, it was still accelerating. There was no doubt now that its intention was to leave the solar system.

"Maybe it won't be able to decipher the message and will think it's just space noise," Alison said to no one in particular.

"It's a narrow beam signal aimed right at them," Lorendo replied, "and if they're advanced enough for what we're seeing they're definitely advanced enough to figure out algorithms and binary encoding."

"I know," Alison said, "wishful thinking."

"It looks like we're going to have first contact whether we want it or not," Knight said. "I figure twenty more minutes for the signal to reach them, say thirty minutes for them to figure it out, maybe less, and then depending on how fast that thing can go, a matter of hours or a day for them to get here. We're going to be meeting them face to face by sometime tomorrow latest."

"It's just one ship," Alison said, "if they are hostile and they start jumping ugly with us it's just one ship." She thought about the F-15 she'd just ridden in and how formidable it had seemed to her.

"They've mastered interstellar travel," Knight reminded her. "Who knows what capabilities they have."

Reinman rejoined the group and they all looked at him. "They're initiating the First Contact Protocol," he told them. "Our military is going on high alert, along with a dozen others, no need to play dead now. But they're keeping it low profile, just in case it is ET out there; we don't want to spook them. Anyway, everything's being turned back on."

"Will we be able to catch a response from them if they send one," Lorendo asked.

"Yes," Knight said and they all waited, spending the next ten minutes or so watching the ship getting further and further away.

"Maybe they have some type of ion drive or pulse engines or something." Lorendo said, "If they push it to an ultra-high velocity before the signal reaches them they may not even hear it."

"I doubt they'd engage something like that before they transit the Kuiper Belt," Alison said. "If they have it they didn't use it coming in."

Reinman glanced at his watch, "The signal should be reaching them right now," he said.

"Yes, they must have received it by now," Knight agreed.

"They're not slowing down or turning," Lorendo observed.

"But they have stopped accelerating," Knight said, looking at his monitor. "They're holding speed."

"Shit," Reinman said.

There was another rise in the conversation level in the pit in front of them and they all looked at Knight. He studied his computer display for a moment then turned to them.

"They're sending," he said, "not an energy beam like the one they used to communicate with one another, they're sending using the same binary encoding system that the signal was sent to them in."

"That was incredibly fast," Lorendo said. "They received the signal, read it, duplicated one of the methods of transmission and replied, all over the course of two or three minutes. That's incredible."

"Can you read the message?" Reinman asked Knight.

"Not yet. They are copying SETI's formulae, but they've got it kind of jumbled. It will take a few minutes."

"They're leaving," Alison said simply and they all looked up at the screens. The alien ship had indeed begun to accelerate again, toward the Kuiper Belt. They watched as its speed kept increasing until finally it was through the asteroid field and gone. The big room was silent with a sense of relief, and of disappointment. Alison wasn't sure which was the predominant emotion.

"The Russians must be pissed," Reinman said.

"This isn't going to improve their moods." Knight waved a hand at his display screen and laughed; Alison didn't think she'd ever heard him laugh before.

"What'd they say," Reinman asked Knight.

"Well," Knight looked at them, "to paraphrase, they basically said; 'Yeah, we know you're there but we have better things to do'".

None of them had a response to that.

HIDDEN PLACES: WILL THE REAL RIPPER PLEASE STAND UP

Chapter One

Verity Quinn was walking along the Victoria Embankment by the Temple Gardens talking into her cell phone. Rather, she was arguing into her cell phone and while she was taking care to keep her voice down she had failed at this several times in the past few minutes. One pedestrian, who was passing when one of these increases in volume occurred, shook her head and made an untoward comment about loud Americans. Verity either didn't hear the comment or more likely chose to ignore it.

"Why must we discuss this every time I'm away," she said into the phone as she reached Somerset House and turned back toward the Temple. She listened for a moment then,

"Because it's my job Brian, and you knew that when we started. If your plan was that you were going to convince me to change the way I live with your charming personality and prowess in the sack you were obviously sadly mistaken, weren't you?" Another moment and then;

"That's the first intelligent thing you've said since this conversation began." She punched the screen to end the call then dropped the phone in her pocket. She walked over to the railing and looked out at the Thames and Waterloo Bridge. Her phone began to chirp in her pocket and she ignored it. Now that she was no longer arguing into a phone the glances she got from male passersby were much more appreciative, she ignored those too. Finally, she turned and headed back toward the Inner Temple Library because that's where Phineas Gage was.

"Either you went for a run while you were out taking your call or your call didn't go well," Phineas said when Verity sat down across from him in the basement room that had been provided for them. She looked at him and raised her eyebrows.

"Your face is flushed, it's not a normal look for you," Phineas explained.

"Oh, no it did not go well." She began to study the papers in front of her then added; "Never get involved with an attorney Phineas, they have no souls." Then she quickly looked up at him. "You're not an attorney are you?"

"I am not," Phineas smiled, "but considering where we are currently sitting it's a bit of an ironic statement, wouldn't you say?"

Verity mumbled something and went back to her papers. There was a large old wooden table between them that was currently covered with old files and pages of foolscap. In the corner was an honest to God microfiche machine that had actually come in handy earlier that day. Phineas went back to the stack of papers in front of him, some of them made of parchment, a few of actual vellum. They were both wearing white cotton gloves.

They were on their fourth day of research at various spots around London, each successive stop leading to the next until they'd finally ended up here, plowing through one hundred and twenty-year-old legal records. They had gotten this room, access to the records, and exceptional cooperation after Phineas had made just one call. Verity hadn't asked him how he'd managed it, or who he'd called, she never did and neither did any of the other members of the team. Phineas kept himself to himself and while he was probably the most intriguing man Verity had ever met, and working for him was amazing most of the time, it was sometimes vexing to think how little she really knew about him.

Her phone call had been right after they'd had lunch and they spent the rest of the afternoon working their way through the records on the desk. For most people being in London and spending all their time rooting through musty old records would have been disappointing to say the least, but Verity was a serious history buff so for her it was extremely satisfying. Besides, she'd been to London many times, on none of her previous trips had she been allowed such access to the history of the city.

The library research fellow had told them that morning that the archives would close promptly at 4 p.m. so by 3:15 p.m. Verity was assuming they'd have to come back the following day when Phineas held up a dog-eared old piece of foolscap and smiled at her.

"I assume that's what we've been looking for," she said to him, a bit disappointed that she hadn't found it.

"It is indeed," he said. "We are done here. Let us head back to the Savoy for a good dinner and a good night's sleep. Tomorrow we will leave for home."

Chapter Two

Dalton Land and Dan Birdsong were the first to arrive in Chicago so they checked into the hotel then spent a few hours on the Navy Pier. By the time they returned to the hotel for dinner Devon Lindo and Verity Quinn had checked in as well. Phineas arrived last after having made a stop in Boston on his and Verity's return from London. Phineas had rented a suite and it was there that they met for dinner at 7 p.m.

Per his custom, Phineas waited until after dinner to conduct business. Once the dinner dishes had been cleared and coffee served they gathered around in the sitting area to begin.

"As you all know, Abbey and Robert won't be along on this project," Phineas said. "Abbey is in Seattle presenting at a symposium on the future of artificial intelligence in society."

"That many computer geeks in one room," Dan laughed, "must be a wild time!"

"Maybe not," Lannie replied, "but I'd love to know what the collective IQ is. I imagine it would be a bit humbling."

"I'm sure it would," Phineas said. "And Robert is doing some advance work for a possible future project; right now he's somewhere over the South Pacific."

"We're not going back to that godforsaken island are we?" Dan groaned. "I promise Phineas, Amelia and Fred were never on that island. All that *is* on that island is heat and coconut crabs big enough to eat you. I still have nightmares about those damn things."

"Robert's trip has nothing to do with Nikamaroro," Phineas said, "and I happen to agree with you regarding Amelia and Fred." He took out the customary file folders that began every project and handed one out to each of them. "Some of you have been busy laying the groundwork for this one," he said, "and Verity and I were just in London tying up loose ends. So, let us begin." He opened the file in front of him and took out an old black and white photograph. It showed a man wearing late 19th century era clothing, standing next to a Grecian column and looking blankly into the camera lens.

"This is one Richard Merle, a lifetime resident of London circa the turn of the 20th century. He worked in that city his entire life as a marginally successful barrister however, he died less than eleven blocks from here in 1903 at the age of forty-one. Verity and I just spent five days in that great city reconstructing the final few years of Mr. Merle's life, and his reason for coming to Chicago."

He reached into the folder again and took out another old photograph, this one of a man similarly posed for the camera, but with nicer clothes and a much more confident expression on his face.

"This is Thomas M. Hoyne, a prominent Chicago attorney from the same period. Mr. Hoyne had a daughter, Susan, who was twenty-two years old during the time we're interested in. She was intelligent and privileged and she's crucial to our project. Unfortunately, there are no known photographs of Ms. Hoyne extant. She died childless in 1971."

He took yet another page from the folder, this one an overhead map of a section of Chicago with an electronic pushpin in it. "This is 24 W. Randolph Street, approximately eleven blocks from here across the canal. You'll find the Oriental Theatre at that address today, however, in 1903 the Iroquois Theatre occupied that space." He looked around at the group, "Does that name mean anything to any of you, other than Lannie, who I tasked with putting together the background for that particular part of this project?"

They all looked around at one another and shook their heads. "Not surprising," Phineas told them, "it's an all but forgotten historical event, one that we will return to shortly. So, let us begin with Mr. Richard Merle, late of London, England. For the purposes of this project we will call him Dick although there's no proof that he ever went by that name." Phineas took a stack of photocopies from his file and placed them in front of him, although as he talked he never looked at them.

"Earlier, I referred to Dick Merle as a marginally successful barrister in London. I'm afraid that I was being generous in that assessment. From what records Verity and I were able to unearth he barely subsisted on what he made as an attorney, apparently he wasn't a very good one. It appears that he augmented his income by being something of a jack-of–all-trades, doing odd jobs for other lawyers, low level investigative work and research, that type of thing. The single thing that made Dick Merle at all significant was that he was related by marriage to Inspector Frederick George Abberline of Scotland Yard. I see by the look on some of your faces that you recognize the name. Anyone care to tell me who he was, excluding you Verity, you were with me in London, and you Dan because while you and I are not avid Ripperologists, we are both very close to that mark."

"He was one of the lead investigators on the Jack the Ripper case," Devon said. "He was probably *the* lead investigator."

"Correct, Senior Inspector Abberline probably knew as much or more about the Ripper murders as any man alive. During our first few days in London I had Verity do a quick background on him so I will let her continue from here."

"Thank you," Verity said. "So, Frederick Abberline spent 29 years as a police officer, first with the Metropolitan Police and then Scotland Yard. The two biggest cases he worked on during his law enforcement career turned out to be two of the most controversial cases in that country's history; the Jack the Ripper murders and the Cleveland Street Case. He's been variously described as an excellent detective and as an incompetent and lazy officer who stole files from Scotland Yard when he left. I suspect the truth lies somewhere in between, it usually does. He retired from Scotland Yard in 1892 with the title Chief Inspector; he was just shy of his 49th birthday. He then spent the next 14 odd years working for the Pinkerton Detective Agency running their European operation." She shifted through the papers in front of her for a moment then continued.

"There are some oddities that I found concerning Chief Inspector Abberline and his career. He did have 29 years in when he retired but still, 49 is a bit young to retire and one would think that if he'd stayed he would have been a prime candidate for further promotion. Of course it's also true that police investigators often retire in order to work in the private sector for more money and at that time the Pinkerton Detective Agency was already world famous. The timing of his resignation was curious though. On the second of January 1892 it was announced in the press that a royal commission was to be appointed to investigate the Whitechapel murders, the Jack the Ripper crimes. Five days later, on the 7th, Abberline resigned from Scotland Yard and apparently, from what I could find, his resignation was considered abrupt." She flipped to another sheet of paper.

"Another thing, the rumors that he'd stolen files from Scotland Yard when he left were just that, rumors, but they were pretty persistent rumors all the same. After he'd retired, Inspector Abberline gave several interviews to the press and he said some interesting things. In an interview with the Pall Mall Gazette in 1903 he suggested that George Chapman aka; Severin Antoniovich Klosowski may have been the Ripper. He also said in that interview that the Ripper could have just as easily been a woman but that 'Scotland Yard is really no wiser on the subject than it was fifteen years ago'."

"In an article in the Evening News not published until 1976 a writer named Nigel Moreland claimed that he'd interviewed Abberline after he'd retired a second time and was living in Dorset. He said Abberline told him that the Ripper case was closed and that he'd 'given his word to keep his mouth permanently closed about it'. He made several additional comments about his superiors knowing certain facts and that you shouldn't look for the Ripper at the bottom of London Society but instead 'a long way up'. Most Ripperologists take this comment with a grain of salt, but if nothing else it does signify that Abberline knew more than he ever said about the Ripper's identity. Abberline never published his memoirs although many hoped that he would. He died in 1929 at the age of 86."

"If we're looking for Jack the Ripper what are we doing in Chicago?" Dan asked Phineas.

"Wait for it," Phineas told him then he looked at Verity.

"That's it," she said.

"All right, I'll pick it up from here," Phineas said. "Getting back to our hero, Dick Merle. Mr. Merle was related to Abberline through his wife, Abberline was her uncle. I found evidence while in London that while they weren't bosom buddies, Merle and Abberline did see one another regularly at family gatherings and such. It appeared that Abberline also threw work to Merle from time to time in connection with his role at Pinkerton's, and on some private matters as well. It's one of those private matters that we're interested in." He looked around the table and no one spoke, they'd all been here before and knew that Phineas would get to it when he got to it.

"All right," Phineas continued, "let us return to Thomas Hoyne, prominent Chicago attorney and his very lucky daughter Susan. Mr. Hoyne was a frequent visitor to London and the Continent; he had numerous business dealings there. He may have owned a house in Baker Square in London; records are sketchy there. He often stayed in a house there in any event. He would apparently bring his family with him on many of these trips and they would enjoy London while he went about his business. I obtained information that Hoyne and Merle knew one another and that Merle worked for Hoyne from time to time in connection with his European interests. Hoyne was also extremely interested in Jack the Ripper and visited the scenes of the crimes while in London. Merle, in regular contact with Hoyne would have known this."

"Did Hoyne know Abberline?" Dan asked.

"I don't think so," Phineas said, "At least there was nothing in the correspondence we found to indicate it. But Hoyne must have known about Merle's connection to Abberline, Merle would have made sure of that. And in late 1902 when Merle learned the identity of Jack the Ripper through Abberline he immediately contacted Merle, who was back in Chicago, and offered to sell him the information."

"Whoa," Devon spoke up for the first time, "Abberline told Merle who it was, just like that?"

"No, I don't believe it happened that way. What I believe happened was Merle suspected that Abberline knew and somehow obtained the name without Abberline's knowledge. It was long rumored that Abberline kept a personal file on the Ripper, an extensive one, right up until the day he died, after which it disappeared. I think Merle somehow got a look at that file, again, without Abberline knowing he'd done it. Maybe Abberline left it somewhere that Merle saw it, or Merle overheard something, or Merle even let himself into the Abberline's house when they weren't there and read the file. We'll likely never know exactly how it came about, only that it did."

"So he may have learned who Abberline *suspected* of being the Ripper," Lannie said, "That's very different from *knowing* who it was beyond a doubt."

"Oh Abberline knew beyond a doubt," Phineas replied. "One of the last things Verity and I uncovered in London was a document at the Temple Library that came from Sir Charles Warren's private papers stating, in no uncertain terms, that only he and three other men knew the identity of the Ripper. The other three men were, like Warren, deeply involved in the case: Sir Robert Anderson, Chief Inspector Donald Swanson, and Chief Inspector Frederick Abberline."

"What about rule number four in your unwritten manual of life lessons," Lannie said, "Three people can keep a secret only if two of them are dead?"

"But they didn't keep it," Phineas replied, "it was right there in the document Verity and I found at The Temple. It's been there for over one hundred years, we were just the first to know to look for it there."

"Well they kept it pretty well other than that," Dan told him. "So who was it, some member of royalty, is that why they kept it a secret?"

"I'm afraid the document didn't say who the Ripper was," Phineas replied, "or we wouldn't all be here. It verified beyond doubt that they *knew* who he was. A second document in the file was a letter from Abberline to Warren in which Abberline tells him that he fears a relative of his, through marriage, named Merle, has learned it as well."

"I assume you're getting to the Chicago part," Devon said.

"Wait for it," Dan told him.

"It's obvious isn't it?" Lannie said. "Merle learns the Ripper's identity and sells the information to Hoyne, so we're here to find Hoyne's personal papers and go through them."

"If only it were that simple," Phineas said.

"Yeah," Dan said to her, "we don't need five people to research some old papers!" He looked at Phineas, "Right?" He kept looking at Phineas so he missed the look Lannie gave him, but he felt it.

"Hoyne never got the name from Merle," Phineas said, "because Merle died before he could give it to him."

"Wait," Lannie said. "He died before he could give it to him, in the Iroquois Theatre fire…eleven blocks from here."

"That's right." Phineas nodded. "So, who's up for dessert and more coffee? I know I could use some."

"Are you kidding, right now?" Lannie said, "Just tell us the rest!"

"I think we need to take a break, and I have to make a phone call to a friend in London."

"It's 1:30 a.m. in London," Verity said.

"Just so, he's a night owl. I'll be back in a few minutes. Order some dessert for us if you would, and another pot of coffee, Kona please." He got up from the table and went into the other room.

"Sometimes I hate him," Lannie said to no one in particular.

Chapter Three

They ordered cannoli's and more coffee and it arrived before Phineas emerged from the bedroom. When he finally returned he sat down, poured some coffee and reached for a cannoli. Lannie watched him eat half of it before she spoke.

"I'm going to throw my dessert at you in maybe 30 seconds Phineas, sincerely."

"Then why don't you start us off," Phineas smiled at her, "fill us in on the Iroquois Theatre fire and then I'll connect the dots."

"Sometimes I hate you," Lannie said to him and put down her cannoli. She slid her file over in front of her on the table and flipped it open. Then she started without bothering to look down at her notes.

"December 30, 1903, the Iroquois Theatre, 24-28 W Randolph Street, the matinee showing of Mr. Blue Beard starring Dan McAvoy and Eddie Foy."

"Of the Seven Little Foys?" Dan, who was an old movie buff, asked her and then smiled.

"I hate you too," Lannie told him, then continued. "The theatre's license was for a maximum capacity of 1,602 patrons. It was estimated later that at this matinee, including standing room, there were between 2,100 and 2,200 people in the theatre, and around 400 employees, stage hands, actors and ushers."

"A whole lot of people in one place," Devon observed, "I hate that."

"Just a few minutes into the second act," Lannie said, "between 3:15 and 3:50 pm, accounts vary, an electric light shorted out at the top left side of the stage and set fire to a muslin curtain. The fire was too high to reach with extinguishers, and there were a lot of very flammable painted set backdrops hanging above the stage, which it spread to very quickly. The theatre wasn't equipped with a sprinkler system or an alarm system or even a telephone. Of the

30 fire exits, many of which weren't marked or were hidden behind decorations, 27 were locked."

"Jesus," Verity said softly.

"Yeah," Lannie agreed, "and it gets worse; of the doors that weren't locked most were equipped with something called a bascule lock which only the staff knew how to operate and they were all either already gone or they refused to open the doors. The ones that someone managed to open swung inward so they were quickly blocked by the panicked crowd. Some of the staircases had locked iron gates across them to stop people in the cheap seats from getting down to the good seats. They were also locked that day even though there were no empty seats in the theatre anywhere. Because it was a matinee and Christmas school vacation, there were a lot of mothers with children in the theatre.

"And finally, there was only one main entrance/exit to the lobby which quickly became clogged with people. 575 people died that day in the fire or out on the street where it was minus 5 degrees, another 30 or so died later in local hospitals from their injuries. The official death toll was 605, but that's an abstract number because some bodies were taken from the scene without being identified and a few people simply disappeared. It's been estimated that the fire lasted eight minutes. It remains the country's single largest loss of life by fire to this day, worse than even the Coconut Grove fire in Boston in the 1940's."

They were all silent for a long moment, taking it in. Devon was the first to speak, "Tell me someone at least went to jail for this," he said.

"The theater manager and a few others, along with several city officials were tried and found guilty on various charges related to the fire, but their convictions were all overturned on appeal. The only person who served a day in jail was a nearby tavern owner who was caught stealing money and valuables from the corpses."

"That just completely sucks," Dan said.

"It does," Lannie agreed, "sadly, I think it also shows that some things never really change."

They all simply sat there for a few moments thinking about what they'd just heard. Finally, Devon looked up at Phineas.

"So Merle was in Chicago to meet with Hoyne, sell him proof of the Ripper's identity and make a lot of money. What was he doing at the Iroquois Theatre?"

"That was one of the things I couldn't nail down," Phineas told them. "I knew beyond doubt that he was there that afternoon, but I didn't know why. It seemed a bit out of character that he would decide to catch a matinee attended by a bunch of mothers and their children, even if he did have time to kill."

"How are you sure that he was there at all?" Dan asked.

"That is where Mr. Hoyne's daughter Susan comes in," Phineas said. "In a moment of pure synchronicity she was at the matinee with two friends. They were seated on the main floor and managed to get out cleanly when the fire started, the extent of their distress was that they left their coats behind."

"I imagine it went a bit beyond that," Verity said. "I'm sure the memory wasn't one of their fondest as they went through life."

"You're right of course," Phineas said. "The thing that makes young Susan's presence at the theater that day so important to us is that she saw Dick Merle there, first in the lobby and then again later leaving the orchestra area and going backstage, just before the play began. Susan knew Merle because she'd seen him numerous times during his frequent visits to her family's house in London to meet with her father. She stated later that she remembered him clearly because he always had a furtive air about him when he met with her father and she considered him an odd little man. She mentioned to numerous people, including her father, that she'd seen him at the theatre that day. In the days following the fire her father took an inordinate interest in tracking down Merle, or his remains. Despite Hoyne's strenuous efforts however, Dick Merle was never seen again, alive or dead."

"If he died in the fire before having the chance to meet with Hoyne, then doesn't that bring us to a dead end?" Dan asked him.

"I've never much believed in those," Phineas replied, "and particularly not in this instance. As I said earlier, it bothered me that Merle would take time out of such an important trip to attend the afternoon showing of a comedic play about a pirate. Then I recalled exactly what Susan had said. She said that she saw Merle twice, once in the lobby and a second time from her seat, going backstage just before the play began."

"He knew someone at the theatre," Lannie said. "He wasn't there to see the play; he was there visiting someone."

"Precisely," Phineas said, "and one of our eureka moments in London was when Verity found a connection between Merle and one Frank Barr, who was employed as a carpenter and set designer at the Iroquois on the day of the fire. How exactly Merle and Barr met isn't known, but they seem to have had mutual friends. On the afternoon of December 30th, having just arrived in Chicago from London and apparently with some time to kill, Merle went to the theatre to see Barr."

"And Barr survived the fire," Verity told them.

"He did," Phineas nodded. "He testified later that he'd been in the basement of the theatre when the fire started and rushed up to the stage to find it already raging. A stagehand also stated that Barr was the one who opened the big loading doors at the rear of the stage allowing a huge rush of cold air to enter the theatre creating a backdraft that shot out and over the seats where patrons were still trying to flee. It was never determined if Barr really had done that and even if he had, there's no reason to believe that he would have known the terrible consequences, he was probably just trying to help. Most of his testimony from his first appearance before the grand jury is lost and when they tried to locate him again in 1905 to interview him further, he couldn't be found. Fortunately for us, that wasn't the last to be heard from Frank Barr. He wrote to friends in England after the fire and told them that he and Merle had been sitting in the basement sharing a drink and catching up when the fire broke out above them. Not realizing how serious it was, he told Merle to stay put while he went upstairs to investigate. He also told Merle that if he got held up and didn't return there was a set of steps in the corner of the basement that led down to an iron door that opened to an old unused tunnel, and that that tunnel would lead to the basement of the building next door. Barr said that he'd told Merle this not because of the fire, he had no idea how serious it was at that point, but because he didn't want Merle sneaking around backstage without him when the performance was going on; that could lose Barr his job. After he'd gone upstairs and did or didn't open the loading doors he realized that the stairs leading to the sub-stage and basement were by then hopelessly blocked by the fire. He assumed that Merle would find his way out through the old tunnel and he left the theatre. What Barr didn't know was that because the tunnel pre-dated the theatre and was not in use, the steel door at the far end had been sealed by the owners of the adjacent building. Also, once Merle entered the tunnel and closed the door on the theater end it would have locked behind him so, that would have been all for Dick Merle."

"You actually think he's still down there," Lannie said, her eyebrows raised, "you think the tunnel is still there and he's still in it, along with whatever proof he was bringing to Hoyne!"

"I don't know it for a fact," Phineas smiled, "but his body was never recovered, he simply vanished that afternoon. I think it's enough of a possibility for us to take a look, and that's what we're going to do."

"If you're right, if he is still in that tunnel, we're going to find out who Jack the Ripper was."

"We are," Phineas was still smiling. "Richard Merle is finally going to deliver his secret, one hundred and fourteen years late."

Chapter Four

Verity and Lannie were sitting at the Peninsula's bar having a drink and catching up.

"So how are things going with Brian?" Lannie asked.

"They're not," Verity replied. "Brian is dead to us; we shall speak his name nevermore."

"Oh that's too bad," Lannie said, "he was such an uptight jerk. I thought you guys were really going to hit it off."

"So tell me, how is Dan in the sack?" Verity asked and Lannie choked on her drink. She put her glass down and got a bar napkin to cover her mouth with.

"How did you know?" she asked after she'd stopped coughing.

"Everyone knows. So, does he know any kinky Indian tricks? You slut."

That evoked another coughing fit from Lannie, to the point that the bartender came over to ask her if everything was all right.

"No it's not," Lannie finally managed. "My friend is an asshole."

"She'll be fine," Verity said. "It's her first day off the wagon and she's going a bit fast." She gave the bartender a smile that usually made men forget where they were. It made the bartender smile back and wander away.

"Everyone does *not* know," Lannie said after he was gone. "Tell me that's you yanking my chain!"

"Yeah, I am," Verity smiled sweetly at her. "No one else knows, except probably for Phineas because he knows everything."

"How do *you* know, did that asshole tell you?"

"Phineas?"

Lannie gave her the look.

"No one told me," Verity laughed, "all I had to do was watch the two of you together."

"God, is it that obvious?"

"Not at all, it's just that I've known you for a long time and I know your looks. You look at Dan like you can't wait to gobble his…"

"Yeah, I get the idea. I'm going to have to watch that."

"Really? I usually close my eyes."

Lannie burst out laughing and put the napkin back over her mouth. The Peninsula was a very nice, very upscale hotel; she didn't want to have to explain to Phineas why she was tossed out of it.

"So why are you even keeping it a secret?" Verity asked her. "Dan's a nice guy, although I've never been big on dating people I work with; if it goes south, there you both are."

"I know, I know, I didn't mean for it to happen. But he is a nice guy and we're together so much. And it's kind of difficult to maintain a normal relationship given what we do for a living."

"How I know that to be true, and at least now you're getting it on a regular basis. We all know how you get when you're not," Verity took a sip of her drink then added, "slut."

Lannie shook her head and sipped her drink too. The bartender came back with a big smile asking again if she was OK and she assured him she was. He put another drink in front of her and told her it was on the house.

"What a jerk," Verity said after he'd left, "gives you a free drink right after I told him you'd just fallen off the wagon. And you'll notice that I didn't get shit. It's because you're a hot blond and I'm just a brunette, that's it you know. Men are scum."

"Yeah, you're a real ugly duckling," Lannie said. "Are you sure no one else knows?"

"I'm sure. If Abbey knew she'd just come right out and say so in front of everyone; social etiquette is not that girl's strong suit. If Devon knew he'd do the same thing for the same reason. If Robert knew he'd probably congratulate you because he thinks a lot of Dan. And you haven't answered my question, why are you keeping it a secret, do both of you want to keep it a secret or just you?"

"We both do. We both think that Phineas won't like it, and that everyone else will start treating us differently. And if it doesn't work out then Phineas will try to keep us on separate projects, or even let one of us go."

"He would never do that, that's not him."

"Yeah, probably, but I just want to see if it has legs first, it hasn't been that long. If it doesn't, then no harm, no foul and we both just move on."

"You really believe you both could do that?"

"We're both adults, contrary to Dan's usual behavior patterns so yeah, I think we could."

"Well, hopefully you won't have to find out, although the odds aren't in your favor."

"Thank you for the pep talk. You're just cynical when it comes to men."

"Because most of them are knuckle dragging Neanderthals. And on that note, looks who's here."

"Good evening ladies," Devon said as he slid onto the seat next to Lannie. "Buy you a drink?"

They both held up their glasses, which were almost full.

"Oh, well then buy me a drink?"

"Lannie will get you a free one; the bartender is enamored of her."

"Phineas pays our hotel bills," Lannie said to him, "you know that, right?"

"Yes he does, with the exception of my bar bill. He puts that on me after my little problem in St Petersburg last September."

"You broke up the hotel bar and put three hotel employees in the hospital," Lannie reminded him.

"And I can't tell you how sorry I was that I missed *that* little adventure," Verity said.

"I wasn't drunk, and those so called employees were muscle for the local small time mob guy who was trying to screw us out of the money I'd paid for access to that facility we wanted to get in to. They tried to strong arm me out of the place, it didn't go well for them."

"I'd go with saying you were drunk, it sounds less caveman," Verity told him.

"We haven't worked together much, but from what I hear you don't take any crap from anyone either," Devon said to her.

"There's a time and place though," Verity said, "and that wasn't it."

"Maybe you just bribed the wrong guys," Lannie said, "it happens."

"Remember that Colonel in Azerbaijan?" Verity asked her and laughed.

"Thanks so much for bringing that up," Lannie said.

"What Colonel? I don't know this story," Devon said.

"We needed access to some military archives from back in the day when the curtain was still up," Verity said, "Usually over there an envelope full of cash does the trick, but this Colonel in charge of the archives took one look at Ms. Land here and decided that he wanted her instead of the cash, wouldn't take no for an answer."

"So what happened?" Devin said,

"All for one and one for all," Verity said. "She did what she had to do. She's a real trooper this one!"

"That's bullshit," Lannie said, "and wipe that look off your face Devon. I didn't do anything other than tell him to shove his archives right up his ass. He wasn't getting me or the money."

"So he took the money," Verity said.

"Those places are the wild west," Devon said, "rooting around in Chicago suits me just fine thanks,"

"So where are we rooting tomorrow?" Lannie asked. "We going right for that tunnel, first thing?"

"Don't know," Devon said, "but he had me pull the schematics for what's under the buildings on the block were the Iroquois used to be. What's that tell you?"

"That I need to get some sleep," Verity said sliding off her seat.

"Me too," Lannie said, "Phineas likes to hit the ground running."

"I think I'm going to stay for a while," Devon said, "not really tired."

"Stay out of trouble," Verity said and she and Lannie headed for the lobby.

"Are you really tired or did you just want to get away from him?" Lannie asked. "I don't think he's such a bad guy, really."

"I am tired," Verity said. "Besides, I figured I'd get you out of there because Dan is probably waiting in your room right now wearing his Spiderman jammies."

"That's only on Saturday nights," Lannie said and Verity laughed.

Chapter Five

They met in Phineas' suite the following morning, but not until mid-morning. They'd each had a message waiting for them in their rooms telling them to sleep in a bit and meet at ten o'clock. Breakfast was ordered in and this time there was Hawaiian coffee because sooner or later Phineas usually got his way.

"The reason we're meeting late is because we're going to have a late night," he told them as they finished eating. He slid several sets of schematics across the table to each of them and jumped right in.

"The Iroquois Theatre was refurbished after the fire and re-opened under a new name," he said. "The building was finally razed in 1981 after having sat vacant for a decade. A new theatre, the Oriental, was built on basically the same footprint and operates there today. I have not contacted the current owners of the theatre because understandably, anything to do with the fire, even this far removed, doesn't sit well with them. Fortunately, for our purposes we don't need them. If you'll turn your attention to the plans in front of you, this is the block that the theatre occupies. As you can see it shares the space with two other buildings, one of which, also fortunate for us, pre-dates the original Iroquois Theatre. The other, the long narrow building along the rear left of the theatre at 159 N Dearborn is the Oliver Building, built a few years after the fire. In 1997 the owners of the Oriental obtained permission, after a bitter fight to preserve the Oliver, to gut the building and use the space to deepen the theatre's stage. They agreed to preserve the façade which is why it still looks like a separate building today."

"The other building, 36 W Randolph Street, The Delaware Building, is next door to the theatre. It was built in 1874, it's the oldest occupied building still standing in The Loop, and it was there when the original Iroquois was built. It will be our way in." He slid two of the schematics to the center of the table and put them side by side.

"These are the floor plans for both theatres, both orientated with their fronts facing Randolph Street," he said. "You can see that the Oriental has a very similar layout to the old Iroquois; the stage is pretty much in the same place; it just extends back further thanks to the extra space gained from gutting the Oliver Building. In both theatres, as you're facing the stage the left side of it abuts the back of the Delaware Building. And you can see that in the Iroquois the stairs leading down to the sub-stage and the basement were in that front corner of stage left. Frank Barr indicates in his letter that the door to the unused tunnel was in this same corner of the basement located down an additional two or three steps. So, it should connect to the sub-basement of the Delaware building in that building's rear right corner, as you stand on Randolph Street and face the front of the building. We need to find that door, get through it and into the tunnel where hopefully we will find Richard Merle."

"And he won't smell too good, I can tell you that!" Devon quipped.

"Do we have permission from the owners of the Delaware building to do all this?" Verity asked.

"We do."

"Then why do we have to work at night?" Dan asked.

"The entire first floor of the building is occupied by a very busy McDonald's restaurant. While it's true that we're going to be in the sub-basement, our activities will very likely generate some noise. Not to mention our coming and going, as necessary. That we work at night was a stipulation of the owners and I was happy to accept."

"Do they know why we're really there?" Lannie asked.

"Not at all, they think we're there researching the fire and looking for artifacts under the old stage. They were not even aware of the tunnel's existence. I got a very strong impression from them that they don't really think it's still there and that we're wasting our time."

"Where do they think we're from?" Verity asked.

"The National Association for the Preservation of Fire History or NAPFH, he pronounced it 'naff'."

"Catchy title," Lannie said.

"I thought so," Phineas replied. "It's a newly registered Delaware LLC, the president and chief reporting officer is one Gregory McGregor."

"A friend of yours?" Lannie asked him.

"I've never met the man," Phineas said. "I have business cards for each of you."

"Of course," Lannie said. "Am I at least a vice president this time?"

"You are the Director of Research and New Projects. A suitably vague title while at the same time impressive sounding. How's that?"

"Works for me," Lannie said, "but next time make me a vice president."

"So what time does Micky D's close?" Dan asked.

"Ten o'clock, Devon is going to line up the equipment he'll need, Dan goes with him. We may find it necessary to go through a wall to reach the door and I'm not expecting it to be easily accessible, especially since the current owners weren't even aware of its existence. Verity, I've lined up a wall penetrating imager for you, it should be here at any moment. Lannie, you and I are going to finalize things with the owners and walk the ground. I want to take a look at W Couch Place, the alley that runs behind the theatre. It's still known as Death Alley by the locals by the way, the stage door is called Death Door."

"What are we looking for there?" Lannie asked.

"I'd like to stage our van there, load and off load from there if possible. There's a multi-level self-parking garage next to it so, if need be, we'll utilize that, but it would be easier if we could use W Couch. It's a walk-through now, but nothing posted there says it's closed to vehicle traffic. I wanted to get some idea if it's normal to see vehicles parked there."

"Is there a show at the theatre tonight?" she asked.

"There isn't, it's closed for the remainder of the week for maintenance, it's the reason we're doing this now."

"Why are we meeting with the owners of the Delaware Building? You said you've already met with them."

"Just to finalize things and make sure they're all on board, I don't want them coming in at the 11th hour saying they need to have someone there with us or anything in that vein. I thought your charming presence would both disarm and reassure them."

"Good thing for us they don't know her," Dan snorted and smiled at her.

"I'll let him have that one," Lannie said to the rest of them, "he gets in so few."

"All right," Phineas stood, "let's get to work. Back here for dinner at seven then we'll head over together. And let's all hope we make Mr. Merle's acquaintance tonight."

Chapter Six

36 West Randolph Street, former location of the Iroquois Theatre, current location of the Oriental Theatre, was in Chicago's famous Loop. It was two blocks from West Wacker Drive to the north and two blocks from Millennium Park to the east. The area was densely commercial and there was at least a half dozen other theatres within a four-block radius.

The block the Oriental was located on was split in half by W Couch Place or, Death Alley. The Oriental shared its side with the two previously mentioned buildings and one other large building that was inconsequential to the task at hand. The other side was taken up with the multi-level parking garage and yet another commercial building. The El ran along that side of the block then turned south one block further on.

They were all sitting in a panel van on the ground level of the parking garage on the side adjacent to Death Alley. They'd yet to see a vehicle parked in the alley itself and Phineas didn't want to risk the van getting towed, so they'd opted for the garage. It was just after 10 p.m. and the McDonald's on the ground floor of the Delaware Building was closed, the employees cleaning up before leaving for the evening. Once they were finished and gone an owners' representative was to meet them by the front door to let them into the building and leave them a set of keys. He was then supposed to leave. It had not been easy to get the owners to agree to that part of the arrangement and Phineas had finally had to sign a binder against damage to the building. Lannie's presence at the meeting that afternoon had helped, as it usually did. Wearing an Armani Collezioni business suit and exuding a sense of quiet professionalism well beyond her twenty-eight years, she had perfectly complimented Phineas' own very formidable presence. Between the two of them they'd had the owners eating out of their hands by the end of the meeting.

Still, as they sat in the van Lannie, at Phineas' request, was wearing nice business casual attire. She would run interference if anyone from the building showed up after they'd started working.

"Those are really nice clothes," Dan commented as he looked her over. "They're probably going to get really dirty you know, once we start going through walls and steel doors and stuff."

"You peasants will be doing all the manual labor tonight," Lannie told him. "I will be supervising."

"How does *that* work?" Devon asked, looking forward in the van toward Phineas.

"There's a chance someone from the building might show up to check on us," Phineas said. "They assured us they wouldn't, but I have a feeling. They liked Lannie so she's going to be ready to head them off if it happens."

"How exactly is she going to do that?" Devon asked.

"With wit and charm and finesse," Verity told him, "all very foreign concepts to you."

"I certainly hope so," Devon replied.

They met Tyler Morgenstern, the owner's rep, by the doors to Micky D's and he let them into the restaurant. Dan inquired about the possibility of throwing together some Big Macs and Verity smacked him on the arm. Lannie chatted with Tyler and smiled and laughed lightly at his wit as he showed them where the access to the basement was. They assured him that they could take it from there and that when they were done, if they in fact finished that night, he would never even know that they'd been there. He reluctantly held out the keys that Lannie took gently from his hand then led him to the door. A moment later he was gone.

"He's going to be back," Devon told them, "if not only to check up on us then to check up on Lannie."

"If he comes back I'll take care of it," Lannie said.

They headed downstairs and the upper basement was what they would have expected: restaurant supplies, old equipment and a very small managers' office that was locked. The restaurant had a fair amount of storage on the main floor so the basement was actually less cluttered than they'd assumed it would be, which was a nice surprise. The sub-basement was a whole different story.

Access to the sub-basement was by a small moldy wooden door located inside a narrow storage room on the west side of the building. The door was locked and looked as if it hadn't been opened in decades. They had to move several stacks of boxes to access the door only to discover that none of the keys on the set they'd been given worked in its lock, including the one Morgenstern had thought went to the door. Devon knelt down in front of the door. He sprayed a lubricant into the lock then produced an old fashioned set of lock-picks and had it unlocked in less than a minute.

The door swung open with a screech of rusted hinges and scraping wood. Beyond it was a narrow set of stone steps leading down into darkness. On the wall just inside the door was an old push button type light switch. Verity reached out and pushed in the upper button with the butt of her flashlight and a single low watt bulb came to life at the bottom of the stairs.

"Ok," she said, "Well that's just so much better."

"Dan, you and Devon find some outlets up here and start running power cords down there," Phineas said. "We'll bring the lights down and get them set up."

They'd brought half a dozen high intensity work lights with them, along with numerous flashlights and three battery operated railroad lanterns. Phineas went down first and Verity followed him. The upper basement had been well-lit and clean with white plaster walls and a tile floor. The sub-basement, which was one big space, was none of those things. It was dark, with a single strand of low watt bulbs running its length, several of which weren't working.

It was dirty, the floor was ancient and cracked concrete, the walls equally ancient brick that used to be red and was now a sickly brown color, and it was damp; Verity couldn't see any mold as she shined her flashlight around, but the atmosphere was definitely humid and close.

"There aren't any spiders down there, right?" Dan called from the top of the stairs.

"Get your ass down here," Verity replied.

A coiled power cord hit the floor at the bottom of the stairs and Dan followed. He had a second coil over his shoulder; he put it down on the floor, found the end of the first cord and attached a three-way outlet to it then plugged the second power cord into it. Verity used a second outlet to plug in one of the work lights and that section of the sub-basement was suddenly flooded with harsh white light.

"Run that second cord down this way," Phineas said to Dan. He had already walked south along the wall toward the far end of the room, pointing his light toward the stained brick wall in the far corner.

Verity plugged in a second work light and aimed in down toward Phineas; it lit up the back of the basement fairly well. Well enough for her to see that the wall back there was solid. She took two more lights and followed Dan. A moment later Devon came down the stairs with a second power cord and most of the rest of their equipment. Lannie was behind him with the rest of it.

"This is lovely," she said as she looked around the sub-basement. "Early American dungeon."

"It could be worse," Phineas said over his shoulder, "it could be wet, or crumbling. All in all, it looks to be in fairly good shape for being almost 150 years old."

"Yeah, and there could be spiders," Dan added.

"We haven't looked that closely yet," Verity told him, "There probably are…big hairy ones."

"I'm standing right here," Devon said. "You shouldn't talk about me while I'm standing right here."

"You are a pig," Verity told him.

Dan laid out his power cord and so did Devon. A moment later they had three more work lights going, all pointed at the basement's rear wall.

"I don't see a door, Phineas," Verity said.

"I didn't think we would," he replied, "which is why we have the wall penetrating gear." He gestured to the rear wall. "This wall abuts the stage left wall of the theatre and the rear wall of the Oliver Building. Since the Oliver Building wasn't part of the theater in 1903 we're only interested in this half of the wall and specifically this corner. I suspect that the tunnel would have connected at or near this corner because of where it had been situated in the old Iroquois." He walked over to the corner and studied the brick for a moment. "The brick here appears to be less degraded than on the rest of the wall so I'm assuming it was added after the building was constructed, possibly after the fire itself. They would have wanted to permanently block off the door after that."

"Hopefully they didn't bother to look behind it first," Devon said, "and remove Dick's body."

"There would have been no reason to," Phineas replied, "it wasn't in use, hadn't been in years; in fact, I think the door was already sealed at this end even though Frank Barr didn't know it. "So," he turned to face them, "let's get set up. Lannie, I need you to go back upstairs and stand watch in case Mr. Morgenstern decides to return, or anyone else for that matter. If he does come back just tell him that it's filthy down here, there are big bugs, and possibly methane gas. If he insists, text me on my phone and I'll come up."

"All right," Lannie said, "but I want to know when you're about to open the door, if there is a door. I want to be here for that." She turned and picked her way back to the stairs and was gone.

Verity began unpacking the wall penetrating unit and setting it up. It was roughly the size of a box of cereal and was simply a square metal box with a flat black face and a small LCD screen on the back. She positioned it at the wall a foot from the corner and began connecting the electrical leads.

"Is that continuous wave?" Devon asked her.

"It's not," Verity replied. "You only need continuous wave to detect movement and if Mr. Merle is actually back there I suspect he stopped moving some time ago. This is a pulsed radar unit that distributes pulses across different bands to detect targets with distinctive reflectivity properties. Different materials reflect or absorb the pulses at different frequencies so, I will be able to tell if there's a steel door in there, or a wooden door, or any type of door." She re-checked everything on the unit then activated it and began moving it slowly down the wall as she watched the monitor. She was moving away from the corner and she stopped almost immediately. She took a piece of chalk from her pocket, reached out and made a vertical line on the wall. She continued moving along slowly and after a few feet stopped again and made a second vertical mark on the brick. Then she moved the device upward, stopped again and made a horizontal line roughly five feet above the floor. Then she stepped back and turned to Phineas.

"There's your door," she said, "Steel, set into concrete. There's open space behind it that's only a little wider than the door. I couldn't tell how deep it is or if anything is in it."

"You're slipping," Phineas told her and she smiled a bit and shook her head.

"Ok," Phineas said, "we have to remove the brick covering the door, carefully because the owners will possibly want it replaced when we're finished. So, one brick at a time please."

Lannie had parked herself at a table at the rear of the restaurant where she could see the doors, but people passing on the street couldn't easily see her. She had her tablet with her and she did some Internet surfing then downloaded a novel and began reading. She'd also brought a small cooler with drinks and snacks. This wasn't the first time she'd sat a static post since coming to work for Phineas, and she'd come prepared. And her spot tonight was downright luxurious compared to some she'd occupied on past projects.

The downside was that it was killing her not knowing what was going on in the basement. Abbey had texted her several times from Seattle and she'd been trading texts with Robert as well because it was killing them, too. The only update she'd received so far was a three-word text from Verity a while ago; *found the door,* that was all.

It was over an hour after that when Dan appeared from the back room. He was filthy, covered with concrete dust and dirt. He saw her at her table and crossed to her, careful to stay out of sight of the windows although it was after one a.m. now and foot traffic outside on the sidewalks had thinned appreciably, as had vehicle traffic on the street.

"What's going on?" she asked before he could open his mouth, "Did you find him?"

"Not yet, we've got the door almost uncovered, an old steel door; after we got through the brick there was old horsehair plaster over it too, we're almost through that now but Phineas called a break."

"Now, are you kidding?"

"Lannie, you're sitting up here reading and eating snacks, we just tore down a big section of brick wall, one brick at a time."

"You're right, sorry. It's just killing me. Robert and Abbey have been texting me all night, it's killing them, too. And you know I'd be down there too, if I could."

"I know that," Dan said. "Phineas said there's an all-night deli at the corner of Lake and North Dearborn, just past the garage. He asked if you could get us some sandwiches. There's also a Dunkin

Donuts next to it, large coffee's all around. I'll go with you to help you carry it all."

"You're a mess," Lannie told him, "why don't you go clean up a little in the men's room first."

The Deli was open, so was the Dunkin's, and when they got back the rest of the crew had emerged from the sub-basement and were sitting at the very rear of the restaurant. They had all washed their hands and faces in the rest rooms, but their clothes were still pretty dirty. When they were all finished eating Phineas produced a bottle of Bushmills Irish Whiskey from the satchel he was carrying and they all smiled and shook their heads.

"You thought I'd forgotten," he said to them as he put the bottle on the table then produced five glasses and put them on the table too. "Now, whose turn is it to do the toast?"

Chapter Seven

It was Verity's turn so she held up her glass and the others did the same, "May we always get what we want and never what we deserve," she said and downed her shot. They each downed theirs then got up to descend back into the sub-basement.

"Can I go back down with you?" Lannie asked Phineas. "It's after two am; no one's going to show up at this hour."

"Be careful what you ask for," Dan told her. "It's dirty and smelly and gross down there."

"There are bugs," Verity added, "pretty big bugs."

"And snakes," Devon said.

"You guys are full of shit," Lannie said.

"Ok, so there are no snakes or bugs to speak of," Verity said, "but it is dirty and smelly and gross."

Lannie looked at Phineas and he nodded. "Just until we get the door open though," he told her, "then I need you to come back up here, just in case. I'd hate to have Morgenstern or someone else walk up on us before we know exactly what we have down there."

They went down through the basement to the sub-basement and Lannie saw why they were all so dirty; there was a jagged edged six by four-foot hole in the wall where the brick had been removed. Beneath that was a layer of yellowed plaster that had been neatly cut away to reveal a door. It was a small door, maybe five feet high and four wide and made of steel. It had once been red, but had faded over the years to a pale rust color. There was a steel bar across the door that fitted into wall brackets on both sides and a drum lock above a rusty doorknob.

They'd pointed four of the work lights at the door so it was lit up as if it were high noon two levels below the Chicago streets. Devon went to the door and after studying the steel bar for a moment grasped it with both hands and pulled up on it. It didn't budge as he increased the pressure, the muscles in his back bulging against the fabric of his t-shirt. After a few moments of this he stopped and stepped back for a moment, contemplating the bar. Then he turned and rooted around in the equipment he'd brought down until he found a small hydraulic jack. He and Dan stacked bricks up in front of the door until Devon could set the jack on the bricks with its top braced under the center of the steel bar. He inserted a large screwdriver into the socket in the side of the jack and began pumping. It only took three pumps before the steel bar broke loose from the rust holding it and popped up almost out of its holders.

Devon removed the bar and leaned it against the wall, off to the side, then hunched down to look at the lock. He turned to look up at Phineas, "It's rusted pretty much into a solid mass," he told him. "Is it all right to just pop the cylinder out of the door?"

"Go ahead," Phineas replied.

Devon retrieved the large screwdriver he'd used on the jack and placed the butt end of the handle against the cylinder lock. He took a long handled hammer from his bag, positioned himself, then swung the side of the hammer's head against the blade end of the screwdriver. Half of the screwdrivers handle disappeared into the door and they all heard the drum lock clatter to the floor on the other side. Devon pulled the screwdriver out and tried the doorknob, which came off in his hand. He put several fingers into the hole were the lock had been, jiggled the door a few times to test it, then pulled hard and the door swung open with an ungodly screech of metal as its hinges moved for the first time in over a century. Devon stepped back and looked at Phineas.

Phineas nodded to him then stepped forward and pulled the door all the way open. He moved the closest work light directly in front of the opening and they all moved forward to see. The light shown down a long, narrow passageway with a concrete floor and brick walls. They could see another door at the far end, identical to the one at their end. The passageway was roughly sixty feet long and almost at its middle, on the right hand side, they could see something leaning against the wall.

Phineas picked up a flashlight and started down the passageway; the rest of them grabbed lights or a lantern and followed him. They all noticed upon entering that the air in the passageway was very stale and much dryer than the air in the sub-basement. And incredibly, there was still a faint odor of smoke. They all reached the middle of the passageway together and stood there in a semi-circle looking down at the body of Richard Merle.

He was sitting with his back against the wall and both legs straight out in front of him. Both hands were in his lap, his head was turned to face the door they'd just come through, as if he was waiting for them, for someone, to come through that door. He had been sitting in that position, underneath one of the busiest cities in the world, waiting, for over one hundred years. They had expected to find a skeleton, if they found anything at all, but that's not what they were looking at because Richard Merle had mummified in the dry stale air of the tunnel.

His skin looked like tanned leather and was pulled tight around his face and his sunken eye sockets. His hair, a mousy brown, was still in place and still combed. He was wearing a Burberry jacket, grey striped pants and brown lace up shoes; they were tattered a bit, but still in good shape. He was sitting on something that they would later learn was his folded overcoat. A bowler hat was on the floor next to him. More importantly, a brown leather satchel was on the floor as well. He'd placed it by his side so that it leaned against his right thigh, as if he'd wanted to keep it very close.

Phineas squatted down next to him and softly patted both sides of his jacket, then slid his hand inside the left side and carefully removed an oversized leather billfold. He opened it and held it under his light, then gently went through the contents. Then he replaced the billfold where he'd found it and straightened up. "It's him," he said simply.

They all continued to look down at him and Verity was the first to speak. "It's nice to meet you Mr. Merle," she said gently, "sorry someone couldn't have gotten here sooner." She squatted down herself and looked at the body closely. She had the most medical training of anyone there.

"Did he suffocate or die from lack of food and water," Phineas asked her.

"I hope he suffocated," Lannie said. "It would have been a hell of a lot quicker."

"There's no way to tell really," Verity said, "but my money would be on asphyxiation. If he'd died from dehydration or starvation he wouldn't look so calm, sitting here like this. He'd probably be curled up on the floor. If he asphyxiated, then he probably just slowly lost consciousness."

"Is anyone going to mention the 500-pound gorilla in the tunnel?" Dan asked. "Can we please look in that satchel? Right now?"

"Of course," Phineas replied, "but upstairs, on a table, and carefully."

Chapter Eight

They were all seated around the same table they'd eaten their late dinner at. Phineas had spread a large plastic evidence bag on the tabletop and placed the satchel on top of it. He'd also donned a pair of cotton gloves. The snap holding the satchels flap closed was rusted shut, he produced a folding knife and carefully pried it loose then he slowly folded back the flap and spread the satchel open.

The only thing inside was a heavy cardboard sleeve a little larger than a standard legal file. It was sealed along its top edge, Phineas used the knife to carefully slit the seal and open the sleeve. Inside was a slim stack of papers, maybe ten in all. Phineas placed them carefully on the table and gently went through them. He chose one and slid it carefully over to Dan, their residence document expert.

"That's a page from Chief Inspector Abberline's personal Ripper file," Phineas said, "or at least it appears to be. What do you think?"

Dan examined the page under his flashlight, then held it up and put the light behind it, then put it back on the table and slid it back to Phineas.

"It's a copy of an original," he told him.

"Really," Devon said, "what did Merle do, run down to the nearest drugstore and use their copier? In 1903?"

"In a way that's exactly what he did," Dan told him. "There were copy machines in 1903, quite a few actually, just not the kind you mean." He turned back to Phineas, "I suspect that Merle made that using something called a Bushnell's Perfect Letter Copying Book. It was a kind of roller, you put the page you wanted to copy between two flexible covers or a 'book' then rolled it up around a wooden rod attached to the 'books' spine. The pressure of rolling it around the wooden rod, along with a slightly damp sheet of muslin placed inside, would copy the text onto a thick piece of paper just like that one. The other thing that gives it away is that, in rolling the document around the rod, some letters at both edges of the document would sometimes smudge or appear a tad elongated, especially if the process were rushed. You can see both effects along the edges of that page. It appears that Mr. Merle had his very own Bushnell's Copying Book, in 1903 he would have paid around $1.60 for one.

"So he somehow got into Abberline's personal Ripper file and hurriedly made copies of key pages," Phineas said. While he was talking he was carefully separating the pages and looking at them. He stopped at one of the last ones, read for a moment and then looked up at the rest of them seated around the table.

"These pages represent Abberline's spelling out, in a private file that he probably never intended for anyone else to see, the Ripper's identity and how he and the other three police officials came to discover that identity."

They all just looked at him.

"But before we go there," Phineas continued, "we need to take care of some business."

"I really hate you sometimes," Lannie said.

"Right now I really hate you too," Verity said.

"In a moment," Phineas told them. "First, we all need to agree that everything we did here tonight stays with us, how we came to be here, everything. At least until we decide how we're going to disseminate that information."

"We're not going to just seal up that tunnel again and walk away, are we?" Dan asked.

"Phineas, we can't do that," Verity said. "We can't just leave him down there like that."

"Of course not, Mr. Merle will at long last get out of that tunnel and hopefully go home. But there are issues here that require our attention. First, we had permission to access that tunnel from the owners of this building, however the spot where Mr. Merle chose to sit down for the final time is not under this building, it's under the theatre, so we need to deal with the owners of the theatre. Also, the scene, the body, and these," he held up the papers, "will need to be collected properly, documented, and verified. That is essential if anyone is going to believe and accept what we've found here. And of course city officials will have to be involved because we are dealing with a body, however old. I have a protocol in place for all of this, but it will take a day or two to evolve so during that time I ask that you let me, and only me, do the talking, agreed?"

They all agreed.

"Excellent," Phineas said. "All right, since besides me Dan is the other resident Ripperologist in this little group and is well acquainted with all the known suspects, I shall let him see the name first, after which he can pass it around the table, to be handled very carefully of course." He slid one of the pages gently across the table to Dan, "The name you're looking for is at the bottom of the page, the very last sentence."

Dan had to keep himself from snatching the page from Phineas. He slid it in front of him on the table, studied the name for a moment then looked back up at Phineas.

"So who the hell is that?" he asked.

Authors note;

Chief Inspector Abberline was a very real person, as were his three colleagues mentioned here. Frank Barr, Thomas Hoyne and his daughter Susan were also real people, although to the best of my knowledge none ever had anything to do with the Ripper case. Richard Merle on the other hand was a figment of my imagination, nothing more.

Unfortunately, the Iroquois Theatre fire was very real. It is today a little known tragedy in the city of Chicago's history and still stands as the most lethal fire in US history.

INVESTING IN THE FUTURE

The man was walking down Summer Street in Boston's financial district. Between avoiding putting a foot in the many piles of horse dung on the street and trying to ignore the smells that assaulted his senses he almost walked right past his intended destination.

His business on that day was with the firm of Morley, Matheson and Wells located at 100 Summer Street in a brand new four story building that had only been completed earlier that year. The firm primarily dealt in investments and estate planning but also dabbled in a few other areas, all having to do with money: making it, managing it and preserving it. They also had a few lawyers on staff which he knew was necessary although he didn't trust lawyers, not here, not back home. He had chosen this firm for this business transaction solely due to their longevity.

His appointment that afternoon was with an associate manager named Finney who had been making the arrangements he'd requested, along with a few side requests. Mr. Finney met him at the door and ushered him to a desk that was second to last in a long row of desks located near the back of the cavernous two story room, a temple of marble and polished wood dedicated to money…and greed.

"We are happy to see you again Mr. Howard," Finney said cheerily. "I trust you are faring well on this hot day?"

"The horse droppings in the street are a bit much," the man replied. "I don't know how you stand it."

"Ah yes, well usually they are not so apparent as you find them today. The street cleaners are on strike you see, haven't been at work for two days now. I'm surprised you were not aware of it; it has been in all the newspapers."

"I've been out of town," he replied, "I only arrived in the city this morning."

"I see. Well, everything is on order for us to complete your transaction." Finney produced a stack of papers from a drawer and placed them on the desk. "Your signature is required in several places I'm afraid. And an outstanding balance of four hundred dollars is required to endow the trust, and cover our fee of course."

"Of course," he said. He took a pen from the ink well on the desk and began signing the documents. There were a bit more than several places to sign and it took him a few moments to satisfy all of them. As he finished signing he handed them back across the desk to Mr. Finney who dutifully witnessed them and returned them to the stack. After the last one Mr. Finney produced yet another, albeit smaller stack of documents.

"These are the deeds to the parcels of land that you've purchased," he said, "along with the documents representing the trust you've established to cover payment of taxes on said land for the next one hundred and fifty years and copies of the documents naming this firm as trustee in perpetuity, or until such time an agent representing you, your family or your holding company should assume that responsibility. And lastly a bill for our services up to this date, of course going forward from today the trust will be in effect so you need pay us no further out of pocket fees. As I've said, the total comes to exactly four hundred dollars. I understand that this is rather a large sum of money however, you've requested a rather long lifespan for the trust to operate so I fear it is necessary."

"That's quite all right," he said, "I've been well informed by your firm all through the process regarding cost and I understand completely." He produced a long leather billfold from his inside suit jacket pocket and took four one hundred dollar notes from it. He placed the bills on the desktop in front of Mr. Finney who immediately made them disappear into a desk drawer. He flipped the billfold closed and returned it to his pocket and neither he nor Mr. Finney noticed the piece of paper that had been stuck to the outside of the billfold and fluttered onto the desktop.

"I must admit," Mr. Finney said as he organized the paperwork and made sure all was in order, "I've never handled a request quite like this one. The land you've had us purchase for you is quite off the beaten path, and to arrange for its stewardship for so long a time, it is a bit unusual if you don't mind my saying."

"I'd heard that one of the cornerstones of your firm is its discretion and respect for its clients' privacy Mr. Finney," he replied. "In fact, it was what made me decide to approach you with this matter in the first place."

"I understand completely sir," Mr. Finney replied quickly, "just so." He finished with the papers and his copies disappeared into the desk. He handed a few more across the desk then provided a leather portfolio to hold them, the firms name impressed into its cover. They both stood then and Mr. Finney walked him to the front entrance then offered his hand which the man shook heartily before heading back out into the odors and equine produced pitfalls of Summer Street.

Mr. Finney returned to his desk and it was then that he noticed the square of paper on the desktop. He frowned because he always kept his desktop immaculate; he would have it no other way. As he picked up the piece of paper he remembered that he'd thought he'd seen something fall when Mr. Howard closed his billfold as they were transacting their business, but it must have then been covered up by the documents they had been reviewing or he would have surely taken note of it and called Mr. Howard's attention to it. He hurried to the front door and out into the bright sunshine of Summer Street but a careful check in both directions revealed that Mr. Howard was nowhere to be seen. Mr. Finney returned to his desk and only then did he unfold the piece of paper and look at it.

A few moments later he approached his managers' desk, sat down, and handed the piece of paper across the desk to him.

"What's this?"

"Mr. Howard, the gentleman who arranged that rather unusual land deal with us was just here and he seems to have inadvertently dropped that on my desk."

"Remind me of the deal you're speaking of."

"Mr. Howard, a new customer, he came in a month or so ago and wished us to purchase several large parcels of land for him far outside the city and to establish a trust to maintain them almost in perpetuity. The length that the trust will need to continue was odd enough but the land he bought was more so, it's almost worthless, in the middle of nowhere. True he paid very little for it, but he bought four very large parcels of what amounts to wilderness. Why, they're all more than forty miles west of the edge of the city."

"Ah yes, I remember, he paid cash as I recall, nothing wrong with that!" He turned his attention back to the piece of paper and studied it closely under his desk lamp. It was green and white and had a picture of George Washington on one side and the word ONE on the other."

"Did he try to pay you with these?"

"Oh no, I believe it was in his billfold and it fell out when he produced the currency for the transaction. He paid me with genuine one hundred dollar bills, the most I've seen in one place in some time I might add. What do you make of that?"

"It's a clever ruse of some kind, meant as a parlor trick or something of that sort."

"It states that it's legal tender, a one-dollar bill."

"Don't be silly. It looks nothing like a one-dollar bill, and look how small it is." He was still studying it under the lamp and finally he looked up and harrumphed, "Look here, this proves that it's a farce of some kind, the date on it is 2015!"

Mr. Finney leaned forward and looked, "I didn't notice that," he said after a moment. "The bill is very small as is the writing. Had I seen that I wouldn't have bothered you with it, sir."

"That's quite all right," the manager laughed. "It is a rather ingenious gimmick I will admit, if a short sighted one. Why 2015 is one hundred and twenty-one years from now and by then I doubt paper currency will even exist!"

Made in the USA
Lexington, KY
16 February 2018